# The Whistling Thorn

## BY

Ronald Jameson

*To John*

*With Thespian Regards*

*Ron AKA Wil*

ISBN: 978-1-291-49301-6

**The Whistling Thorn**

© Ronald Jameson 2013

The right of Ronald Jameson to be recognized as the author of this work has been asserted by him in accordance with the Copyright, Designs and Patent Act 1988.

All rights reserved. This publication may be not be reproduced in whole or in part by any means, electronic or mechanical or any information storage and retrieval system without express permission in writing from the author and/or publisher.

Characters in this story are not based on anyone living or dead.

PublishNation | London

www.publishnation.co.uk

## Dedication

Africa, with its ancient art of story telling, its legends and exotic peoples, has been my inspiration to create this story set in Kenya.

"The Whistling Thorn" is dedicated to my late wife who first encouraged me to write. Also to my personal and Thespian friends; to my editors Rosemary Allix, Jill Hancock and cover artist Tamara Hickie; all of whom have given me the zest and inspiration to write of East Africa and my time there.

## Legend

***The Whistling Thorn*** *of East Africa allows ants to burrow into its galls to make their nests and to patrol and protect the tree from injurious parasites. To return the favour the tree encourages the wind to blow across holes in empty galls to create a whistle to warn ant-eating birds to keep away lest they are impaled on the tree's many thorns.*

# 1.

Africa's Rift Valley, the greatest scar on the earth's surface, burned under a sun undimmed by rainclouds for three years. An unprecedented event. From Ethiopia in the north to Mozambique in the south was tinder dry. Hot air making it difficult to breathe lay as a blanket over all below vibrant morning skies and rainless afternoon broken clouds. Water courses, small rivers and lakes were now areas of crazed mud. *Dongas* were nothing but dust. Dust in clouds followed moving vehicles like ghosts. Moving feet kicked up dust.

*

A twister, spinning dust and small stones up to hundreds of feet pun a path across parched earth with meagre patches of arid grass. It brushed past a flat-topped thorn tree by a large *kopje* with tumbled rock at its base. Under the tree Peter Grant crouched in his safari truck covering his ears against a screech while the truck took a pounding of dust and wind as the twister went close by. Continuing its path it met a cluster of 'wait-a-bit' thorn next to an expanse of crazed mud that was once a salt lick. The dust devil hit the thorn and tried to uproot it. But this time the bush won. The swirling mass lost its momentum and the spinning slowed allowing the tower of dust gradually to sink to earth. Those with exceptional hearing of very low frequencies such as the elephant might have heard the twister moan its last.

Peter stood and brushed dust from a sweaty shirt not having been changed for three days and nights. Also rising from having crouched against the twister was a mixed herd of Grant's and Thomson's Gazelles close by. They continued grazing as though nothing had disturbed them. Taking a loaded movie camera from a padded box Peter mounted it on a sturdy tripod in the back of the truck and wiping sweat from his eyes, made a note of the frame counter.

Now all was quiet. Despite the violence of the twister there was not a breath of wind. Above him in a blazing sky vultures cruising at a thousand feet saw through telescopic eyes the merest chance of a meal. Spiralling down they glided over the *kopje* to land and settle as sentinels on the tree. They jostled for a strong foothold while folding their wings. Nature's scavengers, now in sinister silence occupied front seats in the dress circle to make ready to descend and squabble inelegantly for a morsel of an impending carcase, a 'Tommy' browsing on the edge the herd.

Peter spoke sharply to himself. "Why do this? You idiot! I'm shattered. Three days and nights – but, there we are, I urgently need . . ." A long yawn interrupted his words. He sighted through the lens to where the gazelles grazed in meagre scrub. The Tommies' dark tan and white scuts constantly semaphored their presence and could be seen by a predator at a considerable distance.

"Now where's that damned elusive Bili?" He was alone in the truck and spoke to himself to keep awake. "I think she knows it's me who's been stalking her all the way up from the Mara and is having me on a bit of string. It's not only girls with *two* legs who have been at the witches' brew . . . a-ha! There she is! I shan't let you escape me this time Bili. Sleep or no sleep." A cheetah had come from the cover of rocks where she had a good view of her next meal. Bili, an orphaned cub rescued and reared by hand on his farm and let out six months previously when able to fend for herself was easily recognised by Peter. He knew just about every spot on her, a tuft of hair on one ear and could identify her very individual footprint even in starlight.

Now with long tail straight out for balance and to help a sharp turn in the chase she stood with head stock still. Peter focussed finely on her to see great golden eyes just above the top of a clump of grass. She singled-out a Tommy. Peter pressed the camera's trigger. Film whispered through the gate. He too whispered. "Bon Appétit Bili. And here we go, a nice bit of cash coming up." He imagined the cash sign in the viewfinder. Placing her paws not to disturb even an insect underfoot Bili moved stealthily forward. But then a continuous growling noise getting louder filled the air. The gazelles' ears pricked. As one they ran helter-skelter from the unnatural noise. Bili also ran – eighty yards at sixty miles an hour – but the Tommy escaped. Despite her speed over short distances she was not close enough. Now still, thwarted, puffing and frowning, then turning, she went to cover as the origin of the noise manifested itself from around the rear of the kopje. A Nairobi taxi with loose exhaust, now with horn blaring and brakes screeching came to a halt in a pall of dust.

Peter's expletive "SHIT!" as he aborted the shoot was louder than the vulture's flapping wings as they rose. Gritting his teeth with frustration he leaped from the truck as a girl alighted from the taxi. Smiling and removing over-large sun glasses she stepped forward, a vision in a tight khaki skirt just above her knees, cowboy boots on long model's legs, chequered shirt with a silk kerchief, and white Stetson over honey-blonde hair. He stopped her in her tracks.

"What the hell do you think you're doing?!"

Taken aback but uncowed she answered "What the hell I am doing is . . ."

"What the hell you're doing is being a damned pain in the butt! Whatever possessed you to make a din like that! Are you out of your mind? You have just ruined a film of a very precious cheetah desperately needing a meal – and still not getting it after too many days without. This is Africa, not New York or wherever you come from, and you have shattered my nerves."

"I'm sorry. But it wasn't me. It was the driver when he had sight of your truck. And I am from Houston in Texas."

"Huh! It's got to be Texas . . . You don't sound it."

"My father had us move from Augusta, Maine in 'forty three. He's in Oil."

"A pity your taxi isn't. Sounds as if it will seize any moment." Striding across to the taxi and in rapid Swahili he called to the driver, "Switch that damned noisy thing off. That engine sounds as if it's on its last legs." He wrenched open the scuff-edged door on which was written in faded paint 'Chui Taxi'. The driver got out saying *"Pole bwana*, sorry, sorry."

"You'll be more than sorry if . . ." He took a deep breath and let it out slowly, then turned to the girl. "So, what can I do for you? What's your business, Miss? Mrs?"

"Miss. Della Mitchell. Are you Peter Grant?"

"What if I am?"

"I am a journalist . . ."

"A journalist? First you ruin a film and now you ruin my day. How did you find me?"

Unabashed, she continued. "I spoke to someone at the Norfolk Hotel in Nairobi who knows you and said he knew whereabouts you might be at this time with a bit of luck, and drew a map. I carry a compass and have a tongue in my head."

"You can say that again. You ran out of luck two minutes ago." He shut his eyes to visualise a full roll of film of a cheetah's kill. "Ach!" he said, clenching his fists. Then opened his eyes and looked darkly at the girl again.

Peter had dallied with many a blonde, of whom there was a fair sprinkling in Kenya. This one had presence and confidence. Without make-up, not chocolate box pretty but smooth featured and feminine to her fingertips, she began to affect him as no other girl had on first meeting. He thought that every negative turn in his adult life had been caused by an attractive girl.

"I am very sorry," she said with a mellifluous voice nurtured by Radcliffe the premier Ladies Ivy League establishment. "But I am not to know what you are doing at this precise moment."

"Haven't you eyes? This 'precise moment' as you call it happens to be the end of a damned hard slog. Out here you don't go honking your horn and scaring off every animal within a mile . . . You'd better pay off your taxi – and come over here, I'll run you back" he said, turning his back on her and going to his truck.

"But . . ." The 'but' was lost in the hot air. Telling the driver to wait she retrieved her holdall and camera case from the taxi and followed, putting them down while Peter dismantled and stowed his camera in a padded box next to three guns, a twin Express .577, a bolt action Springfield .308 and a Purdy 12 bore. He picked up two bottles of water and tossed one to her which she caught.

Pushing back a canvas hat over unruly hair he sat in what little shade he could find, on the earth against a front wheel. She looked at the bottle in her hands, looked at him wiping his unshaven face with a scrim choker, shrugged her shoulders and sat on the mounting step next to him.

"I didn't pack cocktail glasses," he said cynically, and took a swig, rinsed his mouth, spat it out then sipped. She copied him, but found no feminine way in which to spit.

With chin in a hand and elbows on his knees he gazed through half-closed eyes eastwards to a line of hazy mountainous hills, his thoughts going to his farm. It lay high and dry. High because the three thousand acre spread lay between six and nine thousand feet on the western slopes of the Aberdare range under the Kinangop, and dry because Kenya's rain had failed yet again.

Water for the farm came from a fall fed by the high rills of the Kinangop under the Dragon's teeth of the Aberdare range that made the eastern escarpment of this part of the Rift. Now all were running low with the fall just one meagre cataract, the resultant flow petering out and evaporating even at altitude. Cattle feed was hard to come by. Banks were stretched. Peter was broke.

Now, with the trifling remains of any cash he possessed in a shirt pocket he was attempting to get a film of a cheetah's kill for which an agent in Nairobi would pay good money. He took a deep breath and let it out slowly. "Damn it. Still no Bili."

"Bili?"

"Yes. A cheetah. It's the name I gave her when rescued as a cub from a dead mother. 'Bili' is basic Swahili for number two. Number one, a male, did not survive."

"Oh! I am sorry."

"Don't apologise. It only makes it worse. I tracked her for three days and nights up from the Mara. She was just about to start her run when . . ." He stopped talking. How could he censure an attractive girl, no doubt another American dumb blonde he guessed who was in an environment she did not understand? But he had to treat her professionally.

Besides being a farmer Peter was also a hunter who helped keep the mystique of the 'Kenya safari' alive. His late father, a prominent hunter, had taught young Peter the skills of tracking and how and when to close on his quarry, and where a client should put the bullet to make a clean kill. But now, at twenty six, he preferred to see East Africa's animals alive and behaving naturally in their own territory, and not displayed as severed heads with decaying manes or dusty horns under an arch of tusks decorating the walls of proud 'sportsmen'. Killing Africa's majestic elephant just for a hollowed-out foot to carry umbrellas and walking sticks sickened him. Now he and his clients shoot the quarry with a camera.

At this time of Kenya's history he should have been very busy taking out clients to photograph the 'big five' in action, but the world was still bemused. World War Two was not long gone. The participants were still licking their wounds. Fifty million young people no longer walked this earth. East Africa now waited with open arms for holidaymakers to turn their backs on the horrors of war and to start the safari ball rolling again.

One thing worried him. Poaching. European and African soldiers were now back from the war and demobbed. Rifles and ammunition could be bought unlicensed on a thriving black market.

He was quiet for some time while thinking of his success in tracking Bili, only to be thwarted by Della's intrusion. She was thinking how unfortunate it was to have got off on the wrong foot, and would he now agree to do what she was about to ask? She had dealt with many a difficult interviewee, and some that had wasted no time in 'coming on' to her. With these latter she had developed a defensive technique and with a general wariness of the male she kept her sexuality under wraps. She had not bargained to find her hunter as being so young. She had expected a middle-aged professional. She would let him speak first.

"So," he said eventually, still smarting from frustration and tiredness, "You reckon you're a journalist. Why would you have come all the way out here from Houston to speak to a Kenya farmer?"

Thinking that no softening technique she used on difficult interviewees would work with Peter in his current mood she began with a direct approach. "I am a features reporter for a newspaper with the biggest circulation in Texas which is syndicated throughout . . ."

"Huh!" he exclaimed with a cynical laugh, "it's bound to be the biggest if it's in Texas."

'Here we go again,' she thought. "Why do you British always think of us over there as boastful and brash?" she flashed in a haughty voice. She was neither. She was a sophisticated New Englander.

"I'm Kenyan. Father was British. You must know, with the war being over this last year or so we get some of your oil-widowed blue-rinsed ladies coming out here to 'do' Africa. Most of them have one night in Nairobi, go to the game park close by and photograph a bunch of bored sleeping lions along with a dozen other taxis crowding them and think they've seen Africa."

"That isn't fair," she countered, "And you know it isn't. – But I have come here for that very reason."

"Oh?" He looked up at her while she spoke, and, craving sleep, moved nearer with his head close to her thighs thinking they would make a pillow. She smelled good. Better than any dehydrated dying animal he had encountered lately. She swung her knees away.

"We Americans know that Kenya is really unique with exotic peoples and animals and hunters like you." A softer, persuasive note crept into her voice. "The likes of you make this country attractive to the tourists." He raised a sardonic eyebrow while she continued speaking. "I have a brief to write a major article and take photographs for a centre-spread and have it syndicated throughout the States to encourage people to come and see the animals here. I have been recommended to find you in particular to take me on a photo safari then I shall write it up and make the very people you describe as 'doing' Africa sit up and 'do' it properly."

"That's laudable, I grant you – but you won't even start to succeed if you go around the bush in a clapped-out rust-bucket disturbing the very animals and hunters you want to write about!" He still could not hide his frustration despite her sincerity. "And why me? You should have gone to my safari agent."

"My editor thought a direct approach would be better, and I am very sorry. I had no idea my taxi driver knew nothing of the open plains."

"And . . .?" he said eyeing her up and down.

"You do not approve of how I dress?"

"You might pass for a barn dance," he said ungraciously. "Why me?" he repeated. She coloured and drew a sharp breath and was about counter his remark and say that he would pass for a hobo. Three days without a proper bath wearing aged canvas jungle boots with frayed lace holes, worn at the knees cords and sweaty shirt that had seen better days did not impress her. But she decided to ignore his jibe and said, "Your reputation has spread further than you think. You are recommended by a number of people in the States including my Editor who was over here last year . . . will you take me out on a safari?"

"If I've been recommended then you must know I do professional safaris only if and when I have the time or the inclination – and through the proper agency." He did not disclose the fact that at this moment he was not able to finance a safari until his farm was in profit, nor could he obtain finance from a strapped White Hunters' Association.

Not knowing this she volunteered, "My newspaper will foot the bill – cash in advance."

"Where have I heard that before?"

She flushed and realised that since her noisy arrival she had responded to his frustration in the wrong way. She had blown it – or had she? She stood smartly, brushed copper-coloured dust from her shirt and from a money belt under it she took an envelope and handed him the contents; a wad of high denomination dollar bills and a letter of credit from Wells Fargo Bank. Unaware of his financial state she said, "The letter of credit will be held by my Embassy until we settle the account. I am told your charges are tailored to the specific job. You will find it is more than enough. The cash is an advance for set-up and running expenses. Surely you can find time for me? You wouldn't want me to come all the way here . . . and return empty-handed?"

He stood stiffly, six inches taller than her, glanced at her appealing face then looked at the money. Three years ago he had held as much and more in a shirt pocket together with a healthy bank balance. But now all those figures were in red. Fanning the notes he made a quick guess as to the amount. His attitude became professional and engaging.

"How long would it take you to get the photographs you want?"

"That's up to you. You must know where and when to find animals and Masai villages. Would a week be enough?"

"Centre spread eh? . . . mmmm . . . I know where to find most species and the Masai clans. Could do it in . . . fourteen days or so . . . plus two getting there and back – unless we have exceptional luck. I have one or two things to do in Nairobi and at the farm. I'll run you back to Nairobi first, then, when I've finished kitting out I'll contact you. Where are you staying?"

"I have a cottage suite at the Norfolk Hotel."

"You don't mind waiting a couple of days?"

"Not if you are serious about it."

"I am – if you're a good enough photographer."

"I held a commission for two years as photographic officer with the US Air Force, and two in Journalism. I think I know how to use a camera."

"But have you been close to lion before? Elephant, buffalo, rhino, leopard?"

"Only in a circus. Never a rhinoceros, leopard or African buffalo," she said modestly.

He knew he would be committing himself to take out a female tenderfoot – not the first – who obviously had no idea of the hazards of stalking on foot when using just a camera on dangerous animals in their territory, albeit covered by his gun. But Della exuded a confidence he had not seen in a lot of girls. He thought fast and looked again at the money, then at her, now with questioning eyes gazing directly into his. It was her eyes and what lay behind them – and the cash – that hooked him. Handing back the dollars and credit letter he said, "Alright then. Fourteen days, open ended, plus film processing. First change those dollars for East African Currency. You'll need to do that before we start. You should have done it on arrival."

"My Embassy will do that."

"And no doubt take a fat commission. They'll do it at the Norfolk desk. They have a licence and will give you a good rate. Mention my name. Then we'll talk turkey and sign a contract for insurance purposes etcetera." He held out his hand. "Deal?"

She took it. "Deal."

While standing close to her and touching and looking into each others' eyes his tiredness seemed to have been momentarily forgotten and his maleness began to assert itself. Something more than just 'deal' passed through their hands that lingered. Hers, long-fingered, supple and manicured. His, firm, capable and giving confidence. She withdrew her hand suddenly. "Thank you, Mr Grant. I am truly sorry about your filming. I . . ."

"Okay, Miss Mitchell," he said with a smile. "You've apologised enough. I'll run you back. He turned and saw the taxi driver sitting on the earth smoking. In Swahili while going across to him he said "You still here? Put that cigarette out and don't smoke in the bush! You should know better. Didn't you know it hasn't rained since God knows when? One damned spark and the whole Rift will go up in smoke and us with it." Peter twisted his boot on the butt and kicked dust over it. "Get in your cab and go back to Nairobi and be quick about it."

"Er . . . Bwana?" the driver stood and held out a hand, Peter looked expectantly at Della who shrugged her shoulders.

"I'm sorry to touch you for the fare. I told him he would be paid only if and when he found you. He won't take dollars, and said the hunter would pay."

Closing his eyes for a second, taking a controlling breath and wondering when the irritations were going to stop, Peter said, "Miss Mitchell, you have very nearly taken one too many chances today." He took a few of his last notes from his shirt pocket and gave the driver his due who waited expectantly. "I know the going rate for Chui taxis, now hop it."

"Tip bwana?"

"Huh! Here," he said handing over another note while feeling a little compassion for a man who probably had never before left his township and Nairobi. "And your *ghari* needs oil and water," he said getting a can and bottle from his truck. "Put it in now. Fuel?"

"Fifty miles."

Peter gave the driver directions to the nearest filling station twenty miles northwards, east of Longanot on a tarmac road at Naivasha. Oiled and watered the taxi needed a push from behind with his truck. With coughing and an explosion or two followed by a billowing cloud of smoke from its exhaust it rattled away over cracked earth and clumps of parched grass in a flurry of dust.

"He'll be lucky to reach the next hand pump, let alone Nairobi!" Peter said, getting down from his seat. "Leopard taxi my foot! That one comes more of a *shenzi* dog. What made you choose him? You took a hell of a chance – a girl alone in an African taxi in the bush!?"

"He's the only one I could find to come this far. And, believe me, I can look after myself. Will you be alright driving? You look tired. You say you were tracking for three days and nights."

"I'll be alright. It's not the first time. I have coffee here."

The taxi disappeared into the heat haze and they were left standing in a hovering cloud of smoke and dust.

Before setting off from the kopje her holdall and camera case were stowed and Peter scanned the surrounding savannah and bushes and clumps of tall grass where Bili might go to ground. But the brilliance of the sun and rippling air together with Bili's perfect camouflage markings made her invisible. Not having seen a blink of an eye or congregating flies he was convinced there was no immediate trace of her. He memorised his position for another foray to find Bili and got back into his seat.

Both now had positive results from their meeting. She was pleased to have accomplished the first step in her quest, and he began to see a light at the end of the tunnel for his immediate cash troubles. With these thoughts in both their minds he set off across the savannah for a long drive on anything but flat terrain to negotiate dry dongas and rock to take the most direct route to Nairobi while looking forward to the future and a successful safari.

But Peter should have known that Kenya did not deal its cards with such abundant largesse, especially in a time of failed rain. A serious negative influence lurked in the wings. Both were unaware that their lives would be imperilled by an event that was, at that moment, unfolding a hundred and fifty miles to the south in the heart of the Serengeti plains.

# 2.

## LEGEND

*Two Masai brothers of the same blood fought continually. They stole fire from East Africa's volcanoes and hurled it at one another. The Great White Bearded Father who lives on the summit of Mount Kilimanjaro punished them and turned them into the brother peaks of Kibo and Mwenzi. They now give the impression of having taken on the mantle of brotherly love. However, they are still vengeful and when no one is looking they spite fire at each other and cause the earth to quake.*

\*

Standing on one leg with foot resting on knee, leaning on a tall spear, with patterned blanket flapping in a choking breeze, shield and *rungu,* the hardwood stick with heavy knob, at his feet, Sekento, a lone Masai warrior looked for all the world at ease. But having been banished from his clan, had six-hundred head of cattle confiscated, and now no longer an elder, he had time to reflect upon the two major misdemeanours that had put him in this parlous state.

He had set out to kill his younger brother Sianka. Secondly he had attempted to usurp his father, Olekowlish; Chief Counsellor, *Laibon* and spiritual leader of all Masai. This was considered to be the greater fault.

Staring south-eastwards into the impenetrable purple distance where mountains became shapeless reflections in shimmering lakes of scorched blood-red earth Sekento's mind's-eye saw an umbrella thorn tree with huge spread under which the circle of elders of his clan, of which he had been one, had debated his banishment. There was to be no redress. No compromise. Finality. The end.

But no – for Sekento not the end. His head was filled, not with regret, but with murderous planning. Ignoring the badly healed livid scar on his arm gained from Sianka's expertly wielded spear during their last encounter he knew that this was not the end of their argument. It had been announced that his brother had been betrothed to Naiyolang, a thirteen year-old virgin, the daughter of the Laibon of the Loita clan, five days by fast foot to the north at Menengai in Kenya. That spelled trouble. Sekento coveted Naiyolang. Was it not his right as the elder son of an important man to marry whom he pleased? He had sought Sianka to tell him it was not negotiable. But Sianka was a renowned expert in the lore of the spear. Sekento had come out of the meeting worse than expected. The elder brother thought there must be another way to eliminate the young upstart.

Sekento knew that if he could possess his father's staff of office, the *Okiuka*, his ambition to take over the role would be incontestable. From the early days of the Masai, the *Okiuka*, fashioned from an ebony club, contained special properties known only to its holder. But it had been lost in Nairobi some years ago at the time of heated meetings with the Kikuyu people since when the habitual enemies had lived in an uneasy peace. Over the years his clan had made efforts to find the Okiuka but all had failed. Sekento believed that it lay in the hands of the Kikuyu. But whose hands? And where? And could not the White Colonial masters have this artefact tucked away somewhere in order to weaken the independent Masai?

Now, since his fellow elders had left him destitute Sekento was more than ever determined to find the Okiuka then take over the clan, exile his father, eliminate Sianka, marry Naiyolang, and show his true strength by uniting the clans and give the white people a taste of their own medicine. With hate in his heart for all things as they were, he stood fuming while a stinging dust devil went swirling to be lost in a clump of thorn.

With these dark thoughts he stood motionless until deciding that he would make efforts in Nairobi to find the Okiuka. How he would do this he would leave until he reached the City. He would find a way. Having inherited some divining skills no doubt he could create his own luck. He decided to go northwards through the Serengeti then across the border into Kenya where he knew of a friendly clan in the Mara that would give him respite while being unaware of his plight. Picking up his shield and *rungu*, with spear at the trail, he turned his face to the north and began to travel the Masai way – a mile-eating lope on tireless legs.

*

The passenger seat of the truck was comfortable, but Della, perspiring, hands clasped showing white knuckles, far from comfortable, did not dare to put her head out of the open window to breathe moving air while half-way up the winding track of this particular old route on the eastern escarpment of the Rift Valley. Had she done so she would have seen below her feet a tyre gripping the very edge of the unstable surface and a fifteen hundred feet almost sheer drop with Peter's door close to vertical rock. One little slip and she knew they were done for. She could not close her eyes while her mind imagined the horrors that could befall her if Peter had the slightest lack of concentration. She was forced to observe the awful, if majestic rock towering above. He could sense she was under stress but continued talking quietly to himself, and she dared not interrupt his driving.

After what seemed eternity before reaching flat ground at the top of the three thousand feet escarpment they alighted. She with a prayer still on her lips stood well back from the sloping edge of the drop while breathing deeply and slowly exhaling with puffed cheeks to ease the tensions of the stomach-wrenching climb. He began flexing his fingers while bending and stretching with controlled breathing. Here the temperature had dropped ten degrees from their meeting place. But even then the plains at this altitude were denying cool air to breathe. It was hotter than Peter could remember. He gave her water and a strip of dried buffalo meat to chew while looking out on the panoramic view and to let tension slip away.

A hundred miles to the south *Ol Doinyo Lengai*, (*the house of God*) the Masai's sacred volcano that coughed up a hot ash cloud every dozen years or so, now just a silhouette through the haze, dominated a group of lesser mountains. The western scarp, some forty miles distant at this point, also hazy in the oppressive afternoon sun, looked remote and yet at times touchable such was the illusion created by shimmering air causing many mirages. In the Valley's heart Suswa volcano to the south lay squat as though to hide its lava tunnels with wall paintings done by early man. Beyond, the lakes of

Magadi and Natron were obscured but for edges of glaring white soda on Magadi, while Natron, stained red with algae, bore small terra cotta mounds which each contained a flamingo egg jutting above caustic, solidifying minerals. Longanot volcano to the north, standing proud, steeped in Masai history and legend was but a distinctive shadow with a sharp rim.

Della had heard that the Rift Valley was impressive, but this view, just a small portion, even in thick haze, left her indelibly impressed. But she kept her camera in its case expecting to get other shots during different times of the day.

"So what do you think of our Rift Valley?" Peter asked her, "Anything as big as this in Texas?"

"At least, we build good mountain roads!" she flashed at his tease. "And what would have happened if another vehicle was coming down?"

"It wouldn't. Odd days up, even days down."

"Oh." She turned to gaze at Ol Doinyo Lengai while imagining a Masai manyatta and warriors at its base. Softly and sincerely she mouthed "Truly wonderful!"

While looking at her profile, now without hat and honey/blonde hair shining gold in the sun he was thinking that after her snappy remark about the road they had just travelled perhaps she was not the typical dumb blonde as he first thought. She turned and got back into her seat.

"Do you drive?" he asked.

"Why, yes."

"Then move over." He sat in the passenger seat. "Take this road north. Keep to the left if anything comes the other way. Be careful of the storm drain. Rather them than us . . . About five miles from here you'll come to a signpost . . . turn off east for Karen . . . that's if the termites . . . haven't . . ." His head fell onto her shoulder.

'Ha! So this is to be my safari boss,' she thought. 'Gone to sleep on me now. Whatever next?' While driving and getting used to the gears, four-wheel drive selector, differential lock and heavy clutch in Peter's surprisingly quiet, well cared-for truck she realised how good a driver one must be to survive on such roads. At the sign to Karen she turned the wheel and on reaching the place that took its name from Karen Blixen the Danish writer who once farmed there she took the road to Nairobi. A heavily corrugated murram surface did not help the steering. Raising dust that followed the truck, first through golden-grassed plains, then past occasional homesteads followed by substantial European residences on either side of the road, with luck, she found herself driving through the outskirts of Nairobi on tarmac approaching the Norfolk Hotel. Here she parked and lifted his head from her shoulder.

"Hey, Mr Grant!"

After the second "Hey!" he hadn't stirred. With a mischievous grin she gave his face a 'wake-up' slap both sides as playful payment for his rudeness.

Opening his eyes and snorting, he sat up. "Mmmm? . . . Mmmm? . . . Whe . . . Where?"

"Nairobi. Norfolk Hotel." The tensions of the day had not dimmed her latent humour – a grin had changed into a look of censure for him having fallen asleep in the presence of a lady, while knowing how tired he was.

"Oh . . . well done . . . have I been asleep? . . . excuse me." He had not noticed or even felt her playfulness and got out stiffly and assisted her down. "By the way, Miss Mitchell, I have an apartment and studio in town where I do most of my developing and printing. It's a couple of blocks from here. Gulzaar Street, south side of Jeevanjee Gardens next to Abdul the Asian boot maker. After the safari I shall process your shots there as part of the deal. I'll be staying there tonight. I am too tired right now for the long drive out to the farm. Call there in the morning and I can show you around and talk through the contract."

"Jee-van-jee Gardens" she repeated. "Very well, Mr Grant, tomorrow." With that came a most engaging smile – a smile that lit up her face and made him think his day might have been alright after all. "Thank you and good evening." Giving him no time for further chat she turned to go.

Twilight descended as stewards carried in her bags. While staring at her back marked with perspiration down the spine of her shirt Peter was aware of the natural swing of her walk – even in the blocked heels of the cowboy boots.

"Now there goes a sight for sore eyes! I wish I wasn't so damned tired. But, with an attractive female tenderfoot in tow I shall be forced to find a few others to join the safari – if only to save my sanity." He did not see her frown as she entered the hotel.

Being a registered White Hunter he was obliged to follow a code of conduct. Single mixed gender safaris where intimate fraternising was possible, if not likely, were frowned upon. It was considered that when hunting on safari, especially with firearms, amorous liaisons could be more dangerous than any of the 'big five' animals. Chaperones and blameless reputations were the order of the day. These thoughts were with him as he drove the few blocks to Jeevanjee Gardens, then having parked his truck in a lock-up at the rear of his studio he let himself in and took a small lift to the top floor apartment. When guns were locked in a steel wall safe, binoculars and cameras into a cupboard, he took his boots off. Not bothering to wash or have his steward fix a meal he flung himself face down on his bed and thought of his behaviour of the day. "Not so good," he said to himself. "I think I might have been rude to her and unkind about Texas. What will she be thinking of me? I mustn't get this tired ever again. Have to apol . . ." He fell into a deep, twelve hour dreamless sleep.

\*

In her cottage suite in a towelling gown and turban after a shower to wash away the all-pervasive dust and perspiration, with her clammy clothes put aside for the *dhobi* and briefs and bra hand-washed and hanging in the bathroom, Della sat at the dressing table mirror while applying moisturiser to face, hands and arms. The lingering memory of the handshake and what passed between them had her worried if he should start making advances when on safari. "Whew. What stinker of a man!" she said to her reflection. "I am not impressed." Then thought that she would be angry if someone was the cause of spoiling her filming, 'but I don't think I'd be that grumpy. I hope he's not that sassy on a professional safari.' Then thinking out loud, "I reckon he thinks I'm the typical American dumb blonde. Well, let him think it. I might then get from him what I really want."

While sitting on the bed and leafing through briefing notes she took from her notebook a folded piece of typewritten paper. She had not been honest with Peter. What she unfolded was the second, most important part of her quest – the major reason why she had come to Kenya. It read:

*Find White Hunter Peter Grant – best shooter and cameraman there I am told – who may be one of a coterie of hunters believed to be licensed to arrest poachers. Is he one? Do not let your holiday article get in the way of your main brief to discover all you can re poaching but be discreet. Your report should hit hard to back up conservationist hotheads here. Uncover all you can. Include ringleaders. Get names – the bigger the better – No one would suspect a girl if you play it right. I rely on you. But be very careful. A lot is hanging on a good punchy story. Liaise with 'you know who' at the Embassy. ED.*

Not wanting such information to fall into the wrong hands she put the note on the fire in the hearth that had been lit to ward off the evening chill at Nairobi's altitude of five and a half thousand feet above sea level.

That she found Peter at her first attempt was a bonus. What she found was a tired, scruffy, sweaty, unshaven, irascible man of about her own age. But she was given the brief and had to contemplate asking Peter for help on the problem although was not quite sure of her editor's wording on the note – "*Is he one?*" Was Peter a privileged hunter or a member of a poaching syndicate? Perhaps the latter? That would be a disaster! Was this why he hesitated at first to take me out? Was he really truthful about there being a cheetah in the bush where he had been disturbed or was he looking for elephants? Was he really filming or was he discovered about to poach? She had found him in a remote part of the Rift Valley where no habitation could be seen. There were guns in his truck and he used binoculars and a long focal length lens on his camera. Was it guilt that made him so angry for so long? If this was the case then he had fooled her utterly. On the other hand she had heard that white people in Africa became deeply frustrated and emotional when rain was late or had failed – or was that an old wives' tale? Was it because he was so tired? Not wanting to think about it any more she dressed for dinner, but the possibility of Peter being a poacher for profit would not leave her.

The last thing she did that night while hugging a pillow in her bed and before sleeping was to chuckle at having slapped his face.

\*

In the dark recesses of a Masai hut, lit only by a small fire that made a smoke ceiling under bent branches packed with mud and dung, Sekento sat on a small stool drinking while in conversation with six other Masai of a clan just north of the border into Kenya's Mara. In the low flicker of firelight their faces looked as sinister as the subject on which they dwelt: "Would the six moran in this group join him to form a small armed band to find his brother, Sianka?" Their reward would be power dispensed by him when he had enough support eventually to usurp his father.

"But is not Olekowlish, your father a great man?"

"He is past his time. He is impotent and not worthy of his office," he lied. "He has weakened over the years, He is called a great man by those who do not know," saying nothing of his own shame on having been banished and of the impending attempt to find the Okiuka.

They were awash with strong drink made from a fermentation of maize and honey prepared by the clan's women. This gave them the careless courage to agree to his plans and now they were discussing the finer details of where they would look for Sianka and what to do when they found him. It would be easier with seven looking instead of just one.

"We must not speak of this when abroad," ordered Sekento. "Word of our intentions can travel faster than our feet can carry us." Discussion was abandoned when females of the clan brought more drink. Diversions were now in order. At sunrise the women left having given their carnal blessings to the men's murderous mission.

# 3.

Does the palm of the hand confuse the fingers?
*(Substitutes are sometimes acceptable)*

Away from the noise and bustle of a waking Nairobi, a much revived Peter was bathed, clean shaven, dressed, groomed and breakfasted. His eyes were clear with no sign of yesterday's tiredness. After choosing lens filters to add to his equipment for Della's safari he went to pick up the telephone in a kitchenette cum-office-cum-utility room to ring the Maitre-d at the New Stanley hotel who would have a list of potential clients to recommend for a small commission. Before he could make the call it began ringing. The caller spoke expansively.

"Ah, Mr Grant. This is Arap Kamau. Would you come to my office and photograph me in my new robes? I am President of the newly formed National Printers Association and one or two other things. I could do with a portrait to dress up the boardroom and you are highly recommended."

"I am about to set out on safari. I could fit you in, say, two week's time."

"I am told you can do these things quickly for those with influence."

Peter knew of Arap Kamau, an educated Kikuyu with fingers in many pies, and saw cash coming his way. "I'll do it as a special favour for you Mr Kamau, this morning. My fee to be paid up front and I'll deliver the finished framed portrait, twenty-four inches by thirty, tomorrow morning."

Kamau hesitated for a few seconds. "Discount for cash?"

". . . Of course."

"I have my robes here at the office. Eleven o'clock is my best time."

"Eleven o'clock? . . . fine. I believe your offices are at the printing works in Racecourse Road?"

"Yes. The first floor."

"Right. I shall be there and set up before eleven. We should be through by twelve and can seal the deal over lunch at the New Stanley Grill if that suits you." Although ingratiating it was Peter's way of getting referrals.

"I knew I could rely on you Mr Grant."

"Eleven o'clock then,"

As he hung up Della came through the front door. "Hello! Anyone there?"

"In the Studio on the right," he called. "Take a pew. I'll bring coffee."

She stepped into a large studio and looked around at the standing and suspended lights and rolled backdrops. Mounted on a wall a framed, panoramic picture of a young cheetah with Mount Kilimanjaro in the background took her eye. The studio exuded comfort and a relaxing atmosphere. With tongue in cheek she draped herself on a prop Victorian *chaise longue*, just crying out for a pose under an aspidistra on a pedestal before a bookcase backdrop.

He came in smiling carrying a jug and mugs on a tray.

"Cream or . . .?" He did a double take. Looking cool she was sitting up wearing a knee-length full khaki skirt, knees crossed wearing calf-length chamois boots, belted bush jacket over a cream shirt, a coffee bean necklace and a cheetah spotted bandana to hold her flowing hair. An arm was draped with fingers casually on her cheek A complete change from her yesterday's image.

"Hold it! Don't move!" He quickly picked up a camera from a cupboard, inserted a slide back, turned on one floodlight and from an angle looked through the viewfinder.

"May I?" he said, and adjusted the set of her head slightly to capture her singular features – good skin, refinement and sophistication with subtle make-up. 'A photographer's dream' he thought. Then after adjusting the camera's aperture he inserted a soft filter. He sighted again. "A bit more energy up your spine to your eyes . . . good . . . straighten your index finger . . . Look straight ahead . . . not at the camera . . . Think of home." Her face changed. The shutter winked. Peter smiled. He had not photographed a face like Della's for as long as he could remember.

"I'd like a copy of that," she said, standing. "Why straighten my finger?"

"You don't want to look as though you are scratching your lovely face, do you?"

'Hmmm,' she thought; 'early morning compliments! Is he sincere?' . . . "Just a dash of cream please." She took a sip while being impressed by his cleanliness, demeanour and sartorial change into what she thought was rather English; blue business shirt, plain yellow silk crocheted tie, twill trousers, polished brogues and tailored barathea jacket. "You make excellent coffee,"

"Thank you," he said, obviously more than just impressed with her ensemble. "I make a few different kinds. Keeping awake; after dinner; this is for mornings. It comes with a sincere apology for being ratty and rude to you and Texas yesterday. I take everything back. I hope I didn't swear? I know it is somewhat late to say so, but welcome to Kenya. I hope your stay here is a worthwhile and pleasant one. Biscuit?"

"Thank you," she said with a wry smile while choosing a plain Bath Oliver. "You damned me to hell a few times, but now I understand why, having seen that lovely painting of the cheetah. I accept your apology. I hope you'll accept mine for interrupting you."

"Yes," he said smiling while she continued. "She's pretty. So appealing. Would it be Bili? The artist has caught her just right."

"Yes. Bili. The artist was my camera."

"Not an oil?" she said, surprised.

"No. Just a bit of dodging and filling here and there when processing with the odd filter to get the effect. One of these days we'll find a way of mounting the finished emulsion actually on canvas. Then it should have a more authentic surface."

"I must get to know the technique. Shall you look for Bili again?"

"Oh, yes."

After another sip of coffee she said, "I have changed the Dollars for East African currency. I mentioned your name at the desk and the chatty redhead girl there gave me a good rate and taking just a nominal commission."

"The girl married to an airline pilot?" he asked.

"There was a framed picture of a man in uniform on her desk. I suppose, yes."

"Ah, good for Susie," he said remembering a bygone fling. "Come and see the darkroom. I suppose you had all the latest mod cons with your Air Force. Getting any kind of equipment here is difficult. Did you fly with them?"

"Yes. I clocked up about a hundred hours," she said while admiring equipment he had made himself.

Both now were chatting comfortably while carrying their coffee mugs. Then, when back in the studio explaining lighting to her she said, "I've bought extra packets of film with faster emulsion than for portraits to fit my hand-held camera. I'm all set to go."

"Er . . . I have a business meeting crop up this morning which goes on into lunch. I am sorry I can't ask you to join me." She showed disappointment. "Then I have to dash out to the farm to burn the midnight oil to tie up loose ends before the rain – we should be so lucky! – and then I shall arrange for a few others to join the safari."

"Oh? . . ."

"It's the done thing. We professionals have rules. I'm sure you understand why. I shall find company for you. But it will not interfere with what you have to do for your article. You shall have precedence in all journalistic and photographic opportunities."

"Er . . . yes. Of course."

"I did say I had one or two things to do, and I can see you are champing at the bit. Eager to go out. Shan't be more than a day. You don't mind?"

"I hope you are not putting me off!"

"Good Lord, no. I am eager too. There is nothing serious I can do at the farm without rain. But I must tie up loose ends with my manager and staff before a safari. Might I recommend a few places to go if you are kicking your heels for a bit?"

"I think I could find my own entertainment . . . thank you."

The genial atmosphere between them when first in the studio had slipped down a peg.

" . . . Would you like to read the contract?"

"Shouldn't you be off to your business meeting? We could look at it and discuss money when you are ready."

"Er . . . Yes . . . I shall contact you at the Norfolk hotel."

"I think that is best . . . thank you for the delicious coffee."

He looked her in the eye for some moments as though he wanted something mended before parting, but not offering her hand she turned and went out of the building.

While walking off to do some window shopping Della began to think that a transformed Peter was quite personable and lacked the offensiveness that must have been due to tiredness and her noisy arrival. And then was reminded of the handshake. 'I've heard of these big game hunters,' she said to herself. 'Perhaps he's just another white hunter wanting to add an American blonde girl to his list of conquests. It's a good thing he's getting others to join the safari, but watch it Della.' She made for her Embassy to liaise with 'you know who' and to ask for introductions and ideas of what to do while kicking her heels.

Peter busied himself with loading equipment for the portrait shoot into his Chevy Station Wagon he used in town, "Della's a bit of alright. But I expect she's just another American blonde with an eye to the main chance. A cut above the ordinary though. I think she's playing it cool right now. So watch it, Peter."

\*

Arap Kamau's office had been recently decorated and had European style furniture standing about including a glass cabinet behind his desk. When arranging Kamau's first pose sitting at his desk Peter noticed a polished ebony staff about twenty inches long with a black jewel set at one end lying on a stand in the cabinet with assorted Kikuyu paraphernalia. He had a slight frisson. His mind flashed back twenty years to when he was a tow-headed boy of six on safari with his father and allowed to play with a Masai boy called Sekento, the son of Olekowlish, the Masai's Chief Counsellor. Peter's father, George Grant had friendly dealings with Olekowlish negotiating hunting areas with him. Both boys became close friends and even at that age were allowed to go out on foot with the warriors on lion hunts. But crucially he remembered that Olekowlish always carried the Okiuka, his staff of office. Surely this was the Okiuka that was lost a few years ago? He remembered the look of it and knew of his father's closeness to the Masai and the research he carried out into the Masai's colourful history. The Kikuyu witchdoctors did not have that kind of thing in their armoury. Most wielded a carved fly whisk. He noticed a small key in the cabinet lock.

After the session Kamau, having the aura of success about him showed him around his business. Peter then had an outrageous idea. He took mental note of the layout of the interior with the presses on the ground floor leading out into a walled yard bordering the sidewalk in which was a wooden door. There was no sign of an alarm system.

At lunch, during which Peter said nothing of the discovery of what he believed to be the Okiuka, Kamau regaled him with how he had clawed his way from one of Nairobi's shanty-towns to become what he was with fingers in many pies with an eye to politics. Money changed hands as Kamau said he trusted Peter to choose the best shot to show off his robes and to make him look handsome.

Peter was thinking that apart from the cash in hand a lunch with Della would have been infinitely more preferable. Della was having the same thoughts with brought in sandwiches, and talking shop with her contact in his office at the Embassy.

On his way back to the studio Peter thought more of Olekowlish and how, without his Okiuka, he would be near impotent in his spiritual dealings. With it he would have full power and the workings of mystery at his fingertips, and more immediately useful, if and when to call upon his powers to attempt to make rain. With it in his hands his exceptional insight to matters beyond the ken of ordinary mortals would be unassailable and superior to that of a Kikuyu witchdoctor; but without it . . .? He sucked his teeth and thought that the article in question ought to be with Olekowlish; not languishing in the office cabinet of a Kikuyu. "Now where can I get a replica made?" he mused. "Ah, yes. I know the very man."

Back at the studio rummaging in a tea chest in the storeroom to find three of his late father's old handwritten research journals he chose the first of the three in which most of the Masai legends were recorded. On finding the legend of the first Laibon – a five-year-old boy who found water during difficult times and was made the first ever Laibon on becoming of age – he discovered a loose page with drawings. In the centre was an ink sketch of the Okiuka with the dimensions written alongside. Underneath, in his father's handwriting was:

*"One is reliably informed that when the five-year-old boy became the first Laibon the Okiuka was fashioned from an ebony club and was carried by him for many years and handed down to those who respected its properties. In properly ordained Masai hands the Okiuka has workings of mystery. In perverse unordained hands – its potential could invert and become <u>very</u> dangerous. I do not myself fully understand it. Its power and spirituality lie not only in the staff itself but also in the beliefs of those that use it, or indeed, those that abuse it."*

"It's identical! I swear that one in Kamau's cabinet is the original! I've not known any Kikuyu carry a thing like that. Masai, yes. Kikuyu? no," he said to himself. Then from a box of dozens of assorted labelled keys he selected two skeleton keys his father had made for emergencies or lost keys; one for padlocks and another for mortise locks. For the first time in his life, much against his conscience he was intending to steal. But then he shrugged his shoulders and decided it would not be stealing. It would be a matter of returning something to the rightful owner.

While processing and printing the proofs of Kamau's portrait and choosing the best pose for the large final print he planned how he would obtain the staff and have a replica made. More processing followed and he hung the final large print to dry. On looking at his watch he saw it was seven pm. In his top floor apartment he changed into dark clothes and soft desert boots, made a flask of coffee and put small binoculars in his pocket.

He drove to Racecourse Road where, opposite Kamau's printing godown he parked in the rear of a small down-market rooming house, owned by a South African ex-railway worker, and paid a few shillings for a room overlooking the road. In the room he turned out the light and looked across to where a watchman had lit a brazier in the recess of Kamau's front entrance and sat on a stool behind it. This was the only light in a dark road.

Peter saw the watchman nodding. He left the rooming house, crept across the road and with a skeleton key opened the padlock of the door in the wall behind which, the yard had bins overflowing with paper from the printing presses, making a heap between two bins. He stood on a bin with a secured lid, leaned over the wall and reset the padlock. Another padlock securing double doors, when opened quietly, led him into the presses. He went up metal stairs and removed his boots in case he had picked up ink on them and padded in his socks to Kamau's office. The mortise lock opened stiffly. The cabinet opened easily. Shining a tiny-beamed torch onto the Okiuka he lifted it from the stand. He could have sworn the black gem at its end winked its approval. Locking the door of the office on his way out he descended the stairs with his boots on, went through and out of the pressroom and secured the padlock. Instead of leaning over the eight-feet-high wall to unlock the door he made sure that all was clear and lowered himself down onto the sidewalk and sped across the dark road to the rooming house.

He drove out to a suburb of Nairobi near the RAF airport where Asian houses and small businesses were spread among trees. Here, he sought Rajat Singh who had made furniture for the Kenya Regiment Officers mess when Peter had been a Subaltern there during the war. It was here another idea came to him. He would have two replicas made. One for Kamau's cabinet and one for himself to join the Masai memorabilia and regalia he had at the farm.

In the workshop Rajat and he exchanged a few reminiscences before Peter said, "Mr.Singh. I want two exact copies of this ebony baton. Can do?"

"Oh dear, Mr Grant Sa'b. Ebony is expensive. Very hard to come by isn't it."

"Oh, come on Rajat. Do your best for old time's sake?"

Rajat went to a stack of various woods at one end of the shed and brought back a rectangular piece of ebony he had put by for a possible occasional table. "This is all I have Sa'b. Rather expensive. I will have to cut two lengths and charge you for the whole piece."

"Well . . . we'll see. Now here's what I want you to do. Make two copies of this ebony baton down to the last minute detail including the gem. I trust you have some black Perspex to copy it?"

"Yes I have jet black, clear, red and green from the RAF surplus. What is this thing and why would you want two copies?"

"All three are for an urgent photographic job. This original you see has an elastic band to identify it. If you can start on them now I'll call back for one of them at twelve thirty tonight and the second one in the late morning and pay you cash. Is that okay?" They bargained until a price was agreed and shook hands on a deal.

Back in his apartment Peter dressed in black tie and tuxedo and drove to the exclusive Equator Club, signed in and saw friends on the dance floor for their usual weekly wining, dining and dancing and went to their table with a bottle of wine. As they returned to their table Peter asked, "May I join you Amelia? I want a word with Reggie when you go to powder your nose."

"As it so happens," she said, "that's just where I was going." At that she got up and made her way to the ladies room. When she had left, he and Reggie sat.

"So what's the latest Peter?"

"Have you been invited to the District Commissioner's house party tomorrow night?" Reggie nodded. "Good. I have a brilliant idea for a dress rehearsal for our double act for the Nairobi City Players' Cabaret."

Five minutes went by before Amelia returned to the table. "Have you two finished nattering? Someone here I'd like you to meet. Found her at the mirror and said she'd like to meet a hunter. I said she couldn't do better than meet the best."

While Amelia was talking Peter looked at the girl standing almost shyly; looking vulnerable yet sophisticated, holding a small, black vanity bag, shortened, thick shining honey-blonde hair; subtle make-up and smiling blue eyes; a short black evening dress accentuating a slim feminine figure; sheer black silk stockings on long legs with high heeled black satin court shoes. He blinked and kept staring.

"Hey, Peter. Don't just stand there gawping. Let me present . . ."

"Della?" he breathed. "How? . . . How on earth . . . ?"

"I say, you two, you haven't met already?" They both nodded. "Well. There's a turn up for the books." She turned to Reggie and said, "Meet Della Mitchell from Texas." To Della she said, "You can't have Reggie, he's mine. Best dancer in East Africa." She grabbed Reggie's hand and led him to the dance floor saying "Better leave them to it if they know each other. Thought I'd made a coup there. Peter can do with a nice girl since that redhead Susan left him for a pilot."

Della and Peter stood for some moments before he pulled himself together and held a chair for her. Under low, amber, romantic lighting he poured wine and they both started talking at once. They stopped and laughed.

"As Amelia said – there's a turn up for the books. Miss Mitchell, you – are – a knockout!"

"Well now, Mr.Grant. You've noticed. What does a girl have to do out here?"

"In your case, absolutely nothing at all . . . Love your hair. So. Why are you slumming it in Nairobi's five-star gutters?"

"Someone at my Embassy made a telephone call and has gotten me temporary membership. What are you doing here? I thought you were tying loose ends at your farm."

"Yes, I should be there now but something's cropped up. I popped in to have a word with Reggie."

"Must be very important."

"As a matter of fact, it is."

"Do I detect a trifle side-stepping here?" she said over-sweetly. "Do you find that burning midnight oil in a nightclub will tie up loose ends at a farm?"

"Touché, Miss Mitchell." He detected ice in her voice. "I find this music is putting honest answers in my feet and not in my mouth. I think we should try side-stepping on the floor." He grasped her hand and swung her past a table onto the sprung floor. "Miss Mitchell, on the dance floor my name is Peter. I believe yours is Della?"

Suddenly she laughed and began to jive to the African band playing an up-beat tune from an American musical film. He followed as best he could and at the end of the number when the music changed to a smoochy blues and the lights dimmed he held her close and they began to move as one. He enjoyed the sensuous merging of bodies but she held off a little until he whispered through thick, silky hair, "Della the delectable dancer."

"Well, now, Peter. You could show some of our root-beer swilling oil riggers a cute pair of pumps."

The way she said it sounded lyrical. He nuzzled her ear and said quietly, "I know a giraffe that would kill for those eyelashes of yours."

"Mmmmm," she murmured and fluttered them on his cheek.

He was about to say something else endearing when suddenly he thought of what he had to do. The spell was broken but his hold on her did not change. Her lithe body was doing things to him. Reluctantly he guided her back to the table. She had noticed the change in him and looked at him in a new light.

"Well, Peter," she cooed, "that was some dance! . . . I wish it could have gone on." Still holding her hand he said, "I too . . . Oh, hell. I . . . I – can't stay, I have a few things to do."

"Do? At this time of night? All done up like a dog's dinner and you have 'things to do'?"

"Yes. Really. I wish, at this moment I wasn't caught up in this something. It is . . . cutting across everything. I am sure it will resolve itself over this weekend. It should be clear by Monday."

"It sounds as though you are trying to put me off," she said sadly. "Should I find another hunter? I have deadlines, you know."

"No. Please. I am serious and looking forward to a good safari."

The music stopped, lights went up and Amelia and Reggie came sweeping back to the table and found them in earnest conversation.

"I shall seek you at the Norfolk on Monday," he said squeezing her hand. "Would you folks excuse me?" he asked. Then quietly to Reggie, "Tomorrow at my place?"

He was about to leave when a broad Southern Irish voice said "Hello there, Peter m'boy. I haven't seen you for months. I haven't had a chance to thank you for that safari you put my way. And who's this gorgeous filly?"

"This is Miss Mitchell from the States."

"Hello. I'm Patrick O'Brien. Pat to you."

She nodded as he took it upon himself to sit at the table with a full glass of Irish whiskey. Della could see that he was drunk.

"I say, Peter, m'boy, you know, you did me a very good turn by putting me in the way of that safari. We bagged all the big five including a buff with the biggest spread since that one of two years ago. Client was very happy along with my bank manager. I can't thank you enough."

"That's okay, Pat. I was busy up at Kinangop. Any time."

"Sure. I'll do the same for you one day. Just let me know. I owe you. I'd do anything for you. Just let me know," he said effusively while raising his elbow. He wore his Irish charm on his sleeve when he was drunk. This charm and drink had cost him two marriages and six children, all back in England away from the harshness of his life in the bush and his womanising. He turned to Della.

"Miss Mitchell, you have a fist name? mine's Pat."

"Yes – Della."

"You want to watch this young man y'know. He'll get you out on safari before you can blink an eye. Now, as for safaris, I happen to be popping out in a day or so, would you be interested now?" he asked, lifting his glass again. But then to Peter, "Don't forget, m'boy, say the word and I'll do anything for you. Anything."

"You're a good sort, Pat." Peter then turned to Della and spoke quietly close to her ear. "I must go. Urgent things to do. So sorry. Monday." He squeezed her hand again, let it slip and left the table. Pat's voice followed him. "Going so soon m'boy? lots of time." Della stared at the space Peter had left and wished that he wasn't so cagey about what he was doing.

While the strains of honey-sweet music from the small stage and an internationally known singing voice drifted down the stairs of the club after him Peter now thought of Della as anything but a dumb blonde. But in any case he could not right now take a journalist into his confidence.

"I didn't know you'd met Peter," said Amelia. "Pat's a hunter too. You'll want to talk." She steered Reggie to the floor again and left her with Pat.

With difficulty Della snapped out of staring after Peter for she had thought that this chance meeting would have helped to get to know him better before embarking on a safari. He was so different from her first impression. And what was this 'things to do?'

"Will y'have a drink, now?" came Pat's voice again. "What'll y'have?" He turned to call a waiter.

"No thanks. No, really. I have some here." She picked up her glass of wine and sipped at it. She was not keen on heavy drinkers, but looking at him again she began to think. Was he a hunter who had licence to arrest poachers? But even if he was she did not relish the thought of spending the remaining hours of the night in the club then breakfast there with a drunk.

*

Rajat Singh was as good as his word and was finally polishing the Perspex 'jewel' in the first replica when Peter arrived at half-past-midnight.

"There you are, Mr.Grant sah'b. Simply exact same size and copy, isn't it."

Holding them one by one Peter discovered that the replica was 'cold' whereas the original had a certain feeling he could not describe. He gave Rajat some of Kamau's folding money for the copy staff and said he would call late morning for the other.

*

From the rooming house window in the early hours Peter looked out and saw the askari talking to other watchmen warming themselves around his brazier. After a frustrating hour of pacing the room Peter saw the visiting watchmen leave and the askari settled down again. Now with a replica baton he slipped across the road, followed the same routine as before, went into the godown and put the baton on the supports and locked the cabinet. He heard a bus go past and when in the yard heard the watchman unlocking the padlock on the sidewalk gate. He dived into a pile of waste paper between two bins and covered himself with a poster, just in time as the watchman opened the door and shone his torch that flashed across the poster missing his feet by a hair's breadth. The watchman went out and secured the padlock. Peter stood and climbed onto a bin near the door, looked over the wall to see that the coast was clear with the askari disappearing into the front entrance. He dropped quietly over the eight-foot wall and sped across the dirt road back to the rooming house for his car.

That morning, Saturday, he delivered Arap Kamau's portrait in an ormolu frame. Arap was delighted with it. The replica Okiuka, nestling on its stand in the cabinet looked no different from the original.

When leaving Racecourse Road, Peter offered up a prayer of thanks then drove out to Rajat Sing who was ready with the second replica. Peter gave him the balance of cash agreed from Kamau's bundle, chatted for a few minutes about times gone past and started back to his studio. Now with the original rolled in brown paper and the second replica both tucked under the rear seat he was blithely confident that all was going well with his plans.

# 4.

Daylight follows a dark night.
*(Fortunes change)*

Two tall Masai moran, bodies glowing under a bright moon and a myriad stars, strode across dry grass. Their hair, matted with ochred mud and goat grease was knotted into a peak with beads in the centre of their foreheads above straight noses. Other strands with plaited beads hung down the napes of their necks. Dyes streaked their faces. Patterned blankets, worn toga-style, swung to their step. Feathers decorated arms and legs and each carried a spear and rungu. One had legs zigzagged in blue and white and carried his staff of office secured through a leather thong around his waist to denote his status as Chief Counsellor and Laibon. They approached the light of amber lamps strung up in trees surrounding the lawn of a sprawling colonial house.

On the manicured but yellowing lawn and wooden veranda of the spacious residence European ladies and men in black and white evening wear stood around laughing, plotting intrigues and planning business deals making up a group of professional Colonials and their wives and girlfriends to welcome an obscure official just arrived in Kenya to take up an obscure post.

While the party was gathering momentum a gong was beaten to announce food. Jostling at a long table in the hall of the house they piled food on to crested plates and collected napkins and forks. Carrying drinks, and with feats of balancing born of much practice at similar parties up and down the Colony, they stood about the lawn and veranda steps eating, drinking and chatting. Occasionally, with fork in hand, lazily they would wave away mosquitoes and flying ants that broke away from the clusters of airborne insects crowding the lights. Silk and lace stoles protected bare shoulders while waving forks protected many exotic foods, some made locally and some flown that day up from the coast in refrigerated boxes; the usual fare at Kenya soirées.

The two Masai appeared on the lawn in their midst. Chatting, laughing and joking stopped. Groups froze and went into tableaux as if a movie had stuck on one frame. But for the primitive songs of cicadas on the night air competing with a 78rpm wax disk of 'The Arcadians' on a wind-up gramophone there was silence.

The District Commissioner, host to the party, halfway up the veranda steps with a champagne bottle, stopped in his tracks then turned to see the two warriors advancing up the lawn. They strode through the assembly looking neither left nor right. Reaching the base of the steps, with sandalled feet set firmly, they raised their spears stiletto ends foremost and flung them to thud at the feet of the host. Both Masai thrust noses forward and challenged loudly in one voice – "SOBA!"

At that point the music came to its conclusion with thorn needle continuing a rhythmical scratching for what seemed like minutes until an unseen hand lifted off the sound box. There was a moment of silence during which two men disappeared into the house to appear a moment later with a pistol and a shotgun as the buzz of surprise now spread among the guests.

The Masai held their ground while the D.C., with easy composure and cultured voice, spoke in impeccable Kiswahili a long phrase that should have meant:

"Good evening gentlemen. You are well met. Was there something . . .?"

Those who spoke Kiswahili well knew precisely what was said. It was subtly impolite. The two armed Europeans came forward and took up positions either side of him. The smaller of the two men, Herbert Smith, District Auditor, carried a Luger pistol in a nervous hand, and the other, Pat O'Brien, held a loaded shotgun.

In protracted silence the Masai and the D.C. stood their ground, but then Smith blurted out, "Look here, sir, shall we take them in?"

"Take them in be-Jases" said Pat with his face breaking into a broad likeable grin. "Let me blow them to Kingdom Come."

The host moved a hand to quell the talk, then stared straight into the eyes of the two warriors. Each looked back at him with an unblinking defiant gaze. He moved forward between the upright spears not taking his eyes off theirs. Descending the final step he moved right up to them and put his face close to each in turn. One Masai seemed to develop a slight twitch on his face. The D.Cs face twitched in turn and broke into a tight smile while the warriors gritted their teeth. Then, as one, all three burst into laughter. The host rocked on his heels and sat on the steps. The 'Masai' flung their hands in the air and collapsed laughing in a heap. In front of the amazed guests the D.C., between gulps of laughter, said "You silly bastards. You mad fools!"

The two 'warriors', now almost helpless, lifted their wigs, showing European hair contrasting against a line of make-up. At once the tension broke. Some guests, including the wife of one of the actors came running forward to greet them with cries of "Reggie! . . . Peter!" From the now crowded veranda someone with a loud, drink-sodden voice said, "Who the bloody hell are they?"

Pat came down the steps. "Peter? Is that you? Well, now. There's a thing. Damned clever make-up. I didn't recognise you. I nearly gave you both barrels!"

*

The party was now in full swing about the house and grounds. An impromptu pounding on a Grand piano in the music room accompanied some risqué ballads and rugger songs while outside an occasional whoop and splash told of yet another fully clothed guest having a sobering swim in a floodlit pool. But not taking part in the festivities, four men sat sipping drinks around an almost bare desk in a large office in the house.

The two men who had livened-up the party by appearing as warriors were showered and removed of elaborate make-up. Reggie had joined his wife who played the piano for the revellers, while Peter, in white tuxedo, sat at the desk on which rested the Okiuka – the Ceremonial Staff of Office of Olekowlish of the Ilaiser Clan, the Senior Counsellor and Laibon of Masai.

Sitting around the table were the District Commissioner, O'Brien the hunter, and Smith the auditor. But standing, staring first at the baton in disbelief then at Peter was the imposing rotund figure of the Colony's Governor, Sir Rupert Stafford. He spoke.

"I'll ask you again, and for the final time, Mr.Grant, how in God's name did you come by this? I saw it when you were play-acting . . . damned fool! Spears at a party. Whatever next. Answer me young man. Where did you come by this? It has been missing for years. Come, man, answer me!"

"It fell off the back of a rickshaw," said Peter casually, showing disappointment at having it revealed to the Colony's Governor who obviously knew what it was.

"Rickshaw my sainted aunt! Do not joke with me, young man. I am Governor here and don't you forget it. Where did this come from? How long have you had it? How is it you have it?"

"Just a day or so," he said honestly. "But that's my story. I brought it here to be authentically dressed. It was a dress rehearsal for a charity show."

Sir Rupert nearly exploded. "Damned fool! If it wasn't so sensitive I'd have you locked up for this. It is Government property and will go into security first thing."

"This is not Government property." Peter said with spirit. "It belongs to the Masai and I am taking it back to them!"

"No you are damned-well not! Don't be impertinent Mr.Grant . . . Frederick," he said to the DC, "Lock-up this Okiuka. I don't want a sniff of it outside these four walls. We've been looking for it for too long. The Masai can go hang."

"But Sir Rupert!" protested Peter, rising out of his seat.

"But nothing, young man. Do it, Frederick."

The DC locked the Okiuka in a wall gun case. The Governor made to go and all rose except Peter who sat. He showed grave disappointment on his face.

"I shall be off now," said Sir Rupert. "Damned fortunate to have just called in to make my number with the new ADC and catch sight of this thing. I shall be flying to Tanganyika at sunrise to see the Governor at Dodoma. Make sure it gets to Government House before then, Frederick. Get it there yourself and make sure no one gets to hear of it. All here are sworn to secrecy. You are to keep your lips buttoned. If I hear anything to the contrary I'll have the hide off the culprit, and I am not joking." He turned at the door and looked at Peter. "You farmers are the absolute damned end. Bolshie lot, most of you. Play-acting with spears and Government property indeed!"

Peter stood smartly. "Sir Rupert, that is not Government property. Bolshie farmer or not, I am a Kenyan. I was born here. I shall be here for the rest of my life. I am not a visitor or just a resident for a few years and then back to cosy old England and a fat pension. I do what I can for Kenya. Not for Civil Service promotion and a Peerage!"

The Governor was stunned. He looked as though he would explode. But a trained diplomat, suddenly he smiled. "That's what I said. Bolshie." To the DC he said, "I shall see you at Government House before six. Frederick – with that Okiuka." He left the room.

As the DC closed the door after Kenya's appointed Governor he said, "If I didn't know better, Mr.Grant, I'd be inclined to agree with Sir Rupert."

"But I was to have taken that Okiuka back to the Masai tomorrow."

"No can do. The Governor is right. The Colonial Office gave instructions last year, that if was found, we were to have it. You are not a politician. Keep your nose out of it. Stick to your farming and your photographs. End of subject. Now, let's get back to what we were discussing half-an-hour ago. You, Mr.Grant, I want you to go to Elmolo Bay at Lake Rudolph to do those photographs; and Mr O'Brien, I want you to go and sort out those poachers below the Mara just over the border. The Tanganyika Game Department there haven't the men to spare."

"District Commissioner," said Peter angrily, "I didn't come to this party just to have that Okiuka stolen from me; or to have to go all the way up to the NFD to take a few photographs while my farm needs urgent attention. I'll get back to Kinangop if you don't mind. I am not in your jurisdiction up there."

"Mr.Grant," the DC said warmly, trying to defuse Peter, "you, as we all know, are possibly the finest photographer we have. Very important human remains have been found south of Elmolo Bay and we need the photographs before the press get wind of the location. You, a Kenyan, would be doing your country a valuable service . . . Go this morning, early." He looked at his watch – "Discretely. Do this for us and we'll be indebted."

"You certainly will! You owe me for purloining that Okiuka!" He pondered . . . he could see more money coming his way. "I'll do it –

for double the fee – up front – plus mileage. There and back is about five hundred."

"And don't forget me, Commissioner," cut in Pat. "I have to go up and recce the Ndoto Hills for a client. I can't go to Tanganyika just now."

On hearing 'Ndoto Hills' Smith looked up, coughed and his face twitched. "Catching those poachers in the south, Mr.O'Brien is more important than a mere recce up in the Ndoto Hills. Your licence puts you on call when not actually on safari with clients. I believe your client is not in the country yet."

"Nor he isn't b'jiggers. Well now . . . I'll tell you what, Herbie," – the auditor winced. He hated being called that – not even Herbert by someone he thought to be his inferior, or who was not a civil servant. Pat smiled. "I'll tell you what. I'll do it – for double the fee."

Smith thought swiftly, looked at the DC and nodded his head. Frederick raised an eyebrow. "Are you sure, Smith? Double fees? Plus mileage? Both of them?"

"It is within the contingency budget."

"Very well." He turned to the two hunters. "I do believe you two are a couple of con artists. I'll allow it just this once – if only to get you both out of my hair and get these jobs done. Write the cheques Mr.Smith."

"Make mine payable cash," said Peter. "Write what you like on the counterfoil."

Although he was most meticulous when auditing official accounts, for reasons best known to himself Smith did not hesitate to write two cash cheques and passed them to the DC for his counter-signature.

The meeting now over Peter put his cheque in a zipped leather wallet while he and Pat went to the rear of the Residency to the compound where Pat kept his safari vehicles and where Peter's car was parked before the 'play-acting'. Peter was grinning from ear to ear and softly laughing.

"So what's the joke, Peter? There's nothing to laugh at. Why did you allow them to take that thing from you? Where did you get it anyway?"

"Pat, you wouldn't believe it if I told you. But I will tell you this . . . at sunrise this morning our charming Governor will be the proud possessor of a useless lump of wood! I'd love to see his smug face boasting to the Colonial Office that he has the Okiuka. That one is a replica I had made. The original is here in my car! I didn't expect Stafford to be at the party, but he was so stroppy I put on an act and let him believe it was the real thing."

"Some act!" said Pat. "That's twice you fooled me."

"Now I can get it down to Olekowlish. It's he that needs it – not some Colonial official to play politics with"

"For Christ's sake! That's a hot potato you're playing with." Pat said laughing. "I hope for your sake no one ever finds out."

"Ah, but you see, I am a Kenyan. I was born here. I do what I can for Kenya. Not a stiff Englishman who thinks he owns the place while living in that monstrosity of Government House."

Both of them were laughing when Peter reached his car. Pat said, "But wait, you can't go to Tanganyika right now when you're off to El Molo Bay"

"Oh, shit! I was so happy to have fooled Sir Rupert I forgot. Now I shan't be able get down to Wemberi to give it to Olekowlish for some time. I am supposed to start a photo safari on Monday . . . too much to do."

"Do you remember what I said at the Equator club? I'd do anything for you since that safari you put my way? Well I believe that particular bunch of poachers are operating between Wemberi and the border. Why don't I take it for you? I have a rough idea where Olekowlish has his manyatta."

"But that's out of your way. I couldn't lumber you with that."

"If you remember we both have a double fee. It's really no problem."

"I don't know. I had so wanted to talk to him. Did you know I used to be close to him and his elder son? My father let me loose sometimes to play with Sekento when we were nippers and in the area."

"I've never actually come across any of them. I've heard of them though. Who hasn't? Let me do it for you. I owe you. Then both of us could kill two birds with one stone and you could get your photographs – and your safari."

"Pat, we've been colleagues and friends for years. I trust you, but this thing is precious. Precious to me and the Masai. I promised myself I would deliver it personally. Olekowlish has to have it a.s.a.p. I'd go tonight but for two things. I accepted this Elmo Bay job for immediate cash. I know the importance of it and it has to be done quickly before anyone gets to hear of the discovery. Also this safari I have shaken hands on. I can't let down my client. It means more cash money and the farm needs a cash injection right now. If it wasn't for the lack of bloody rain I'd – Oh, hell, Pat, What the blazes am I to do?

"Well, Peter, my boy, I thank you for that trust. Yes, you can trust me to deliver that thing for you. I'd do it for you because of those safaris you've put my way since you took to photographing instead of getting trophies for clients. I can't think of anything else I'd rather do for you."

"There is another thing, Pat. Delicate subject. Can you, er, stay off . . ."

"Stay off the whiskey? Of course, Peter, my boy. If you let me do this for you I shan't take a drop till the job's done. Nor when I get at those poachers."

"Do you think you can, Pat?"

"Of course. I swear to drink nothing but water from now till I've delivered your precious article"

In his time Peter had come across a few alcoholics, and had heard this statement a dozen times – "I'll not touch a drop more until . . ." Could he trust Pat? Peter thought for some moments. The El Molo job and the safari would take at least two, perhaps three weeks and he did not want to jeopardise the cash from either source.

"Okay, Pat, you're on." He reached into his car and gave Pat the Okiuka now wrapped loosely in brown paper. "I don't have to remind you, Pat. Be careful and don't let anyone else have it. Just Olekowlish. Give my best regards and tell him I'll be down soon."

"That's okay, Peter, my boy. I'll take care. Just water. Now you go and take some brilliant photographs. Oh, You can do something for me. That American girl Della. She's somewhere about. She came here with me. Could you do the honours and tell her I am engaged?"

"Of course, Pat. It'll be a pleasure." Pat went to his vehicles in the compound to find his safari team who no doubt were skiving somewhere. Peter went back to the party.

At the poolside he found a dry towel and sat on it at the end of the low diving board with a cool drink while watching the noisy revellers and three men surface diving. One came up with a cry of "eureka!" – he had found the monocle dropped by a Peer of the Realm. Peter mused how easy it was to be distracted from the main purpose in this glorious country. At that moment the diving board on which Peter sat moved to the tread of light feet. He was about to turn when the person knelt at his back and put hands over his eyes. In an exaggerated Texan drawl the person said, "Y'old real stinker. Y'all is some actor. You should be in li'l ol' Hollywood!"

"I know those hands and that voice. Hello Della," he said without turning. "What brings you here? Slumming again?"

She released her hands and stood, and both laughed as he turned.

"Wow!" He was stunned. She was bare footed and wore an *haute couture* bright pink trouser suit, turning the heads of swimmers and those by the pool.

"Slumming is right," she said. "Someone was kind enough to invite me. Seems you've been too busy. Is this what you mean by 'things to do'?"

"Well . . . er . . . Yes. If I'd . . ."

"No excuses now, Peter. I don't know what sort of people you are out here, but my escort seems to have deserted me. First, I don't get asked by someone who turns up anyway and then I get asked by someone who decides to disappear without an apology. You know him. The Irishman who came to the table in the Equator Club. Pat O'Brien – says he's a hunter – when you disappeared. Remember? He was the one with the shotgun on the steps."

"Yes. Pat is a hunter. One of the best. I doubt you'll see him any more tonight. He's off on a trip at dawn. He asked me to run you into town."

"What? Why is everyone dashing off and leaving me? That sort of thing doesn't happen in my country. There we have good Southern manners and politeness"

"In Houston? That ostentatious dockyard?" There was no malice in what he said. He was smiling. "Perhaps men there haven't much to do except hang about and be polite. This happens to be a busy country."

"Busy? After what you and your friend did tonight? You jest." She also was smiling. "Look around you! And that's not a nice thing to say to a young lady about her country folk. Busy? Ha! I think you're all so 'busy' you could do with cooling off – especially you!"

Laughing, she stamped on the sprung board dislodging him. He started to fall and grasped her bare ankle and both toppled, he with tuxedo, and she with a pink flash and a shriek, into the deep end.

They came up together. She laughed, splashed him and began swimming away. He too laughed, shook his hair back and said, "So that's your game, is it?" and swam after her. She might have had the advantage of surfing in the Texan Gulf breakers, but he had won a race in the sea the length of Malindi beach – all four hotels, for a bet. Now he was hampered with shoes and jacket while she was bare-footed and bare-armed but he caught her at the shallow end, lifted her out and carried her mock protesting and laughing to the house.

He put her down on the steps and both were acutely aware that her suit was now showing her body through the only two other flimsy items she wore underneath.

"You had better go to the ladies room and get dried off. The dhobi is on duty tonight and clothes will be cleaned and ready to wear in half an hour. You'll find towels there."

"I have a change of clothes in my bag. How about you?"

"I'm okay too. I also have a change. My safari gear is with me. I'm off up country in an hour."

"What? You off again? What is it with you? First I had a boring sandwich lunch yesterday because of your 'business meeting' then you leave me to go off to your farm which is obviously not truthful because you couldn't have been there for five minutes. You turn up at the club in tux, then you leave me standing, or rather sitting, then you don't invite me here but turn up just the same and then when you are around you decide to slip away from me just when this party is getting under way! What sort of a man are you?"

"I hope I'm not one of your Southerners who seem to do nothing but be polite. Some of us have things to do. I told you. This is a busy country."

Now her smile had gone. She was put out. She pouted and frowned. "Furthermore you throw me into a pool with my new outfit on, and now look at me. Soaked with a new hair-do all spoiled." She looked daggers at him.

"Steady on Della, if you remember it was you who stamped on the board and put us both in the oggin, nevertheless . . ." She went to speak . . . "Nevertheless," he repeated masterfully, holding her shoulders and stopping her, "I think it was fun. Don't you? You are fun." He moved close to her and spoke intimately. "Now, before I begin to tell you that you have a gorgeous body, lovely hair and fantastic eyes, you are going off to the ladies room pronto where you'll find a Somali woman who will do your hair, repair your make-up and see that your outfit is laundered properly. I shall be in the drawing room in forty minutes with a hot drink waiting for you. Forty minutes. Okay? Or would you rather stand around here and listen to your teeth chattering and catch your death of cold?"

Open mouthed, she said submissively "Oh. Alright." But stood looking at him with wide eyes.

"Then go!" he said in a stage whisper.

As she went he called after her "And put some shoes on or you'll get jiggers!"

Peter went to towel down and change into safari clothes with a comfortable woollen cardigan, gave his evening clothes to the dhobi and waited for Della in the drawing room with hot coffee laced with honey. He looked at his watch and when the minute hand reached the forty-minute mark he mumbled that she was bound to be late, but just seconds later she walked into the room dressed in jungle boots, with American army fatigues tucked into socks, plaid shirt, a bandana holding her newly dressed hair. Wearing no make-up she carried a bush jacket over a shoulder and put her holdall and camera bags gently on the floor.

"You don't do things by halves here. My outfit looks as though it was straight off the rail and folded in tissue paper and the colour hasn't run . . . That lets you off the hook for a new outfit."

"Oh?" he said, looking at her with a raised eyebrow, "That's nice to know. Here's the hot drink I promised. Wrap yourself around that."

"Nice fire. You are right. It can get cold here, even in Nairobi."

"Just here at this spot we are six thousand feet above."

"So" she said while sipping coffee, "You are off to the wide blue yonder again. Where to this time?"

" . . . The wide blue yonder."

"Sounds intriguing . . . When do I get my safari?"

"Soon. It's just a one-off job. I was commissioned tonight by the powers that be. I should not be more than a day or so, then I'm all yours."

"I think I had best come with you or I might lose you for ever. May I? It would be useful to add to my article. It could start our safari."

He thought quickly. He would love to have her come with him – just the two – but then, whatever he thought about their growing familiarity, she was a journalist and would not shirk her responsibilities. He knew that discretion would have to be the better part of ardour such was the confidentiality and urgency of the job he had to do. It could not be combined with a pukka safari.

"Before either of us gets embarrassed about this trip I shall have to refuse. The Authorities here have commissioned me for this urgent job and the local press will have precedence. They do the syndicating. I'll make sure you are the first to get copy on the release date. Pictures and all."

"What's the job then that's so important?"

"Sorry. I have to be discreet."

"Oh." She was disappointed. "Could I come just for the trip? I'd keep my mouth shut about whatever it is you are doing."

"You, a journalist, keep your mouth shut?"

"Don't you trust me?"

"What can I say? It is a job I have to do alone, Della. That's my brief. As much as it would be most enjoyable – desirable, I cannot ask you to come."

She frowned. "Why is everybody putting me off? You're doing your best to make me feel redundant, and Pat O'Brien disappears without even explaining what he's doing. What is it that's so urgent that both of you leave me here like last year's cast-off."

"I'll run you back to town."

"What's wrong with me? Do I smell? Do I talk too much . . ?"

"Della, it is nothing to do with you. You smell divine and I love your voice. Believe me, it is what we have to do here. I have to do an urgent Government job, which, if you did but know, will keep you, and people like you in business. Pat also has a job. He has to go off and find poachers. Finding them and looking after the game instead of slaughtering it for a pocketful of ivory."

At that Della looked up. "Poachers?" she asked without seeming to be all that interested.

"Yes."

If only I had known, she thought; did I miss an opportunity at the club when Pat offered to take me out? . . . "So when is Pat off?"

"Soon I think. Why don't you ask him? He's not far away. Mind you, I doubt he'll tell you. He does that sort of thing alone. That's his brief."

He was not sure he should have mentioned Pat and his intentions knowing he would not countenance a journalist going with him on an anti poaching mission. His methods when catching them were known to be unorthodox. Also to deliver something as politically sensitive as the Okiuka of which no one, especially a journalist, should have the slightest sniff.

"What do you mean he's not far away?"

"His trucks are in the compound here being loaded for the safari. He starts from here."

"Ah," she said non-committally.

A steward came and handed Peter his clothes now cleaned and pressed, and announced that breakfast was ready.

"Come Della. Full Kenya or Continental? Then I can run you into town."

After a 'Full Kenya' she excused herself while Peter went to the poolside where he expected to find the District Commissioner to pay his respects but the DC was already on his way to Government House.

Peter collected his Chevy from the compound and drove to the front of the house to wait for Della. After a while he thought she was being a long time and went back into the house without finding her there. He searched as dawn was breaking but she was nowhere to be seen. Not a little peeved he decided to call it a day and drive back to his apartment and pick up extra photographic equipment for the job in hand.

"She's a grown girl and can do as she pleases I suppose. I can see she's disappointed about her safari and found a lift. What a pity. I was beginning to like her. Ah, well, I'll see her back at the Norfolk. She's bright enough to get a lift into town" he said to the steering wheel. "Let's get to the bank and cash this cheque then up to El Molo country before anyone gets wind of those bones."

\*

In the cloakroom Della had a glint in her eye and was considering the lead that Peter unwittingly had given her regarding Pat and poachers. Here she was, she thought, right at the heart of the administrative centre that was trying to stamp out poaching, and a licensed hunter about to go out on the job to boot. What luck! If only Pat O'Brien would let her go with him she would see it at grass roots level without having to go cap in hand to the Game Department and through official channels. But then, Peter had said that Pat, if asked, would likely refuse to have her with him on such a safari and she had to think of what to do. In semi darkness as dawn was breaking she went to the compound in the grounds of the residency and saw a truck being loaded by a team of half a dozen Africans. Among their Swahili chat she heard *"Bwana Obrien."*

She crept past a black Buick saloon, a big Ford and an ex-service Jeep, and when the group of Africans were at one side of the service truck she climbed in after her bags and found a place to hide behind a stack of rolled tents. Further things were put in the truck while she was wondering what Peter would think of her, but she was not about to turn down a chance like this, for after all, this is why she came to

Kenya. In any case he wouldn't be back for a few days. It might be that poachers would be found and she would be back before Peter returned.

Less than five minutes passed and she heard Pat talking to a few of the team. "Now lads, is everything aboard? Then let's be having you. *Pesi pesi* now. Jump to it!" With good-natured shouting and jostling the safari team clambered into the service truck where she was hidden. The truck started and followed Pat's Jeep to leave the DC's boma and head for the road that took them past Nairobi then to descend a tarmac road on the Rift escarpment and go west across the Rift Valley. With the swaying of the truck it was not long before Della was asleep in her hollow behind the tents.

She woke later in daylight as the truck rattled over a bad stretch of road to find herself looking into the face of one of Pat's men. He hauled her up. The others were surprised and after a short discussion they were about to stop the truck. She did not want Pat to know of her presence just yet so she smiled sweetly and said in a few simple words with accompanying mime. "Jambo. Shhh. I come for bwana. He not know now. At camp I tell him."

The one who discovered her spoke reasonable English and understood her perfectly. He rattled off in Swahili to the others the gist of what she said adding his own interpretation of what this memsa'b and the bwana were about. The team immediately got the drift, knowing full well the reputation of their bwana when it came to women, and made appropriate noises. For the rest of the run the team sang songs while Della tried to cope with embarrassment and wondering what she was going to say to Pat.

They stopped that afternoon when reaching a tributary of a low river on the Kenya side of the border into Tanganyika. As soon as Pat's tent had been put up and he was alone she went to him.

"Where the blazes did you come from?"

"Your service truck. I stowed away."

"That was not a clever thing to do."

"You walked out on me last night. That wasn't so clever."

"You refused to let me run you home after breakfast at the club."

"It is not safe to be driven by a drunk driver."

"But you are here now. Does that mean you have changed your mind about us?"

"Don't flatter yourself. Frankly I don't abide men who drink too much. I'm not chasing you all over Africa because I want you as a boyfriend. You're not my type in that department. I look after myself."

"Now that's a pity. Think what you could be missing."

"I know precisely what you think I would be missing . . . I do want your help though."

"Well now, you chase me all the way out here for my help and nothing else?"

"That's it. Yes."

"What help is it you want then? You could have asked me in Nairobi."

"There, you . . . might have refused."

"I still might, if you'll only tell me what you want."

"Very well, Mr.O'Brien. I've come this far so I'll put my cards on the table."

"Please do Della – and it was Pat last night."

"Pat . . . I am a journalist. I am here with a commission from my editor in Houston to investigate poaching. I am told you are on a safari to look for poachers and have authority to take them into custody. I would like to be with you when you discover them . . ." The look of incredulity on Pat's face grew deeper as she continued speaking. "An interview with a poacher could well lead to uncover the ringleaders."

Pat took a deep breath, shut his eyes for a moment and then, "Holy Mary Mother of Jesus! How naive can you get! Your editor needs his head looked at. Does he think that a chit of a girl can come all this way to a place that you'll never in a month of Sundays understand, expose a racket that's been going on since man has been carrying the jawbone of an ass as a weapon and discover who the ringleaders are? He's barmy!"

"Surely it's not that difficult a thing to do?"

"Della, for God's sake come down to earth."

He knew he wouldn't mind a feisty lass with him whom he was sure he could tame, but he could do without a journalist with him on any pretext. Not when he was looking for poachers because when he did catch them his methods were not the sort of thing that the press should see, and certainly not on the other job in hand for fear of the cat being let out of the bag and upsetting Peter and people in high places. The Kikuyu chiefs, he knew, should they learn of this, would rub their hands with glee and relish the opportunity to start something with their sworn enemies the Masai. Furthermore, the Colonial Office would go bananas, knowing they had been duped by a mere farmer who would then be in serious trouble with the Governor and the Kikuyu.

"It's not just a handful of dear little misguided chaps with spears and a big chap with more savvy who flogs the spoils to a ship's captain in Mombasa. We are talking big bucks here. It is a million-dollar industry. Since the war the place is swarming with unlicensed surplus guns and ammunition just for the taking. Some gangs are using automatics and spraying herds of elephant probably just for two measly twenty-pound tusks. It's a nasty dangerous and bloody business. People get hurt. The game department here lost men hand over fist before they got the message and started shooting back. The bosses are hungry for the money the tusks bring in and will go to any lengths to get it."

"What you say is not what we hear in America."

"What I say is only half of it. If you want ringleaders I reckon you'll have to go back to Nairobi from where most likely it is controlled. Look for people in high places and the extra rich and let them start proving how they got it – then pray you come out of the other end alive. It is bloody monstrous that a newspaper editor many thousands of miles away throws a strip of a lass into the deep end all that way from home. No. For that reason alone I'll take you to the nearest *duka* where there's a bus to take you back."

Della was not a little put out by his outburst. Although Pat painted a picture far worse than she had been given to understand in Houston, she did realise there was some danger.

"I take your point Pat, but surely you'll let me come and just observe. I can stay out of trouble. I shan't get in your hair."

Pat shrugged his shoulders, looked at the sun then turned on the charm.

"I can't send you packing right now. The boys are making kongoni stew for supper. D'you fancy some?"

"Yes please."

"Where do you expect to sleep tonight?"

"I could get my head down in the truck."

"For Christ's sake that sort of thing went out with Karamojo Bell," he said laughing. "I'll have another bed put up in my tent." Then with typical Irish humour, "Can't sleep with the boys – they'd put you in the cooking pot in small pieces after having had their way with you." He reverted to his 'seriousness'. "It's too dangerous for a girl to be out by herself on safari. I'll look after you."

"And I suppose 'looking after me' is what you intend doing if I sleep in your tent?"

"The thought hadn't crossed my mind," he lied – almost sincerely.

"I'm afraid, Mr.O'Brien, that two dances in a club breathing alcohol over me and only half a party with someone who's more than half drunk doesn't qualify anyone for that sort of caper. I came out here to see a hunter at work. Not sleep with him. I'm not that sort of a girl. I don't sleep around. Furthermore, the American services trained me in unarmed combat. I've seen off a gang of circus roustabouts before now."

He knew he could cope with anything in a skirt on safari, but somehow, he respected this one. She was class. He called for the boys to fix a tent for the memsa'b and be quick about it.

"We shall have supper at sundown, and regarding what you propose; I'll sleep on it and decide in the morning what I should do with you Della."

"Thanks, Pat."

*

He was first up in the morning before dawn. After a wash and shave in a canvas bucket he dressed in a tough shirt and threw a goatskin coat over his shoulders to keep the morning chill off his back, and he went from his tent to a blazing fire to accept a mug of hot tea from the watchman.

After sunrise the camp breakfasted on beans, bacon and tea, then the gear was struck and stowed away. He took Della to one side.

"It is no place for a woman to be on a hunt for poachers, but if I do smell something and decide to go after them on foot you must promise to stay in the truck with the driver and one of my chaps who will be armed. Do not use your camera while the hunt is on. The slightest noise can be heard at two hundred yards. Only afterwards if I say so."

"Thanks, Pat. I'll be careful."

"This morning you travel in the service truck with the boys," he said, "It is ten miles or so to the border where you will stop and wait for me. I now have extra paperwork to sort out which will take about five minutes. I shall follow on and meet you at the border post."

He was letting her believe she was going to witness a hunt for poachers, but had decided to leave her at the border in charge of police there. She could then take the daily bus to Nairobi. Thinking she was on the right trail Della went happily to the service truck and sat in front with the driver who started up and drove off.

Pat sat in his Jeep and habit made him reach for a hip flask. He suddenly realised what he had promised Peter and put it back. He reached for the water. He poured some into a plastic beaker and drank half of it. He shuddered. It had no taste. Now he was in a typical alcoholic's syndrome. He tried another mouthful, shuddered again and thought that a little drop of whiskey in the water would do no harm. He drank the laced water, took a deep breath and stared at nothing for a full minute. The token whiskey in the water was beginning to do its work. The memory of his promise became hazy. A further minute went by. He poured more water and laced it heavily. The memory of his promise had gone. A second later the flask was at his lips. He drank two good mouthfuls and watched baboons that had come inquisitively close. He threw the empty beaker at them and they stood back. While he drank another mouthful he heard rhythmical grunting and footfalls in step. The baboons ran. He finished another generous swig from the flask as seven Masai appeared running through the bush.

"Perhaps they can direct me to Olekowlish's manyatta," Pat thought. He got out of the jeep, hailed them, and as they arrived he spoke in the OlMaa tongue.

"Greetings. I see you well. Come and drink. I have water." The seven Masai clustered around him and accepted water from a gallon container he carried. "Any of you fellows come from Tanganyika? Wemberi side?" he asked jovially, the whiskey taking effect.

"Eeeeeh. This man, our headman. He comes from Wemberi side." Sekento looked up. "Yes. I come from there. What would a white man want to know about that place?"

"I have business with a great man there."

"Who is this great Man?"

"He is called Olekowlish. You may know of him."

Sekento's eyes flickered but one of the men in the group said, "We know that man. He is the father of this, our headman here."

"Ah. So I am speaking to the right person. You are the son of Olekowlish?"

"I am the elder son. Sekento. What is it you want with my father?"

"I have some business with him."

"My father seldom has business with white people. What is this business?"

"It is private business. For him only."

Sekento's eyes flickered and his brain worked. "I have come from my father. He is indisposed. I am here in this place to conduct clan business for him. It is better we conduct your business here, and I can speak to him when I return there."

"But this business is for me and Olekowlish urgently and privately. It is for no other."

"But, my father is indisposed. He can see no one until the time when he is healed. You will have a wasted journey. It is better you tell me this business. If you speak our tongue you will know that there is no separation between father and elder son. We have the same dealings. There will come a time when I shall take my father's place. This indisposition of his may make that time come soon. If he were here he would agree to my doing this business." Pat was thinking through the whiskey. He did not want a wasted journey. And Peter had said he knew Sekento as a child, and he knows the Masai better than I. "Have you proof that you are his son?"

"Here. My father's mark." He touched the vermilion triangle dyed on the breastbone.

"I see it well."

Pat's thoughts were now unclear. Should he give the staff to Sekento to pass on, or should he insist on taking it himself? But then, Olekowlish was indisposed and he would have a wasted journey. Another swig of whiskey convinced him that Sekento was a decent fellow. "I have something precious for him . . . Will you deliver it safely?"

"What is this thing?"

"I have it here," he said reaching into the Jeep and lifting it out in loose wrapping from behind his seat. "It must be delivered safely . . . It comes from your childhood friend Peter Grant." On saying Peter's name he remembered his promise and had remorse at letting Peter down. "No. Forget it. I shall deliver it." Still holding it he asked another question. "After passing the three kopjes by Lake Manyara how many miles east of there do I travel to find . . ."

The question was unfinished. Sekento's eyes had flickered again when he saw the loose parcel in Pat's hand. The jewelled end of the staff was exposed. Immediately recognising the Okiuka, with a swift movement he seized the precious staff leaving Pat holding the wrapping. The Okiuka was now in unscrupulous hands. Peter's father was right. Instant power and evil consumed Sekento. A strange "AAAEEEHH!" came from him. What followed was only a matter of a split second. Pat looked up, but facing a low rising sun, hardly saw the lightning thrust of Sekento's spear. Pat then had a curious feeling as the honed, four-inch-wide blade entered through his ribs to appear out of his back. It was when Sekento withdrew the long blade Pat felt the awful pain.

His body went into spasm and he sank into the dust and he heard vaguely the shouts of triumph; the noises of the Jeep being ransacked; his kit being thrown out; his own clothes tossed over his inert body and the beginning of a chant that faded as the Jeep was started and driven away.

In great pain and with paralysed back and legs and fading eyesight Pat managed to cry out "Peter . . . dear friend . . . sorry . . . so sorry!" – a cry heard only by baboons. He then grasped a brittle twig that was lying against his hand. He managed to begin to scratch some straggling letters in the dust . . . S . . . E . . . K . . . At this point the twig broke and with barely any feeling now in his fingers the . . . E . . . N . . . hardly discernible as letters, was all he could manage. The attempted T was just a straggly line as his hand and eyes failed. Meanwhile his other hand was attempting to make the sign of a cross where the pain was and his lips were trying to say many times "Hail Mary full of grace, the Lord is with thee, pray for us sinners now and at the hour of our death . . ." A desperate final gasp came from him followed by the escape of air as he sank into painless nothingness.

A mile away the service truck went merrily along with the sound of a happy song sung on the dusty air by the safari team with an excited Della believing she was on her way to expose East Africa's growing poaching problem.

# 5.

It has gone wrong as a donkey's neck skin.
*(This thing is odd and does not fit)*

The noisy game of *Bao* played by one of the safari team and a guard while squatting on the ground outside the border post, was jangling Della's nerves. At dazzling speed each player slapped and scooped black and grey stones in and out of parallel hollows in a long wooden board to complex rules. The swiftness of the two players' moves overlapped that brought cries of encouragement or derision from the onlookers. Both expert players gave no quarter and what had started as a game of planting and capturing the opponent's seeds had developed into a game of buying, selling and rustling cattle.

When the game had been played for an hour without a conclusion, during which time Pat had not appeared, A perspiring Della got down from a hot cab and went across to the driver, one of the noisiest and excited of onlookers.

"Why are we waiting here?" she asked him. He was paying more attention to the game to than to Della. "Can't we go ahead?"

"No m'sabu," he said, not looking at her. "We wait for the bwana. He has papers."

"But it has been a long time. He should have arrived by now."

"Yes m'sabu. A long time."

"Something may have happened. Shouldn't we turn back?"

"He will come. The bwana always come when he say he come."

"I think we should wait no longer. He does not come. We should go back and look for him."

"But, m'sabu, the bwana say he come," he said while still looking at the play.

"I know what he said. He said he would be five minutes. It is now an hour."

"Yes."

"Then why not go back and look for him?"

Resigned to the interruption he turned to her. "He say he come here."

"What if he does not come?"

"But he come. He say he come."

Irritation was turning to frustration. She was sampling what she thought was intransigence but it was simply a case of the extraordinary patience inherent in Africa's nature. If it were meant to be, then the men would wait all day before they would think their bwana to be held up for any reason. He had said he would arrive. His word had been given. Not yet understanding African native logic, although she should have equated this trait with that of the American Indian of the plains, she drew him away from the game and spoke slowly and carefully.

"If the bwana was here and waiting for someone who was late, would he just wait here for a long time just twiddling his thumbs or would he think it better to go back and find that person who may have trouble?"

The driver had a vision of his master twiddling his thumbs as Della had just done and thought it to be very funny. "But the bwana is not here."

"Yes, I know that," she said through gritted teeth. "Who is head man?"

"I head man."

"What is your name?"

"Joseph Sikule, m'sabu."

"Well, Joseph Sikule, I am a close friend of Mr.O'Brien. You should do as I ask."

"If you speak for the bwana . . ."

"I do, Joseph. It is better we turn back and look for him."

"The bwana be very angry if we do this."

"I shall be very angry if we do not! You leave the bwana to me. He'll not be angry with you."

Joseph quietened the noisy group and told them they must return to the camp. Upset because their game had been interrupted, they picked up the board and, complaining, climbed into the truck. Joseph then swung the vehicle to head north on the track back to the camp of yesterday. Della expected to meet the Jeep on the way, but for all the ten miles they saw nothing but a troop of baboons among rocks.

At the vacated camp there was no Jeep. In its place was a scattering of Pat's personal gear. The men jumped down and scattered baboons picking at the debris. They found Pat's Mannlicher rifle, shotgun and ammunition and looked for the Express. Joseph turned up a corner of what he thought to be a heap of clothing and uncovered the booted foot of his master.

"M'sabu! He called. "M'sabu! *Kuja!* Come!" He removed what covered Pat.

Her hand went to her mouth as she stared at Pat lying on his side in a pool of drying blood from a gash in his chest and another in his back crawling with insects. Joseph knelt, held Pat's head in his arms, and wailed, rocking on his knees and shedding tears, oblivious to the insects "Bwana oh bwana! *Anakufa! Anakufa!* – He is dead! – He is dead!" Della stood transfixed. "Oh my God!" was all she could say. In her time with the US Air Force and as a reporter she had seen bodies in mortuaries or accidents when she knew what to expect, but not like this. Not someone she had known, however briefly, however likeable. She now felt isolated, many miles from home, surrounded by Africans, vulnerable and frightened. Then the journalist in her took over. Retrieving her camera from the truck she went back to see Joseph pointing to the Jeep's tyre tracks. These she photographed. They could be seen going east through the dust. The marks were neither regular nor straight and there were places where the wheels had spun showing the result of inexpert use of clutch, accelerator and steering. Then she turned to Pat and took a series of shots from different angles with a few close-ups.

Joseph turned to the watchman. "Kimani, where be the big gun?"

"The gun for elephant not be here at all. Maybe it go for Masai along with Jeep. I been seek it when you cry. I not find at all. Other guns are here."

"We believe it to be the work of Masai, m'sabu. We see here the marks of sandals belonging to Masai. What we do now m'sabu?"

She took a deep breath and thought. "We ought to go back to Nairobi . . . with . . . everything."

"What we do with bwana?"

"Why, take him to Nairobi of course."

"We not bury him here?"

"No. We should take him and his things back to the District Commissioner in Nairobi. We report to him what we have found."

"It would be better to bury him here."

"I know it to be better in this heat, but the bwana is – was – an important man." It took all six men to carry and lay him surrounded with personal gear to stop rolling with the motion of the truck. All were subdued during the journey back and there was no happy safari song to sing, just a long repetitive lament.

They stopped at Narok to refuel from jerricans where she bought bananas and bottles of cola for all at a *duka*. Della decided to go the police post and report the death. Meticulously the sergeant put details into a report book while telling her the inspector was out dealing with a *matata* and would be back at sundown. She decided not to wait.

The journey from west to east across the Rift Valley was something she would have enjoyed in different circumstances. From a high point she could see directly across to the long hazy outline of the Aberdare range without knowing she was looking almost directly at Peter's farm under the Kinangop peak about fifty miles distant. On crossing the Valley they passed south of Longanot volcano with its west side sweeping down from a high peak of its rim to Hell's Gate. Along the road they were forced to drive for five miles in dust raised by an open truck with the trunk of a large, full tree chained to the back dragged along slowly to grade the road.

It was eight o'clock and dark when they rolled into the compound at the DC's residence. The watchman shut the gate and sent a messenger to the house. Della and the driver were taken to an office where Smith, the auditor, met them. While giving their story urgent telephone calls were made. The driver was sent back to the compound where Pat O'Brien's body was put in an empty garage.

"Come inside, Miss," the auditor said. "I am about to dine." Looking at her trousers with just a touch of distain he said, "Join me. You must be famished after your journey. You may clean up in here. The police inspector will have a word with you when he has finished with the Africans. The District Commissioner is in Nairobi."

After cleaning dust from her face and brushing her hair and clothes she went to the dining room where another place had been set. After the meal Smith dismissed the staff, poured coffee and asked what brought her to Kenya.

"Father has done well in oil and manufacturing and gave me this trip so that I could photograph the animals."

His assumed pleasantness during the meal then disappeared. "Miss Mitchell, why did you go along with Mr.O'Brien?"

She fended off an awkward question coming out of the blue. "I just thought I'd like a trip out."

"By yourself? No chaperon? With a man who has a known reputation among women?"

"I'd say his reputation, God bless his soul, was that of a first class hunter. That is the only reason I went with him."

"That leaves us in a quandary. We happen to know he was not on a regular hunting safari. We can only surmise that you were with him for some other reason. Pleasure perhaps?"

"No. That's a nasty thing to say to a visitor to your country. I'm not that sort of a girl. I look after myself."

"Be that as it may, Miss Mitchell. You'd have an apology if only you'd tell us the real reason for your visit here. We know you met O'Brien at the Equator Club and that you came with him here to the party. What can we believe from that?"

"You seem to know a lot about me, Mr.Smith."

"We are professionals here. We know from where and when you came. Please let me see your passport." It was not a request it was a statement.

"Heck," she said under her breath, knowing she had to.

"Hmmm. As we are informed. Journalist. Freelance? Staff?"

"Staff."

"Purpose of visit?"

"I was asked those questions at your customs desk at the airport. I am to book a professional safari with a Mr.Grant and then to travel and take notes for my journal. I have a three-month visa."

"We do not take kindly to journalists who travel, no doubt singly. This is not America. The aboriginals here are of a different nature from those you know. There are many tribes here of different historic origins and no love is lost between them. That makes it dangerous to do as you please and gives us serious problems. No journalist in my recollection travels alone without a definite purpose."

"Is not a proper safari a definite purpose?"

"Ah, yes. But then? A journalist with two months on hand after an official safari? There must be a more serious purpose to your visit. What is your real reason for being here Miss Mitchell?"

She said nothing.

"You know we can have you out of the Colony tomorrow if you do not give us a better reason than what you say?"

"You'd have the American Embassy and an influential newspaper down on you like a ton of bricks if you attempted that. Bad publicity for your precious Colony."

"No doubt. But the authorities here can guess at only one reason for your going out with O'Brien – that of sampling the sleeping habits of white hunters. That would make interesting publicity for you."

"How dare you! You are an ornery S.O.B. to say such things!" she said indignantly.

He knew what that meant. His face muscles tightened. Her remark hurt him. "A son of a bitch am I? You give me no choice unless you tell me the real reason for being here. It is as simple as that. Reason? Or damaging publicity? Make your choice."

"My Embassy will get to know of this." But she knew that only one person at her Embassy knew she was here to dig out poachers but could not officially help her. She was in a cleft stick.

"Your Embassy has no jurisdiction over what we publish here. They, and you, could be highly embarrassed."

She thought she would call his bluff. "Well, go on then. Or are you in a position not to be able to? You are not a policeman."

"As it happens, Miss Mitchell, I am senior to the police here. They do not determine my actions. It is I who brief them."

It was a shot in the dark from him, but Della knew nothing of the set up of the Administration here. There was nothing for it. She could not face that kind of publicity. "I am here to investigate ivory poaching."

The auditor had a cup of coffee halfway to his mouth when his face blanched and the knuckles of his fingers turned white. He froze for a second then recovered and became normal again.

"You did not state this on your visa application?"

"No."

"Why not?"

"It was thought it might have been turned down."

"You are right. It would have been. We do not countenance international snooping into our affairs here. We are doing all that it is possible to stamp out this vile trade ourselves without the so-called help of do-gooders from wherever they come."

"I am told that poaching has reached such proportions here that there must be someone or a group of people controlling it. Since the war the spread of ivory even into the Americas is getting too big for our country not to take notice. Now that I am here, I can only help you people. Do you not reckon it would be a good idea to give me your blessing and let me get on with my job?"

His once pale face was getting redder. "No, Miss Mitchell. I do not think it a good idea. Not in the least. You have come here under false pretences, which give us sufficient grounds to recommend immediate deportation, but we shall have to wait a while. There is another serious matter. The death of O'Brien has to be investigated. We cannot just accept the word of an African driver and an American woman journalist and let it go at that. Depending on what the police have to say, I shall recommend you be held until that investigation is concluded."

"What has it to do with you? Are you a policeman? Are you arresting me?"

He ignored her question "The police officer should have finished with the men by now. He'll have words with you . . . more coffee?"

"No thank you. If you'll excuse me I'll go to the cloakroom."

While washing her hands she spoke to her reflection the mirror. "Dammit dammit dammit! Della, old girl, you are in a fix." She realised that now she was known to the authorities. Her editor would not be best pleased; but this Mr Smith was certainly a strange one, she thought, he's not what he seemed since first meeting him and definitely turned nasty when poaching was mentioned. She then remembered what Pat had said at the camp – *Go back to Nairobi and look for people in high places* . . .

"No. Can't be. Not him. He's only a pen pusher. I'd better play ball and get myself out of this mess."

When she went back the police officer was with the auditor and they broke from a quiet conversation.

"Chief Inspector Andrews, this is Miss Mitchell."

He nodded and looked her up and down with cold, watery pale blue eyes.

"American is it?"

"It's written all over my visa." He raised an eyebrow and waited. She bristled. "Yes. American. Mitchell. Della. Twenty-four. Single."

She looked at his bland face and thinning fair hair and decided he could be anything between thirty and sixty. His stare was most intimidating and he did not blink. She wondered if he slept with his eyes open.

"I am told it was your decision to turn back at the border and look for O'Brien."

"Yes."

"Smart move."

"But I . . ."

"Your passport?"

The auditor handed it to him and he thumbed through the pages.

"Hmmm . . . first time here?"

"Yes."

"Come with me, Miss" he said, standing and putting her passport in a pocket.

"Am I being arrested?" He said nothing. Thinking she would help her case she said, "If it is of any interest I took some photographs of Mr.O'Brien before he was moved." She wound back the negatives and took the cassette out of the camera back, sealed and handed it over to him.

"I shall want copies," said Smith. "As there was a fee involved I need evidence for my files."

"You'll have copies first thing. I shall get forensics straight onto it," said Andrews. "Come with me now Miss. Questions to be answered. Not here. In town."

"Am I a suspect then?"

"Until we find the murder weapon and the culprit we have only your word and of six of his boys of questionable intellect as to what you say happened."

"You can't think I would be ghoulish enough to take photographs after . . . ?"

"It takes all sorts."

"You are out of your mind, Inspector!"

"Chief Inspector," he said smartly. "Now come."

As she turned to the door she did not see the look that passed between the two men.

Now with the Chief Inspector in a police Land Rover driven by a burly African sergeant she was driven to Nairobi's police station, an unattractive functional building, and was taken to a room with bars over a small high window, a trestle table, two chairs and a filing cabinet. He took off the Sam Browne he wore with a revolver in a holster and hung it over the back of his chair.

"How far did you get from the Mara camp?"

"We stopped at the border post to wait for Mr.O'Brien. It was about ten miles."

"Who decided to turn back?"

"I did. We'd still have been there now if I had taken notice of the men. You must know we stopped at a place called Narok on the way back and I made a statement to the police there."

"No" he said with concern. "I did not know."

He turned the handle on a wall telephone and called for the duty officer. An Asian Inspector came in.

"Contact Narok on the teleprinter and tell them to relay immediately the statement by Miss Mitchell regarding Mr.O'Brien. Also get a report from the Mara border guards – that is if they are not asleep."

"Yes sir." He went to the wireless room.

"Before I say anything more of this O'Brien business – I understand you did not make a full declaration of interests on your visa application."

"We, that is my editor and I, thought we could accomplish what I came for without."

"And what was that?"

"To book a safari with Mr Grant,"

"And?"

Realising the Auditor must have told him she admitted she was here also to investigate ivory poaching.

"We brook no interference here Miss Mitchell. We've enough on our plate without foreign journalists wandering about asking impertinent questions and getting into trouble. Keep your nose out of it. The police here have sufficient evidence of what goes on in the poaching industry, for that is about the size of it. It is a dangerous enough business without foreigners coming here and getting hurt." He sat back and thought for a moment without taking his eyes off her. "Did Peter Grant suggest you go out with O'Brien?"

She was surprised at the question. "No."

"Sure?"

"Absolutely."

"Be very sure. It does not do to deceive us."

"I happened to stroll over to where Mr. O'Brien's truck was being loaded in the Residency compound and overheard the men saying that he was starting a safari to look for poachers. I took the opportunity to stow away in the service truck when the men were not looking."

"How many boys?"

"Six I think."

"Are you sure Peter Grant had no hand in this? I was at the Residency and saw you both at the pool."

"Yes I am sure. Anyway, we parted company after breakfast at the house party and I'm not likely to see him again for some time. He said he was off on an official safari."

"Did he say where?"

"No."

The door opened and the Asian inspector brought in a sheet of teleprinter paper.

"No reply from the border post sir."

Andrews nodded, read the transcript from Narok and passed Della a report form and a pencil.

"Write a report of what happened at the Residency and how you came to travel on that safari and from then on."

"I'll use a pen if you don't mind. It can't be rubbed out and altered."

Andrews looked at her sharply, but shrugged his shoulders. "Please yourself."

Used to brevity in her reporting she recorded the bare facts quickly, without embellishment. She slid the paper across to his side of the desk. He read and compared it with the report from Narok.

"Sign it." He sat and sucked his teeth then looked up at her with emotionless eyes.

"Miss Mitchell. I shall impound your passport and visa for two reasons. One: we shall carry out further investigation into O'Brien's death. Two: you entered this country on a false premise and you will be recommended for deportation as soon as our enquiries are done. An appeal cannot be made. You must stay at your hotel until your passport is returned when at such time you will be taken to the airport to board an appropriate flight – that is if you are clear of O'Brien's death. Here is another form for you to sign. You are being bailed on my authority. Your newspaper is to stand surety. You will report here twice a day and sign the book. Eight am. and six pm. Where are you staying?"

"I stay at the Norfolk Hotel."

"Charge any lengthy stay there to your newspaper. Perhaps they won't send females on fools' errands in future. Have you anything further to say?"

Della though that he must be a misogynist. "No."

"Inspector Patel will run you over to the Norfolk. Do not forget you are on bail pending the result of enquiries, and remember you are an alien. If you try any Yankee tricks here you'll stand out like a sore thumb. Jail would be the next step."

He turned the handle of the wall telephone and Inspector Patel appeared with hat and car keys for the drive to the Norfolk Hotel.

When in her banda at the Norfolk Hotel she relapsed into American Air Force cursing but it developed into near tears. "Now, Della old girl, *Nil Desperandum*." She stepped under the shower to calm herself, dried, fixed her face and hands with moisturiser, asked room service for a sandwich and coffee that arrived. Then in her bed she turned out the light and punched a pillow and burst out: "Dammit! Me! Della Mitchell! Number one suspect of a murder!" sighed and murmured "What a mess." She then hugged the pillow and let out a cry from the heart, "Oh Peter, Peter! Why did you not let me go with you!?"

# 6.

HANAFDI.
*(There is no such place. The settlers' tongue reduces
The Northern Frontier District to The N.F.D.
An Edwardian Cockney prospector left his mark by saying –
"I won and lorst a fortune hup in the Han-af-di")*

A pall of dust followed Peter's safari truck leaving a hovering streak for half a mile behind. Before settling it hid an apology of a road. An apology owed not by the road gangs, the most recent of whom were Italian prisoners-of-war from Abyssinia now gone back to Italy; but apologies owed by African weather patterns. Even without rain extreme night-time cold and daytime heat had split boulders that lay randomly about the rutted, potholed and corrugated track. Choking dust flailed up by pounding tyres laid an ochred film over Peter's canvas hat, eyelashes, ears and down his back where sweat patterned his shirt. It filmed the sunglasses he wore.

Negotiating a rising hairpin bend he came to the escarpment road out of the forests of the northern foothills of Mount Kenya where the approaches to the Northern Frontier District were laid out below him with the glint of sun on tin roofs at Isiolo. Further, trees watered by Buffalo Springs and the Uaso Nyiro river cut an olive swathe across the beginnings of the desert.

It was late afternoon when he reached the old fort station at Archers Post and stopped outside the ADC's house. This house, as many others, was built by long-serving prisoners from the place of incarceration euphemistically known as King George's Hotel. The prison officials often won the contract for their meticulous work in building official's houses. The inmates, some qualified building workers, while paying attention to the smallest detail, were outside the barbed wire daily in charge of an armed trustee for as long as it took. They had their daily ration of *posho*, and went back to the barbed wire each evening. For some it was as though they took the 6.20. each day for a nine-hour shift at the office.

The ADC's head steward, an Embu tribesman in a spotless *kanzu* and fez met Peter and said the bwana would be here shortly. Five minutes later an old open Chevy soft top coupé came boiling up the winding drive and parked under a tarpaulin nailed to trees. Three fierce looking Rhodesian ridgeback hounds leapt out of the rear seat and came bounding and barking to Peter to lick the back of his hand.

"Down! Down!" called the ADC and the dogs went obediently to their kennel. "Hello old boy. Potter's the name. Nigel Potter. First things first. Must wash. Dusty don't you know. Be with you in a jiffy," he said with an upper-crust accent one could cut with a knife. He went off to his ablutions.

Fifteen minutes elapsed before Nigel emerged, tall, slim, slicked-down dark hair, immaculately dressed in a cream linen suit, college tie and lovingly polished Chelsea boots. "*Chai tafadhali!*" he sang out, *(tea if you please).* The steward brought two silver pots on a silver tray, one with Green Gunpowder tea and the other with Earl Grey, also on the tray were cold sliced lemons, Jacob's assorted biscuits and the steward's famous drop scones with butter and a pot of ginger preserve. It was put on a table covered with an immaculately laundered and starched Damask cloth that bore the faint stain of the local water's minerals.

Nigel's first claim to be eccentric was, that with a screwdriver he 'requisitioned' a coin-in-the-slot door from a railway station ladies waiting room to use as his own lavatory door to a ventilated long-drop over which was his beautifully polished mahogany brass-bound thunder box.

"I've converted the door to take all coins. It does a good trade in dimes and pennies when inquisitive Americans and Europeans visit me, but then, you see, I have to spend some myself when I get Montezuma's revenge. Funds go to a water-boy. The *posho* is monotonous today. Waiting for a parcel from Fortnum and Mason don't you know. Sent up by Mammy wagon all the way from Nairobi. Frightful mess when it gets here. Bath Olivers all broken. Can't be helped though. Blithering blighters do try. How's tea? Hot enough?"

"Yes, thank you," said Peter sipping Earl Grey and munching a crumbling hot scone dripping with liquid butter and ginger preserve. "Kept busy up here, Nigel?"

"You know what it is. Blithering Somalis send raiding parties down here. Cattle, women and fodder. Usually go back loaded. Locals have the frighteners put on them. Lovely lot the locals. Trust them as far as they can throw their blithering spears. Excruciating fun."

That night they dined steaks of the *kongoni*, the best of the four legged game, marinated in lime juice and brandy with home grown vegetables piled high around the meat. Tinned peaches and condensed milk with Kenya coffee followed.

Peter made up a camp bed on the veranda and strung up a net from the eaves. Before he had time to get inside the net it was peopled by three oversized chameleons making hay with long tongues among the many flying insects that attacked a hanging oil lamp.

After breakfasting the next morning on scrambled eggs, coffee, toasted scones and honey, Peter drove in one stretch up to the south-eastern tip of Lake Rudolph, later to be given the name of the local tribe of Turkana, but always 'The Jade Sea'. When he reached the lake it gave him an unpleasant welcome. It had conjured up the *Kharif*, a wind that moaned all the way from the Ethiopian Danakil depression. The wind was hot, the ground was hot and the host's filtered water at the secret location was hot.

"Must be lonely up here without visitors," said Peter.

"One has to discourage them in my profession," the anthropologist answered. "Too many hangers-on want to get in on the act. Pretty bleak here, though. That's a discouragement in itself. I've made myself comfortable and eat well. Plenty of good fish. An occasional friendly face turns up. Thanks for the beer. I see you have field cameras. Mine are only medium format." They talked and worked in the heat and had a painstaking day with screens and reflectors fighting the wind and dust. During a long lull he got the job done, packed his things, and wanting to get back home quickly said farewell to his companion.

Travelling at night for the inexperienced was folly. This was the time for animals to be up and about when an accident, however trivial, could prove fatal in many ways. A truck stopped by hitting an animal could stay unnoticed for weeks. Only occasional supply wagons came this way.

This night animals were out in their hoards that slowed him down. At daybreak he arrived at Archers Post and went directly to the ADC's house to find he was in his office. He asked the steward for a jug that he filled with lime juice, laced with sugar and salt for Nigel's paraffin refrigerator. He left a note: '*May you never have leaping red-knees in your thunder box. Peter.*'

In Nigel's office his African assistant, filing clerk, floor sweeper, general factotum and now tea maker, gave a wide berth to the main desk under which Nigel kept his three Rhodesian Ridgebacks when not on the back seat of his Chevy. They started barking furiously as a sweating uniformed African policeman came up the drive on a bicycle to deliver an envelope. The dogs were silenced but looked malevolently at the wary policeman while Nigel read the contents of two buff forms. "There is no answer," he told the policeman who said "Sah!" and threw up a parade ground salute with an almighty stamp of a bare foot that started up the dogs again. He leaped onto his bicycle and sped away with the dogs barking at his heels.

"This one's for you, old chap." said Nigel as he handed Peter the official message form. In the ruled lines was the curt message:

O'BRIEN KILLED WHILE SAFARI MARA K/T BORDER STOP JEEP AND EXPRESS.577 MISSING STOP RETURN NBI DIRECT STOP DC NBI END

"Good God!" Peter said. "Killed? Pat? I can't believe it! Was it an accident?"

"I don't know, old boy. Haven't told me. I'm not to know what happens outside my little parcel but I have been told to look out for O'Brien's Jeep. Anyone with half an eye could spot it a mile off with his logo on the door. I expect you know there's a move afoot by maverick Masai in the Rift to stir things up a bit. Seems there's a bit of a feud going on down in your neck of the woods. I'm sorry about O'Brien if he was your friend. Never met him myself."

"I think I ought to get back to see if I can do something."

He left Archers Post and headed south for the dusty red escarpment roads among the northern foothills of Mount Kenya then climbed and drank in the cool crisp mountain air contrasting with the hot khaki coloured desert he had left. On reaching home he threw off his clothes and climbed into a huge Edwardian enamelled cast iron bath full of steaming water, lay back, relaxed all his muscles and promptly fell asleep.

# 7.

One finger without a thumb does not kill a flea.
*(A person is helpless while alone. Unity is strength)*

He woke with a start. The now cold bath water reached his chin. A wall clock told him he had slept for four hours. He pulled the plug and leaped under a hot shower.

After a meal Peter collated detailed records from the notes of all the photographs taken at Elmolo bay that took until nightfall. He was sweating with a headache when he went early to bed. A stiff dose of quinine did not stop a restless night and he woke from a fitful sleep in the morning before dawn when Kinyanjui brought him fruit juice and coffee. A hot and cold shower left him feeling better but his eyes were bloodshot.

Just as it was getting light after breakfast he went to the farm's garage and workshop where his head mechanic was finishing work on a pickup that had been up on chocks for a year.

"How's it getting on, Bosco?"

"Nearly finished, bwana. The rear suspension now has new springs and engine has new head gasket with decoke, plugs and points. Wheel bearings are good and all filters changed. I will finish timing then test."

"Good. Don't forget the antifreeze. After that give the safari truck a service. I shall go to Nairobi soon. If you think the pickup's alright I'll go in that."

"It will need something to keep the back steady."

"Put a toolbox on as well as safari gear and a box of my army survival stuff and throw in this camouflage net under the tarpaulin for good measure. It will make a good hide if I go out photographing. Safari tyres and two spares okay?"

"Yes. All six new."

Before seven o'clock Bosco returned from the test. "All okidoki bwana. I just check the head bolts while hot."

The pickup's smooth running over bad roads while driving down to Nairobi impressed Peter. He pulled up at his studio where he processed the films he had taken of the relics at Molo Bay, and when dry, drove with the prints out to the D.Cs boma. The D.C. was in Nairobi's law courts and Herbert Smith greeted him. Peter spoke first.

"What's all this about Pat O'Brien?"

"The injuries he sustained and the Jeep missing suggest an attack and not an accident. We do not know who the culprit is yet. The police are investigating."

Tea was brought in and poured for them by a steward. When he had gone Smith said that Peter was late back. "You are lucky to catch me. I am off on a fact-finding tour and the Chief inspector wants to see you.

"What would he want to see me for?"

"He can tell you that when he returns from his investigation at Narok."

An open file on Smith's desk revealed photographs clipped to the paperwork and Peter said, "Aren't they shots of Pat O'Brien? May I see them?" The file was passed across the desk.

There were seven prints. "Good God!" he sad, "that looks like a spear wound. Straight through and out the back!" In all there was no sign of the Okiuka. On one print he saw a small twig in Pat's hand and close by there were faint marks in the dust just discernable by means of shadows from an angled sun. A jeweller's loupe from his shirt pocket revealed to a professional eye what a lay eye would have missed. A very indistinct S . . . E . . . K . . . then an almost indiscernible E . . . fainter still a N . . . then a straggly, curved line – Perhaps an attempt at a T? . . . SEKENTO! . . . Peter froze. Here in the photograph Pat was revealing who had killed him. Surely not that jovial six-year-old boy he had played with as a child? Twenty years had passed since he knew him. A lot could have happened in that time. Surely Sekento would have had no reason to kill Pat except to steal the Okiuka. He said nothing of what he was thinking and affected a bland face.

"Have you all of his effects? Are there any clues?"

"The police report that all of his effects were recovered, except for the Jeep and his heavy gun with ammunition. Nothing else was missing. It was fortunate he made a comprehensive list."

"We all do when kitting out."

"You had better hold yourself in readiness for the Chief Inspector."

"I shouldn't worry on that score. I'm easy to find."

"Now, regarding what you went north for, I take it you took all the snaps required?"

Peter winced at the word 'snaps'. For all his important work he used field cameras with half-plate glass negatives on which the minutest information could be recorded. He nodded and laid envelopes on the desk with coded prints and listed details of co-ordinates, date and time.

"The negatives?"

"In my safe at the studio."

Smith stood. "No doubt we shall requisition them. You'll be informed. I have work to do. You have been paid your fee. I shall be away for a week or so. I shall be up-country on a fact finding tour."

"Anywhere interesting?"

"Nowhere that would interest you."

Peter shrugged his shoulders, said good day, left the DC's *boma* and made his way into Nairobi. "Sekento!" he thought while on the way there. "Pat, dear old friend, you shall be avenged. I don't care what it takes."

When nearing the Norfolk hotel he slowed. Here was an opportunity to speak to Della. He parked, and found her in a lounger by the pool wearing a swim suit under a towelling wrap with an oil salesman chatting her up.

"Hi, Della!" Peter called.

"Peter! How lovely to see you!" She turned and with a head movement dismissed the salesman. "Now we're on first name terms Peter, have a drink." She turned and signalled to the waiter. "What are you drinking?"

He spoke Swahili to the waiter who nodded and went to the bar.

"What was all that?"

"I've ordered a repeat of what you are drinking and a lime juice with sugar and a pinch of salt for me. It's a good quick cure for a headache."

"I thought you were looking peaky. I have a different kind of headache and my cure is better they say. Not quicker – better."

"How come you have a headache? Here you are, swanning around Kenya's premier hotel, lazing by the pool looking absolutely stunning with nothing to do but eat, drink, work up a tan and slay all the male chancers."

"I should be so lucky," she said glumly.

"Hey. What's the problem?"

"First I . . . I want to apologise for leaving you after breakfast at the Commissioner's house party."

"I wondered what had happened to you."

"I'll tell you if you forgive me first and not tell another soul."

"Sounds intriguing. I'll forgive you if you let me buy you lunch."

"It is me who is apologising. Have this one on me."

"Could not think of it. This is on me. I have an account here."

The drinks came and she signed the chit.

"I shouldn't take too much of that stuff. It'll rot your socks."

"It's only one in a while." She secured her wrap and suggested they go to her cottage where they would have lunch. "I don't feel like being gawped at by hoards of people right now."

There she went to the bedroom and changed into a skirt and blouse. Lunch came and she toyed with a poached trout while he had Limuru duck.

"So what's all this about? What's troubling you?" he asked kindly.

"It's Pat O'Brien."

"Pat? You know then?"

"Yes."

"I didn't realise you knew him all that well. How did you get to know? It's not long happened. I was told over the wire."

"It's . . . it's that I went out in his service truck from the compound. I saw him at camp and then later . . . such a mess."

"Why on earth . . . ?"

"I'm sorry I walked out on you at the party. I'm sorry you had to wait for me for nothing. When I excused myself I went to see Pat's truck loaded and I stowed away in it. You must think me awful to desert you like that when you'd been so nice to me."

"What possessed you to get in the truck?"

She paused for a long time while he waited for her to speak. She waved a fork over the remains of a fish on her plate then put it down firmly.

"You might as well know now as later and from someone else. That safari I'm to have with you, yes, is for the feature article, but my newspaper gave me the brief to uncover as much about poaching as I could. I was going to pump you for information to lead me to any of the hunters who are licensed to arrest poachers. You let it slip that Pat was going out on such a trip. I saw my chance at the party and took it."

Peter stared into her eyes. She coloured. He reached across the table and held her hand. "I'm sorry. It isn't often I get used."

"That's what I apologise for. Things would have been so different if I'd not been such a fool. I should have put my cards on the table when I met you, then perhaps this wouldn't have happened to Pat."

"Don't blame yourself for that." He wondered if Pat had revealed the real reason for his safari and wondered if she had wind of the Okiuka. "Then you must know who killed Pat and why?"

"No. I don't. That's the whole mess. We stayed overnight at somewhere called The Mara where he let me stay and fixed a tent and a meal. In the morning he said I could observe what went on at a hunt if I stayed in the truck and only took photographs if anyone was arrested. I rode in the truck that went off first and he said he'd follow in five minutes. We waited an hour for him at the border and turned back." She shut her eyes and took a deep breath. "That's when we found him – where we had camped."

"I'm so sorry. I've been to the D.Cs *boma* and saw some photos of Pat. Who took them?"

"I did. A journalist with a camera will always use it whatever the situation. Then we brought him back and reported it."

"I happened to see those shots when talking to Herbie Smith. "They were good and sharp. So what are you up to now?"

At the mention of Smith's name she thought swiftly. She was not about to say what had really happened to her since returning and that she was on bail. It was likely she would lose his sympathy and then drop her. She wanted him to be supportive at this time.

"Well, I am just sweating it out here for a bit. The trouble is there's too much going on at this place for me to concentrate on writing about my initial impressions. I've dropped the investigative side of things of course. I don't want to upset anyone."

"Too much going on here? Lazing around the pool, an occasional swim, clicking your fingers for the odd drink, lunching on poached trout, life must be hard."

"Your trouble is you're not a journalist. No demanding editor. All you do is plant things in dirt in a farm I've not seen and slide off to goodness knows where every so often . . . I take it you really do have a farm?"

"Yes, I do."

"Big? Small?"

"Medium . . . about twelve . . ."

"Twelve acres?" she cut in. "I thought you said you had a farm!"

"Sorry, we don't shout our heads off here like your Texan cattle farmers."

"Nobody would shout off their heads for twelve acres."

"Twelve - hundred - hectares."

"Twelve hundred hec . . . Oh . . . That's Three thousand acres!" She stared at him with wide eyes.

"Around about that. Want to see it?"

"Well, yes. I'd love to – but . . ."

"Come then."

"What, now?"

"Now. Might cheer you up."

She bit her lip and thought. She would be expected to sign the book at six and knew she'd be in trouble if she did not. But then, if she could get Peter to ask her to stay there she could report to the police in his district.

"Where is it? I mean how far?"

"It is up on the Kinangop. A few hours driving."

She did not hesitate. "Give me five minutes."

While she packed her holdall she thought 'ah well, in for a dime, in for a dollar'. "Do you mind if I bring my things?" she called from the bedroom. "I am told not to leave anything about."

"Of course. That's the form here. Keep your essentials with you and always be prepared for any eventuality."

When they got to the pickup she turned to him. "I haven't booked out. I take it you'll return me in one piece, unless you're a sly one and going to take me into darkest Africa then sell me into the white slave trade?"

"I should be so lucky! I could make a fortune with you! . . . You read too many penny dreadfuls and schoolgirl magazines. I'll return you in one piece," he said with a laugh. "If it looks like getting dark before we start back I'll put you up at Kinangop's favourite five star hostelry and bring you back in the morning."

"Oh? What's it called?"

"Dysentery Arms."

The light conversation went on like that as they went through Nairobi's suburbs and left tarmac for a dirt road to Thika. She was feeling much happier now that he had turned up and they were laughing together. So different from their first meeting.

They did not stop at Thika. On passing the market there she noticed large pineapples as big as men's heads in neat pyramids six feet high; plantains and bananas by the hand; citrus fruits with mounds of vegetables and nuts. Africans swarmed among the traders with a few white faces buying for their households while passing half a dozen male sewing machinists treadling furiously to make khaki shorts and shirts for the tribesmen and European type dresses for their women.

"Quite a place," she said.

"One of the biggest markets outside Nairobi."

"What happened to your truck? Strange to see you driving a run-around."

"My truck's being serviced. Always is between long runs. This old warhorse has been resurrected from the great garage in the sky. It's only a two litre engine but it's had a lot of work done. Good power for a pickup and a good clearance. It could turn out to be handy on dry roads. It hasn't a four-wheel drive but it's in very good nick. Reliable and economical."

"It travels well."

"Yes. New rear springs. New safari tyres. It's loaded with spares and a few other things."

They turned north and climbed on a murram track through villages, farms and forest until they reached the township of Kinangop. It appeared to be the usual dirt street of *dukas* – large and small stores, a garage and wayside traders. Not unlike a remote station at home she thought, except for the unique mountainous terrain. He then turned left and down into a minor track to a tree fixed with a white harrow disc painted with just GRANT. Here he turned left again into a long drive between tall jacaranda trees alternating with bougainvillea, across a concrete bridge over an almost dry stream then came to a clearing where he stopped.

Della's eyes widened as she took in the scene. To her left a great two-storied house of early Victorian style with Colonial overlay stood with a stone colonnaded wide veranda with dry wisteria climbing the columns. Wide steps led up from a gravelled front with cropped grass planted randomly with low shrubs. The imposing studded teak door, imported from Zanzibar, was closed. A typical Georgia cotton plantation house crossed her mind. She looked to her right and had a pleasant shock; laid out before her was the floor of the Great Rift Valley four thousand feet below. To her right, Longanot, an old volcano in the middle of the Rift stood stark and sharp-rimmed in the late afternoon sun. Beyond she could see the glint of water on pewter and pink lakes, and the western wall of the Rift rising to Mau Summit. Then turning her gaze west and south the mile-high western escarpment appeared as a shelf of books loosely toppled showing ancient fault formations. Suswa volcano, squat and hiding old lava tunnels and primitive paintings was backed, well to the south, by a group of hills dominated by Ol Doinyo Lengai volcano. The floor of the valley, although having many faults, from this distance looked smooth and covered in golden grass.

"Fancy waking up to this every morning!"

"It is a fancy that never wears thin. Come."

They got out of the pickup and walked to the left of the house along a path that took them to the rear. Through a line of trees a picturesque fifty-foot waterfall now trickling instead of gushing occasionally sparkled in shafts of sunlight through trees.

"I shall build a dam down stream from the falls one day. It will hold water for a dry year."

Further, they went past a filtered, tiled pool on one side of a large lawn. An African in smart kanzu and fez came from the house and stood at a respectful distance.

"Bring tea, please Kinyanjui."

"Welcome *m'sabu*," he said to Della and returned to the house as Peter led her to a table and chairs on a paved court at the back of the house. Dotted about were standing iron baskets with multi coloured shrubs. Soon after they sat Kinyanjui came with the kitchen toto, similarly attired, carrying a laundered white damask cloth, trays with tea in two silver pots, bone china ware with lemon and hot drop scones, a tray of nuts and dried fruit.

They ate and drank while looking out beyond the lawn to the forest climbing up to a sheet of drifting cloud now hiding the Kinangop peak. Mingled with the subdued sound of the waterfall there were a few echoing noises coming down from the heights.

"I have seen a handful of grand American ranch houses in my time but this just about takes the biscuit. When was it built?"

"My father had it done in the twenties."

"Are any of your family here?"

"No . . . There's only me now . . ."

After his long pause, tactfully she said, "I could sit here all day."

"Forgive me for not showing you in the house right now. There'll be an opportunity after the safari. Shall we see the farm?"

"You bet."

They walked back to the pickup and drove down through trees, past farm buildings where a dry track took them into coffee that spread down contours from eight to six thousand feet. Lying back from fields of rain-starved maize and sorghum in a horseshoe of trees was a substantial bungalow with, beyond that, a brick house for servants.

"Our farm manager who lived here did not return from the war. I found a middle-aged ex farmer up from South Africa to take his place but who stays mostly up in Kinangop where he has friends. He looks after the spread very well and despite the reputation of the Boer with Africans he's very good with them and gets fine work from them. He's strict and fair. I let this house now and then, but I would like a permanent resident there." He was aware that the sun was getting low. "I'll run you back to Nairobi."

Della knew she would not make the six o'clock deadline to sign the book and remembered she was in for a dollar as well as a dime and asked him if she could take up his offer of the 'Dysentery Arms'. "Seems churlish to have you run me all the way to Nairobi, anyway, I'd love to wake up to the best view I'm ever likely to see in a whole lifetime. I mean, look at it. That volcano – the distant hills and lakes – and those volcanoes in the south. It's – awesome."

"I might have a better idea. The hotel at Kinangop can hardly be said to be peaceful at the best of times. People go there to do anything but relax and you won't get the five star treatment as you do in town. Let's walk."

While walking to the servants' house he asked her if she wanted a night of peace with no one whooping it up in the swimming pool at the Norfolk.

"That would be nice."

Approaching the brick house he called "Tobias! - *Hodi?*" (*May I approach?*) and a smiling African came out. "*Karibu bwana.*".

"How is the house?"

"The house is all clean. Also the linen is come back from the *dhobi.*"

"Are the other things done?"

"Yes. The frij is working good and everything is prepared."

"Is it fit for m'sabu to stay?"

"Yes."

An African woman then came out of the quarters dressed European style.

"Ah. Wanjui. How are you?"

"I am fine, sir" she said in good English, for she had been a teacher before marrying.

"Will you go to the house, light the fire and get the hot water going and prepare it for m'sabu Mitchell. She is to stay."

"Yes. Welcome to home, m'sabu."

With Della in front and Tobias in the back he drove back up to the farm buildings.

"Do you drive?" he asked her.

"Have you forgotten I drove your truck when you slept on my shoulder like a bushed bison?" Then she remembered slapping his face and tried to hold back a grin. "Yes; anything from a Harley Davidson bike to an army transporter with trailers," she said, gesturing with an over-casual air and a laugh.

"Now who is shouting off her head?" He laughed which brought a playful punch from her. "Licence?"

"International; American Civil; American Forces."

"I take it you'd like to stay at the house?"

"You bet. Thanks. Er . . . a little matter of . . ."

"We'll talk about that after the safari."

At the farm buildings he asked Tobias to collect food from the cold store for the m'sabu for a short stay, and said he and Wanjui were to look after her. Tobias went off leaving them standing looking at the view over the Rift. They watched a descending red sun lighting the tip of the high point of Longanot that glowed with a copper coloured halo immediately taking Peter/'s thoughts to those of the Masai and the Okiuka. He was about to tell her he would be away but thought better of it.

"You have use of the house and pickup for however long it is before I organise our safari and we go out. No telephone there. Wires and poles were brought down by elephants last year. If you wish to dash into Nairobi for anything Tobias can show you the way to the bottom road that leads to Town. There's a good map in the driver's door pouch and it has all the spares you'll ever need and two full jerricans of petrol and we'll fill her up. I shan't need it."

"Well, that's extremely nice of you. That's very kind. So it isn't the white slave traffic after all," she said with a grin.

"Watch it. There's still time," he said, returning the grin.

"You are a star!" She quickly kissed him. It was just a peck, but she was as surprised as he at her action.

Now grinning as though the cat had been at the cream he watched her drive smoothly away; then turned and walked in the gathering dusk up to his house. It was twilight as he went through the door.

At the Manager's house Della put the pickup under the roof of a lean-to and stepped out to look across the Rift. She was less than a degree south of the equator and with the sun seen approaching the horizon was aware of the speed of spin of the earth's circumference. The sky in the west was turquoise while the sun was sinking through streaks of orange cloud that moments ago were pale peach. The vast panorama of the Rift floor sparkled like a gold-washed carpet. Then the whole sky turned red-gold. Gradually it became a duck-egg green followed by an apricot streaked blue and red warm glow. An emotional welled up in her while overcome by the beauty of the continuing sunset. "Ooooh!" was all she could say. The sun, now changed from a yellowish orange was a deep vermilion and with a bulging bottom sat on the horizon for a few seconds then slipped out of sight as it had done for millions of years. Now the sky was lit only by emerging stars in the east while the afterglow of an invisible sun gradually faded. Then it was dark. She stood, transfixed. Then shook her head quickly and went through the front door. With her back against it she said quietly, "How the heck am I going to put such an exquisite experience into just plain words that my readers would understand, or even believe." She turned on a light that started up a generator. A clock on a mantelpiece pointed to six thirteen. She made an omelette at the wood-burning stove and began to make notes. Feeling tired from being at a higher altitude than Nairobi she went to bed. Switching off the final light stopped the generator.

That nigh she slept dreamlessly like a baby while hugging a pillow.

# 8.

## LEGEND

*A rock resembling a Masai girl once stood tall in the Serengeti.*

*A beautiful untouched Masai girl of fourteen years was on her way with an entourage to wed the son of a renowned Counsellor. The caravan was waylaid by drunken rustlers, her retinue killed while she was raped. That night a great storm struck with such force the legs of the rock crumbled. But the torso and head now stand erect in debris to signify the upright dignity of Masai women in adversity.*

*If any ESELENGAI (Young virgin) is again raped a storm beyond measure will rape the land and the stone will fall, causing pestilence to strike.*

In the small hours Peter woke sweating and took a dose of quinine. After a restless night he was up early though and went to the farm garage where the safari truck was waiting, clean and thoroughly serviced. He checked his list and left a message for the farm manager that he would be out for a few days, then drove down to the bungalow where he was met by Tobias to say, "m'sabu she say she is to be at Nairobi to see a bwana called Agent. I show m'sabu the bottom road."

"Oh. Thank you Tobias. When m'sabu returns say I understand. I shall visit her soon." He turned the truck and drove up to where a jacaranda-lined drive took him out onto the road running through Kinangop town. While thinking it strange that his safari agent had not been approached to book a safari through the usual channels he thought it fortunate that she had gone off to Nairobi at this juncture allowing him time to go south to find Sekento and recover the Okiuka. He put his foot down.

*

First he went out to his safari bearer's *shamba* at Kiambu to find him sitting outside his father's rondavel among maize fields. Njoroge put on a much mended and shortened army overcoat and shrugged his shoulders without enthusiasm when Peter said they were off the see the Masai.

Two hours later they crossed into Tanganyika to negotiate the Serengeti plains. Here the temperature gauge in the cab had climbed to over 35°c and Peter was sweating. Skirting Lake Manyara leaving the Rift's wooded escarpment and the Ngorongoro crater in the west he eventually came within a mile of the home of Olekowlish. He found a rise in the ground with rocks and bush in which he hid the truck.

"Njoroge, I have come to chat with a friend. He is in the *engang* beyond that kopje. I should be back before dark."

"Be careful bwana. Animals are fierce at that time."

"Yes Njoroge, I know. It might be novel to stay overnight with the Masai!"

Njoroge was not impressed. Peter started out and reached the engang in good time. "*Hodi*" he called. A call of "*Karibu*" invited him in the enclosure. Cattle was being brought in by boys who returned his greetings as he sought an elder. Greetings were exchanged in OlMaa as Peter was taken to a thorn tree under which three older men sat on stools.

After the preliminaries Peter asked if Olekowlish was in his hut. He was told that the great man was attending a meeting called by the elders of the southern clans.

"He may be returning – one day – two days."

"Ah. Then I shall return in two days." Not wanting to seem discourteous, he made small talk. "You are a popular engang here. You have many visitors."

"Eeeeh. We have visitors. Visitors are welcome."

"For sure. Whenever I come here you make me welcome."

"You remain brother to us since being a toto."

"You have visitors from Kenya?"

"Yes. We have women from the Loita. We are arranging the final details of a marriage."

"Is it a Kenya girl to be married?"

"Aiya. It is a fine girl. She is Nkidong clan of high blood."

"Who is the lucky warrior who is to have a Kenya Masai girl?"

"He is not here. He has been summoned to come. He comes from Kenya also; Nakuru side, but he was born here."

"He is known to you?"

"Aiya, he is known. It is Sianka the second son born to Olekowlish. The firstborn of the second wife. It is he who has been chosen according to custom for this marriage."

"Ah, yes." Peter paused. "The elder son of Olekowlish – Sekento – is he here?"

The question was met by silence. "Is Sekento here? I wish to speak with him."

Again, silence. After exchanged glances one of the elders turned to Peter.

"We do not speak of him now he has been banished from the clan."

"Banished?"

"Aiya. For serious misdemeanours."

Peter now realised that having been banished, possession of the Okiuka would put Sekento in a position of power. He was now sure that was why he had killed Pat for it. And now, as legend would have it; and as written by his father in his journal, the Okiuka, in fraudulent wrong hands, spelled danger.

While they sat and talked of other things women served him a mixture of milk and blood. Then a few women escorts and Naiyolang, the intended bride appeared. She was stunningly pretty by any standards and had a devastating smile. Her teeth remained unfiled, head half-shaved, and for a thirteen-year-old virgin, was youthfully formed with classic grace and dignity befitting the Hamitic people descended from biblical times, and had an immediate feminine attraction that would stir the heart and loins of the most celibate of men.

"Lucky the man who husbanded her," Peter thought unashamedly.

She was here to have the final rituals explained by Olekowlish, who, although of a different clan, was her great uncle. Peter knew that Masai girls were married as soon as child-bearing was possible, and when nature decided this activity to be over, another young wife would be sought to continue child production in order to counter a high mortality rate. However, promiscuity among the young was growing and the old rule of celibacy before marriage was dying, but for a girl to become pregnant before circumcision and marriage was still outlawed and carried great shame, not only to her, but also to her family.

Peter was finding it hard to keep up the conversation because he began to feel unwell with a blinding headache. Persistent flies bothered his damp-with-sweat face and he was invited to sit in one of the huts for shade. There it smelled strongly of goats urine, cow dung, woodsmoke, human sweat and rotting skins. Smoke from a small fire in the hut kept the flies at bay. The smell and a quickening fever overcame him and he collapsed in a stupor while shivering and sweating profusely. One of the men stripped him of his clothes and wrapped him in a blanket. On seeing a festering mark low on Peter's leg he showed it to one of the women. "Look, here is the mark of the tic. He has the fever of the tic. You know what to do."

While Peter was drifting in and out of unconsciousness his leg was treated with the sharp edge of a knife to cut and scrape the place where an infected tic had buried itself. Fresh cow dung was then applied to the wound while his body was washed with diluted goats' urine and an unpalatable liquid was poured down his gagging throat. Then he was left in the dark of the hut to drift into oblivion.

The evening wore on into night that came with the cold of the plains and a cloudless black sky brittle with icy stars. The old people conferred, made a decision that no white man must die in a Masai engang to bring dire consequences to them. Two elderly women were brought to lie either side of him with blankets to keep him warm and let the fever run its course the Masai way. The evaporation of sweat, if let to cool the body too rapidly, would have serious results. The fire was stirred and the women lay next to him now wrapped in a cocoon of blankets. Peter was burning while outside it was freezing. As the fever deepened he dreamed. Not the gentle dreams of the peace and beauty of Africa, but of confused harsh dreams of savage violence and dust.

At the truck Njoroge was concerned for Peter. He had expected him back before nightfall, but as it was now well into the night he decided not to venture out. Peter would be back in the morning he decided.

\*

After a second comfortable night in bed in the house on Peter's farm Della rose before dawn, drank a glass of water, ate porridge and honey, drank coffee and drove the pickup with headlights dipped on the track shown to her the previous day through the lower reaches of the farm to meet the Nairobi/Nakuru road. Following Peter's advice to be prepared for all eventualities she had taken the precaution of stowing her holdall with a change of underwear, dried food from the larder, camera, two dozen rolls of film and her notes together with cash and binoculars, also a four gallon container of water with purifying tablets.

On the way down she was telling herself that ahead was another day in the metropolis when, given other circumstances, she could be up country sampling Kenya's famed scenery and animals. When reaching the main road she flicked on the headlamp beam to read the signpost as a matter of course, left and south to Nairobi; right and north to Nakuru. She was about to turn left when lights from a vehicle approaching from the south lit up the road. She decided to let it pass before pulling out. A black Buick right-hand drive saloon went by at no great speed while her own headlights lit up the driver at an open window who glanced towards Della's lights.

"Good Heavens! That was our Mr.Smith from the DC's place, I swear." She was picking up Peter's habit of reducing long titles to initials. "I wonder what a pen-pusher is doing out at this hour?"

She sat with thoughts of what Pat had said about going to Nairobi where there might be people in high places mixed up in the poaching racket and remembered the auditor's reaction when she told him of her brief and his immediate refusal to let her carry on with her work. This led her to the convincing thought that Smith was involved. A civil servant in a main administrative centre would be a good cover and he'd have access to inside information. And wasn't that Buick in the DC's compound? "I'd stake my winnings on last year's Kentucky Derby against his sweaty little socks that he's my man," she said out loud. "I don't trust people with small feet and, by jingo; I bet he wears no bigger than size six. That does it Della my girl. To heck with Nairobi and that boring book to sign." She had a glint in her eye. "I can't miss a chance like this." The journalist in her overcame any thoughts of the penalty she faced of not signing books. She turned right and drove with dipped headlights, keeping the Buick's rear lights at a respectful distance.

\*

Outside the engang in which Peter lay unconscious, under a waxing moon, seven Masai led by Sianka, stealthily circled the enclosure. They found a low breach in the thorn and, one-by-one, eased through. As ghosts they stole around the outside of the huts without disturbing the cattle or dogs. Sianka made for the designated hut where he knew Naiyolang would be sleeping while the others spaced themselves to keep watch.

Sianka was drunk and tripped over a sleeping woman acting as a guard inside the entrance to Naiyolang's hut. She woke with a start and squealed. "Quiet!" he hissed, picked her up and hit her hard across her face. She collapsed to her knees with her hand over a bleeding mouth. He picked her up and kicked her to go staggering from the hut straight into the arms of one of Sianka's guards who, being as drunk as his leader, put a hand over her mouth and nose to quieten her. He took the struggling girl behind a hut where he lay on her. She struggled vainly for breath as the man dislodged her clothing with his other hand and raped her. Before he was satisfied she was dead.

In the hut Naiyolang woke suddenly and sat up. "Who . . ." A hand clamped over her mouth. "Quiet girl. It is I. Sianka. Your father has refused to have me as your husband. He has acted against custom. He has chosen Sekento who he thinks is a strong leader. I have come to claim you before that murderous brother of mine gets anywhere near you. He is on his way here and comes with followers for a fight. Whatever the outcome he shall not have you as a maiden." With that, he tore the blankets from her. She tried to turn aside from sweat, a stranger's reeking body and breath thick with strong beer. But Sianka, eight years older than her, pulled her down. She lay passive and hurt as his clumsy, drunken actions filled her with numbness and loathing. She lay bruised and broken and it was some minutes before he drew away. "You say nothing of this, girl, or you die." She fought against his hand on her mouth but he was strong. You do not speak of this. If anyone hears of this, remember, you die. Give your word."

Not understanding, she nodded.

"Say it!" he said while releasing his hand.

Too numb to call or scream she whispered, "I give my word."

Sianka and his followers slipped away from the engang as quietly as they had come. They sought a low, bush-covered donga a mile to the south and hid there to await the arrival of Sekento and the return of Olekowlish.

Peter lay still while his fever raged. One of the women got up to go to relieve herself. Behind a hut she discovered the body of the raped and suffocated woman. She went straightway to Naiyolang's hut where she found her sitting outside in the cold, silently weeping. The broken girl responded to the woman's arm and cried heavily on her breast.

"Come, Naiyolang. Come into the warm. You must not stay in this cold."

Naiyolang shook her head and sobbed.

"Come" the woman insisted and took her to where Peter lay. "Lie here. You will be warm. Who did this terrible thing? and who killed Mushoke?"

Naiyolang kept silent. Her sobbing had turned into a vacant stare.

She was laid next to Peter and covered with blankets in place of the two women who went to where the dead girl lay, then to the hut of one of the elders. Other elders were woken and women began a subdued wailing. Men were detailed to look for intruders, and while the commotion went on through the night Naiyolang was ordered to keep the white man warm. She sobbed herself to sleep lying alongside the unconscious white man. In her sleep as the sun lightened the eastern sky she snuggled closer for warmth but her blanket was disturbed and their naked bodies touched.

*

Della followed her quarry along an undulating road through the townships of Naivasha and GilGil for it to become daylight and to switch off lights. When approaching Nakuru there was traffic to negotiate and she allowed vehicles to get between her and the Buick. In the town's wide main street she saw him swing across to park nose-in to the front of the Stag's Head hotel where he got out, locked the Buick door and went into the hotel's main entrance. She drew into a garage to top up with petrol, check the oil and water and to park in a side road near the railroad station where she had sight of the Buick. Here she recorded the mileage and set the trip counter. While munching on biscuits she studied the two maps left in the pickup and was surprised to find that Peter had pencilled in secondary tracks where none were printed plus game areas and possible camp sights. One map covered all Kenya while the other, all Tanganyika.

Oblivious to being followed, Smith ate a typical Kenya breakfast of kedgeree, mixed grill, coffee, toast and honey. Della complemented her meal of two biscuits with a mouthful of coffee from a flask.

*

The dawn came, dry as any other. Elders went to the hut where Peter had been put and discovered Naiyolang lying close to him with disarrayed blankets and traces of her vaginal blood on his thigh. This was calamity. The Masai women thought the worst. Then again, if the white man was to die he must not die in a Masai hut, especially while lying with a Masai girl. He was grasped by many hands and taken some distance away from the engang, dropped unceremoniously close to a bush with his shorts, shirt, boots and a blanket thrown over him. The Masai left him there to die.

His dream while being carried was that of flying over the Nakuru lake. But then he fell into the shallows and was assailed by many wings flapping him. He tried to fend off the flamingo while a noise in his head grew to resemble that of an express train in a tunnel. The flamingos faded but for one that flapped its wings in his face He struggled from a long way down with moments of blackness and buzzing alternated with blinding light until his senses burst into daylight. Njoroge was kneeling over him slapping his face and calling softly "Bwana Peter, bwana Peter . . ."

Peter tried to get up on an elbow and was promptly sick. As he gasped for breath Njoroge held a water bottle to his lips from which he drank greedily. He took a deep breath and his head cleared.

"Njoroge! Where am I?"

"A long way from home, bwana."

"You are joking. How far?"

"*Huuko!*" Njoroge turned his face to the north and jutted out his chin to its fullest extent to determine the distance.

"What am I doing here? What happened?"

"You have been sick. I heard from some Masai you had been at the village."

"What village? Where?"

"A mile. Over there." His chin pointed.

"Where am I?"

"Lying on the ground naked."

Peter bit back a retort and laughed weakly.

"I can see that, you mutt. Help me on with these shorts." In shorts, boots and jacket he stood and staggered with Njoroge's arm about his waist. "Is there water here?" he asked, finishing the bottle.

"None. There will be water at the village."

Peter could not collect his thoughts and left himself to Njoroge who supported him to the deserted engang. He had no recollection of having come here, nor why, nor what happened. Njoroge found a calabash full with clean water and Peter drank deeply. The water containing green and white stones tasted good and smelled of herbs. They sat in the shade of the surrounding thorn.

"I must have come here for something, Njoroge. What was it? Where is everybody?"

"I do not know. You did not come back last night."

"What place is this?"

"Tanganyika. Wemberi side. You came here to talk to Masai. I came down to the village. But there had been trouble there. There was fighting. I spoke with some as they left the village. They said you had been here and other Masai came to cause trouble and you were put to bush. Masai from Kenya also fled as still more Masai came for trouble. There has been killing. A Masai girl. There was much fighting. Some were hurt. All have fled." They did not speak for some minutes. "You look sick bwana."

"No sicker than I will look if we don't get the hell out of here. Where is the truck? We did come in the truck?"

"On a rise. Two miles."

Peter took another mouthful of water from the calabash with the green and white stones. "Stones?" he said, "what would they be for I wonder?" Then forgot about them and staggered to his feet. Njoroge returned the calabash to the place where he found it.

"Your hat, bwana. I find it."

The two-mile journey back to the truck mercifully was blank in Peter's mind. He collapsed a few times but Njoroge got him there as best he could. When there, Njoroge made a jug of lime juice, sugar and salt and helped Peter get some of it down. It revived him for five minutes but he fell again into a stupor. Njoroge then heated water, stripped, washed and dried his boss and friend and put him in a camp bed in the back of the truck. Njoroge was now in a quandary. Should he stay here with Peter until he was better or should he take him back to Kinangop to recover? He did not fancy staying too close to the Masai and decided on Kinangop. He drove speedily and carefully all the way.

\*

An hour after Della had parked Smith came from the hotel, reversed out of the parking space and drove past her. A safari hat obscured her face, and she let him have a few hundred yards with two vehicles in between before pulling out and following.

When leaving Nakuru on a murram road the intervening cars turned off while the Buick picked up speed and went out of sight beyond a rise. Slowly topping the rise Della looked at an empty road. She put her foot down for some miles, and when coming to a fork with the left track rising into hills and the right track going down towards lower ground she realised she had lost him. Here she wished that she had taken lessons from the Comanche in shadowing technique. She was at a loss as to know what to do. Taking out binoculars she stood on the back of the pickup. The rising road revealed nothing but a foreshortened view of treetops shrouded in mist. The lower road while disappearing into dry scrub also revealed nothing. On raising the glasses higher she whistled and took a second look without them. In the distance she could just discern a sheer cliff many miles long reaching into a hazy sky. The beginnings of shimmering heat waves made the cliffs sometimes indistinct and distant, and at others, close and clear enough to pick out features.

Realising she was in the middle of the Rift Valley she took in the hugeness of it all and felt very small. On scanning the lower road again she saw the telltale signs of dust some miles ahead and hoped it was the Buick. She started up and turned into the right fork and drove for half-an-hour when she approached a wayside garage set back behind trees where an African was fuelling a covered Bedford truck from a hand pump. Standing by the Bedford was an ex-army open six-wheeled troop carrier with a group of variously dressed Africans climbing aboard. She caught sight of a dilapidated sign over the garage bearing the place name of Mogotio, and then saw the Buick at the other side of the pump. Beyond the garage was fork road with a copse of trees in the acute triangle in which she hid the pickup hoping the garage mechanic had not seen her. Here she stood on the back of the pickup and waited. Whichever road the Buick took she would know which to follow.

Five minutes and a mosquito swarm passed before she heard the whine of the six-wheeled carrier followed by the Bedford and saw them drive past her on the right, eastern fork. But she could not see who was driving or any white faces. The Buick did not appear. Getting frustrated and annoyed with assorted flying insects she jumped into the cab and drove back to the garage while thinking up an idea. She pulled a scarf up over her nose and drove through the trees to the pump. While there she saw the Buick half hidden in a workshop and an African pulling a cover over it then closing big doors. She punched the horn and the African came to her. Putting on an accent and deep voice she believed to be that of an upper class Kenya Memsa'b she asked if the bwana from Nairobi was still here. "He forgot papers dammit," she said, waving her own notes. "I've come all this damned way here with them. Filthy dust. Enough to choke one, what."

"Sorry m'sabu," said the African shaking his head. "Bwana has gone with Chief Thukuru."

"Where, dammit?"
"Safari *kubwa*. Maybe you catch for him at Maralal."
"All that way?"
"*Ndio* m'sabu."
"You best fill me up then. Important papers."
"You no catch for him on that bad road. You no got four-wheel drive. He has proper ghari. You best take this road. This road better for small ghari."
"Right you are."
"That be six shillin' fifty cent, m'sabu."
She handed over two five-shilling notes. "Filthy dust what!" she shouted as she took off northwards with back wheels raising dust.

When she was out of sight over a rise she pulled in, wiped her forehead, drank some more coffee and with a smug chuckle thinking she had fooled the African. "Chief Thukuru eh? Another big fish? Looks as though I might be on the right track." What she did not know that as soon as she drove away from the garage, the African, who was puzzled by the obvious bad accent and unusually large tip, walked over to his small office, lifted a telephone and called someone for the second time in an hour and quoted the pickup registration number with a vague description of its woman driver.

Consulting the map Della could see that Maralal was some distance along the way she was heading but with a turn east then north to take her around Lake Baringo with another track up to Maralal. The track that the carrier and the Bedford had taken, Della decided, must be little used and chosen to keep Green and the Chief out of sight, but would join her route later near the lake. Folding the map she started for the long drive.

Now used to the right-hand drive she found it comfortable to travel fast on some sections remembering that Peter would 'iron out' the corrugation, but had a hard time keeping her eyes on the road and not look at the glorious scenery. In places she had to crawl and negotiate rockfalls where fierce daytime heat and night frost had split rocks.

The signpost at the turn-off east down to the Baringo lake lay with a sad face in the dry storm ditch having fallen to termites. Without hesitation and with a childish feeling of exploring the unknown she went east into descending scrub and before long rounded the south of the lake where she saw many birds in the shallows. Steam rose from hot springs. She stopped briefly to take photographs and to chew on dried fruit and nuts with a cupful of water and swore she would come to this place again some time to admire one of the most beautiful lakes in the Rift crowded with birds and hot springs.

With long shots of the springs and close-ups of birds safely on the negative roll in her camera she washed the windscreen of a sticky mess of flattened insects and pressed on in the hope that she would beat the two trucks to Maralal. Coming to a junction she took the road that climbed the eastern escarpment. It was here she came quickly to a halt. From behind a copse of acacia came many elephants in line about to cross her path. She took a chance, switched off and slid out of the door and leaped up into the back of the pickup with her camera. Crouching over the cab she took a shot of the line then a number of close-up shots including babies as they past her almost brushing the pickup and near enough to be able to touch her with their trunks. It was obvious to her that the great beats smelled no more than hot metal and oil that posed no threat. Counting them as they filed past with trunks linked to tails, babies and all, she stood amazed at a count of eighty-three. The last of them unhooked his trunk, dipped it and she managed to get a shot of the bull's trunk turned back over its head before he showered dust all over its back, the truck and her. She did not mind for she got back into the cab and clapped her hands with excitement. "That's one for the article!" she cooed. "I wonder if Peter could have found me that many!" Further on she came across a pride of nine lions with the males standing off all waiting while the dominant male, maned and huge, took his fill of a recent zebra kill. She took more photographs and close-ups, this time from the cab with a long lens. One of the females, on seeing the pickup came closer but stopped and snarled as Della took a close-up of just her head. "Oh, heck," she said, "life out here is exciting! But I mustn't stop any more; I could miss who I am after. "Bye, Bye lions," she called, but she had to stop more than once again to photograph leaping impala, gazelle, buffalo and a female baboon cuddling her baby while being groomed by her male. Fearing she would not get to Maralal before her adversaries she pressed on. She need not have worried. The two trucks carrying the Africans and Smith had stopped for their daily *posho* – a maize porridge wrapped in large leaves. Smith had salt beef sandwiches packed for him when at Nakuru.

Having now climbed onto a small plateau she stopped briefly and looked back through binoculars to see two specs on the road raising dust. "That's my boys! If I can keep this up I'll have time to recce Maralal before dark." Climbing further she arrived on an undulating plateau with hills to the northeast and plains to the southeast. A couple of miles further she had to stop while an enormous herd of hundreds of hump-backed Boran cattle attended by small Samburu boys wielding long sticks passed by and she took a shot across a sea of curved horns in hovering dust. Following them were two tall Samburu, dressed traditionally in shukas, and showing the same nonchalant, aloof arrogance of the Masai. She photographed them, and unaware she had done so they came to the pickup, looked at its smiling occupant with disdain and continued walking hand-in-hand into the dust raised by the cattle. What assailed Della were the overpowering sweet smell of the cattle and the curious milky woodsmoke smell of the men.

While driving on and remembering her last visit to Maceys in New York she thought "That pong no doubt suits their women out here, but I reckon I prefer Fabergé or Chanel."

# 9.

The lion will go deep into the jungle if it eats a deaf ear.
*(Ignoring advice can lead to danger)*

Maralal was not much different from what Della expected. A few brick and wooden buildings with corrugated roofs scattered away from the main street that consisted of dukas, an African beer hall and market where Samburu cattlemen gathered, a garage and a police post. At the end of the town on the outskirts an hotel with wooden bungalows and *bandas* was set right back among trees. She drove through the dusty street and stopped on the road half a mile past the town on a rise. Wiping her brow and neck she decided she would have to find a place to camp and still have sight of the arrival of the two trucks with Smith and the Chief. There was a small hill rising into others that had good trees and short grass in which she decided to camp.

As she folded the map a horseman wearing old cord trousers, high chamois boots, check shirt and bush hat appeared from a cultivated field and came riding up to her. She had no chance of driving off as he stood the horse in front of the pickup. He tipped his hat.

"Good afternoon madam. Are you lost?"

His accent was that of a Boer from the Orange Free State in South Africa.

"Er, no thank you."

"Are you looking for me?"

"For you? No, I think not," she said feeling uneasy.

"Then why you stop here?"

"A breather. Why do you ask?"

"Because the last time this blerry truck was up here, I was driving it."

"But this isn't your truck. It belongs to . . ."

"I know who it belongs to. That young scallywag Peter Grant."

"Why, yes. He gave me the use of it."

He got down from the horse, came to her and opened the cab door.

"Let me introduce myself. Eghardt Pretorius. Eggy to my man friends, Pretty to my lady friends. I was hunting partner to George Grant, young Peter's father when he was alive."

At this the unease left her. He held out his right hand. His left arm was crooked without much elbow movement with a jagged scar showing from under his short sleeve to his forearm. She got out and grasped a strong fist.

"Good day. Della Mitchell."

"You're from America?"

"Yes."

Eghardt was not tall, had rugged, pleasant looks for his fifty years, a snub nose, dark, greying curly hair, swarthy weathered skin which she took to be a deep tan, smiling dark brown eyes and a stocky body with hard muscle. His speech while thickly accented was courteous and charming.

"What brings you up here?"

"I thought I'd see northern Kenya before I go back."

"Ach man, you couldn't have chosen a better place. Alone?"

"Yes."

"Be careful. Best to travel in groups. Look after yourself missy. Where are you staying for the night? The hotel?"

"No. I'll be camping. I thought up that hill."

"What? '*Old Nyoka*'? (*Old snake*) You'd certainly have company up there. Place is lousy with snakes. Can't stay there. You stay with us. Me and m'Frau will look after you."

"But I . . ."

"No buts. If you friend of young Peter you friend of us. Come. Turn around and follow."

He leapt easily back into the saddle with reins in his left hand with the right one on his thigh and waited for her to turn. She had no recourse but to accept his courteous offer and she followed him back towards Maralal.

A quarter of a mile before town he turned left, crossed a concrete platform straddling a wide storm drain and took a path that ran between trees. Following, she was struck by the beauty of the low sun throwing beams through the dust raised by the galloping horse. A clearing appeared and he waved as he passed a sprawling wooden bungalow with iron roof crowded with wisteria growing up from the supporting poles of a wide veranda. A woman sat there dressed exactly as Della had seen in old pictures of the South African pioneer with button boots, ankle-length skirt, severe blouse, stiff apron and bonnet. The woman looked up, raised a hand and followed the pickup with her gaze as it went after the horse around to the back of the house and past a huge shed in which was a sawmill with piles of rough planks and tree trunks.

He dismounted and gestured her to drive into a wired compound and park next to a long articulated logging truck while five big Ridgeback dogs greeted him. Two other mean-eyed smaller dogs, thin and scarred, skulked silently looking on as the five eagerly grouped around their master. As Della got out of the cab the dogs faced her and growled.

"Heel! Down!" he said and swore in Afrikaans at them. They all sat. He spoke loudly the Swahili for friend, *rafiki!* then turned to her. "Stay still. They friendly now." Then he took them one by one across to her to smell the back of her hand while giving their names as one would count in Swahili, *Moja, Mbili, Tatu, Nne*, and *Tano*. One by one she made acquaintance with the fiercest pack in East Africa, trained to look after him and his family to the death. Della said the other two looked like prairie dogs.

"They *Shenzies*. Best lion hunters this side of Nakuru. Used to keep them hungry to make good hunters, but they get good food now they pensioned off. Come, the pickup is safe there. No intruder come near my dogs. They stay on the stoep at night to scare off leopards. Come to the house."

Annie Pretorius came from the kitchen smoothing down her apron as they entered the large drawing room. Now without the bonnet she looked less severe with dark eyes and hair, as tall as her husband and with the same engaging smile.

"Velcome to Langlaagter." Her accent was very deep.

"Now sit please," he said "and drink Cape wine." He breached a bottle of the finest vintage from Stellenbosch in the Cape. "You notice two things. First, my dearest Annie is one eighth Hottentot and was my father's lackey. I stopped him beating her and brought her up here before the war when I met George Grant. Second, somewhere back in time my Dutch blood was mixed with Bushman I think. Van Riebeek started something down there in the Cape he could not know what three hundred and more years could do. We do not have that problem here in Kenya."

"My country has a similar history and had a civil war to change attitudes. Are you still hunting?"

"No. You see why. I cannot hold a big gun too well. I shoot only for the pot with a long barrel Colt 38 special from the back of a horse. I tell you that George Grant was a good man. A lion had my arm and from thirty yards he shoot the blerry thing between the eyes two inches away from mine. He was the best shot. He should not have died. He and Peter's mother they both die. And what they die of? She die of blerry influenza and he die from heartbreak. Two good people gone from my life." He quickly changed from frowning to an engaging smile. "Welcome Della. Welcome to Langlaagter. That was the name of our dorp in the Frei Staadt. Young Peter, now, how is he a friend of yours?" She told him how they met, and the ensuing chat went easily before a log fire.

After dark during a superb meal served by a quiet Samburu servant she found Annie to be charming, elegant and self educated, having read and could quote from most of the Victorian novelists, the Afrikaans bible, and was well up on astronomy and basic science. She did not explain that she was born one of nine daughters of a Boer farming couple who, to turn a miserly penny, hired them out as domestic servants instead of sending them to school.

"Our two sons are at Edinburgh University. Jannie will become doctor and Noah a teacher. Our daughter Fiona is at the Kenya girls' high school. I miss them."

"So do I, Sugarbush. So do I," he said with deep feeling.

As the meal progressed Della almost forgot why she was at Maralal. After coffee that Annie served in the large, comfortable drawing room with décor of the Cape Dutch she was shown the guest room. Della said she needed to get things from the pickup. Eghardt took her out to the compound where he switched on lights to flood the area and the sawmill. Light spread past the sheds to a wire boundary fence. She had a shock. The Bedford and the carrier were parked the other side of the wire.

"What are those vehicles?" she asked him.

"I expect they belong to someone staying at the hotel. Sometimes they let hunting trucks park there away from the front."

"Where would they hunt up here?"

"Not here. All around used to be for hunting but it is now reserved for tourism. Samburu country. Hunters go north from here. At one time it was allowed in the Matthews range and the Ndotos. Not now. They are heavily forested and full of game. Playground for poachers now, especially the Ndotos. Hunters go north to the desert."

Unknowingly Eghardt had given her the information she needed. She wondered how she would follow her quarry, if poaching was their purpose, and what if they were to stay here for another and perfectly legitimate reason? What if they left during the night? She knew she could not up-sticks and creep out now with the pickup behind locked gates. These thoughts were with her as she picked up her things. "Eghardt?"

"Call me Pretty. You lady friend now."

"Pretty, is it safe to stay out here for a few moments? It's a lovely night and I adore the stars, and look, there's a brilliant moon rising. Will I be safe?" Her mind was working overtime.

"That's okay. You better have Tano on the lead. She a big pussycat with lady she knows and *khali* with strangers. She not let harm come to you." He called Tano who came bounding across and licked Della's hand while he secured a leather lead to the dog's collar. "If you sense trouble just whistle. They will come."

While Eghardt took in her things she walked around the house with Tano and nonchalantly went across to the wire fence. From there the sawmill was hiding the compound and the pickup. "Come Tano," she whispered, crawling under the wire and up to the carrier. From a pocket she took a folding knife and telling Tano to sit she felt the rearmost tyre on the back axle. It had a good broad and deep tread and she gouged two deep V cuts into the high part. Before going around to the other side Tano bared her teeth with fur bristling and growled softly. She silenced her with a finger and crept under the truck's body with her. An African came to the carrier, climbed aboard and lay down heavily. Soon he was snoring with a strong smell of African beer. She then crept around to the other rear tyre and gouged one cut in that.

"Two left, one right" she said to herself. "Whichever way they go now I might have a chance of following them." She took Tano back through the wire and around the house once more, slipped the lead and said goodnight to all five dogs, each in their own kennel on the veranda.

In a cosy room with a log fire in the hearth, she slid between the sheets.

Unable to keep Peter out of her mind she thought a nice cuddle would not go amiss. Then she hugged her nighttime pillow. She could not understand why she constantly thought of Peter while determined to keep men at a distance. She sighed and fell asleep. But she dreamed that Peter was angry with her for driving away in his pickup.

\*

Back at the Farm, Peter lay in a hot bath. Part of the fever he knew was caused by dehydration. He counted himself lucky that Njoroge had done what he did. "I owe him," he said as he inspected the scar on his leg where the tic had burrowed in. "How the hell did I miss that?" he said.

The Masai had performed timely, crude surgery, and the wound was healing nicely from having been covered by cow dung. Ingested natural medicine, made with a base of cows' urine containing generations of anti bodies had expunged the illness.

While contemplating his luck he suddenly remembered why he had wanted to see Sekento and Olekowlish at the engang and swore in frustration at having missed them. His memory of anything else that had happened there was never to return. Now he was more than ever determined to have the matter of the Okiuka put right but was at a loss to know what move to make next.

"Ah, well, I'll sleep on it. Might get some ideas tomorrow. I'll take a horse out early and pop down to see how Della's getting on."

\*

Della's bed was so comfortable and so deep was her sleep she woke as the sun's rays burst through curtains pulled back by a young African girl.

"Good morning madam. Chai for you."

"Mmmm?" She slowly woke then sat bolt upright and realised where she was. "Oh. Thank you."

The girl smiled and nodded. "You sleep too well, madam. The baas lady say let you be when we see you so fast asleep at sun-up. The time is now eight. You finish tea then you take bath. Baas lady say you breakfast with her at nine."

Now wide awake, Della replaced the pillow she had been hugging and wondered if the two vehicles were still the other side of the boundary wire. She stepped out of bed and looked through the window from where she could see the sawmill shed and up the hill but not the place where the vehicles were parked. She turned to the girl and said what a lovely morning it was and asked her name.

"My name Beauty, madam."

"You are not from here?" she asked, detecting the same accent as Eghardt and Annie.

"Oh, no, madam. I come from Langlaagter with the Baas and Lady when I was pikinin. They take me from bad home and give me good life here. I work for the Baas Lady and she teach me many things."

"Well, thank you for the tea and I shall join Mrs.Pretorius at nine."

Beauty left with a curtsey and a smile. In the bath Della knew she must be polite to her hosts. It wouldn't do to go rushing off after they had been so hospitable.

Breakfast was pleasant and relaxed with a woman who had the social graces and was pleased to have another female to talk to. When finished and the table cleared by Beauty they went to the veranda with coffee where they began to 'put the world to rights'. They saw Eghardt drive up in a tractor and trailer stacked with fence posts taking them to the back of the house.

"I know Eghardt will ask you to stay over. It will keep us company and we can show you the hills."

"That is very kind. I hate to say, but I have a deadline to meet. I work for a newspaper and am writing a travel article and it is my intention to cover the north of here."

At that moment Eghardt came and joined them for coffee. "Did you sleep well?"

"Never better. I was so comfortable I overslept."

"I have been up to the forest sheds overseeing my boys splitting fence posts. We start early here. You'll be staying over for a few days of course?"

"I would love to. I could not wish for a nicer offer. I am very tempted, but I have been explaining to Annie that I do not have the luxury of time. My newspaper has deadlines and I have to go north. I have never been so happy and relaxed while being here. It was my good fortune that you recognised the pickup." Inwardly she was not relaxed. She was thinking of the two vehicles.

"I see you have a job to do. You must call again sometime but not before you tell that young scallywag Peter to come up here. Not for five years have I seen him, not since his ma and pa died."

"I can vouch for him being a scallywag! He's a big boy now. Seems to work very hard at some things."

"We all work hard here. Good country. Work hard, play hard."

Beauty came out and while collecting the coffee things Annie told her to be careful with them. "Wash them properly my girl and stop moping about that boy. I am sure he is up to no good. It is a good thing he is gone."

"But, madam, he say he gone for small time. He say he be back and marry me."

"You'll not marry till he comes here and we speak. You do things right and proper. He keeps bad company with those other boys in the truck. I should like to know what he does first."

"But he say he be rich soon."

"How he get rich? Does he work? Does he steal?"

"I not know madam, but when the two trucks go at daybreak he wave to me and say he come back with money."

"So that is what you were doing when I called for you this morning! I hope you do not sleep with him."

"Oh, no madam. He want me to, but I say we marry first like good Christian."

"I want no pikinin running around here or off you go my girl. Now you forget this boy and do your work. You be a lazy girl when he comes up. Not the first time. Off you go and wash platters then do floors." She turned to Della. "She is a good girl until this boy showed his face. I cannot think he makes an honest living and I hope we have seen the last of him now those two trucks have gone."

Della smiled and was thankful that the information she hoped for had come without asking. She did not show her impatience to get away but she knew they had four hours start whichever direction they went.

That morning time came to say farewells and with a parcel of food she drove out of the compound and waved as she passed the house to go under the trees and out on to the road. She turned north while guessing that would be the way to go. She thought that Smith and the Chief would not have come this far with a truck full of Africans for no reason and turn back.

It was about five miles along the deserted road that she came to a dry watercourse crossing the road. The clear tracks of the carrier's marked tyres showed in loose sand. She stopped to take water and dried fruit and mopped her brow wishing she had a Comanche with her to help her trail.

\*

Half an hour after Della left, Chief Inspector Andrews, in response to signals received, driven swiftly and well by his African sergeant in a police Land Rover, stopped at the Hotel at Maralal.

"I have time for lunch here. Collect me in one hour."

"Yes sah," the driver said opening the passenger door, and for the benefit of anyone who was looking he threw up a parade-ground salute that Andrews acknowledged by raising a swagger stick to his cap. The sergeant then eased his two hundred and twenty five pounds of muscle and paunch back into the Land Rover and drove away to the African beer hall where, by intimidation, he would get free beer and choice of a woman for a 'short time' as was his habit. He had earned his promotion to sergeant the hard way with many postings and was a bully in handling suspects and prisoners. Of the Jaluo tribe he was six feet tall and had a terrifying fist that won him each fight he took on.

In the hotel dining room Andrews sat alone at a table apart from other guests. On returning to Nairobi from investigations regarding

Pat O'Brien at Narok and the incident scene, he had collected papers and read the cryptic messages from the garage at Mogotio. He calculated that he would apprehend Della before she caught up with Smith and Chief Thukuru. He reckoned that an American not used to a right-hand drive on these roads would drive slowly. Although pleased she had revealed her whereabouts by being a bad actress, he was puzzled to know how she knew of the movements of Smith and Thukuru. He speared another forkful of steak and fastidiously chewed it thirty two times – one for each tooth – before swallowing.

*

At Kinangop Peter woke at sun up and was greeted by Kinyanjui with a sealed envelope by a runner. It contained a request to contact his friend, Steve Harris, the police inspector at the Kinangop post. After a good breakfast he went to the stables, saddled a hunter and rode down to the Manager's house. A bright dawn had spread over the Rift as he went to the veranda. From the saddle he called "Hello the house!" There was no reply and Josiah came from his dwelling.

"You call the m'sabu, bwana?"

"Yes, perhaps she's asleep."

"Oh, no bwana. She not here. She not come back."

"Not . . .?"

"Ndio bwana. She not here. She go to Nairobi and not return."

"Did she say why?"

"No. She not say. She go to Nairobi and not return."

"You have the spare key?"

"Yes. Here."

Peter dismounted and went inside. He noticed her holdall and camera gear was not there. What few things she had left there were put neatly away in a drawer and he found no note or clue as to why she was not there.

"Perhaps she has a good reason," he said as he locked the door, but he was worried in case she had had a misfortune with the pickup. "Send a note up to the house when she returns." He mounted and trotted up to the house then took the drive through the trees and turned on to the dirt road up to the Kinangop police post. Steve had just finished inspecting his small force of African policemen and was reading a file when Peter walked in.

*"Leti kahawa!"* Steve called, "or would you like something stronger than coffee?"

"Coffee's fine. No hard stuff this time of the day."

"Take a seat Peter. You look bushed. Heavy night?"

"No such luck. Bad trip this time. Touch of the wobblies. Got back last night. What's cooking? Anything interesting?"

Steve tapped one of the two files on his desk.

"You have a new girl in tow, then?"

"What? Me? A new girl? I wish. What are you on about?"

He tapped the file again.

"You are a cagey one, Peter. As soon as she's in trouble you shack up with her at the farm."

"What the hell are you talking about?"

"Ah. Here's coffee. How do you take it?"

"Black and honey if you have it."

Steve did not say anything until dust was cleared from their throats. He seemed a little embarrassed.

"I have to impart wisdom from the C.I. Peter. Sorry to have to tell you but your girlfriend from across the pond has gone AWOL. Nairobi's had a call from a reliable contact. She's getting into deep water. I read here she's skipped police bail."

"She's done <u>what</u>?"

"Didn't you know? The C.I. bailed her on a false application for a visa. He's impounded her passport. It says here you've hidden her at your place and given her transport. The pickup registered number was traced to you."

"What a lot of cock you talk, Steve. It isn't like that. I didn't know Della had been bailed. As for hiding her, my staff knows she's at my old manager's house down by the mahindi fields and I'm told she went to Nairobi to see her agent. That's not hiding."

"Agent my foot. She was supposed to sign the book at eight each morning."

"Sign . . .? Bloody hell! So, what is she up to?"

"Can't tell you that. Wheels among wheels. According to the C.I. you are aiding and abetting. He reckons you know where, who and why, and wants to see you when he gets back."

"He can take a running jump."

"Off the record, there are others who would help him off the starting block to do just that. On the record though, whatever you or I think of the situation does not count. C.I. Andrews is the governor. The girl and O'Brien are his shauri. I'd hate to see you get into trouble Peter, but I have my orders."

"Damn! What a girl! Plausible and convincing. I'd like to know what she's up to."

"Whatever that is, don't get involved. The C.I. won't let trifles stand in his way."

"Why can't he come up here?"

"He's busy at present with the Pat O'Brien debacle."

"A sad affair. I'd like to get my hands on whoever did it. Any clues?" he asked, knowing full well it was Sekento.

"I haven't. But I have been told to look out for O'Brien's Jeep with a Masai up front." He took a sip of coffee. "Look, Peter, you know the country like the back of your hand; where would a Masai with a jeep hide himself?"

"Not on a recognised route, that's for sure. So does your file tell you what Pat was doing down in the Mara?"

"After poachers I'm told. Off the cuff, Peter, we'd like to pick your brains. Our chaps down at the Magadi post missed the culprit, Jeep and all. Apparently he was on his way north from below the border with a few others in combat array. Can you throw any light on how he eludes us?"

"One minute you want me to go cap in hand to the Almighty and the next you want to pick my brains? I'd tell you all I know, Steve, but I don't know much. I've been away for a few days."

"Can I ask where?"

"I did a photographic job for Nairobi's DC. When I took the prints back he was at the law courts but Herbie Smith is looking after them. Why don't you ask him? He has a file on Pat's murder."

At the mention of Smith's name Steve looked up. "He has a file? An auditor?"

"I think he has one to clear Pat's effects. If you want to see him he told me he's off on a fact finding tour."

"Is he now!?" Steve first had a puzzled frown that turned into a half smile. "A Fact finding tour, eh?"

"That's what the man said. But when did you hear about the police at Magadi missing the jeep?" asked Peter.

"Yesterday. A.P.B."

"All I can do is to keep a lookout and let you know what turns up."

To let Steve know was the last thing Peter had in mind, however friendly. He realised that if Sekento was coming north and had passed Magadi only yesterday then he knew where he was likely to be. He made his excuses and thanked Steve for the coffee.

"I'll be off. I'll see Andrews when he gets back."

"Keep your nose clean Peter. Things are . . . well, things are."

Peter galloped back to the farm, put the hunter to stables and went to the garage where the serviced and loaded safari truck was ready and waiting. While making a quick dash to Nairobi he decided that as Della had gone missing and was wanted by the police he would now concentrate, not on organising a safari for her, but to make a serious effort to find Sekento. "Dumb blonde? Ha! I should cocoa!" He skirted the town centre and made for the Ngong road.

While driving he was thinking he might know just about where Sekento could be. Also Peter wondered how the smiling six-year-old boy, his childhood friend, could have turned out to be a murderer. And what Olekowlish his father would think of his son.

"I hope that if I ever have a son he turns out better than he has. Not just one, but two stroppy sons. Hope the old boy's all right."

# 10.

## GOD'S WISH CANNOT BE PUSHED
*(Nobody can dispute God's intention)*

The 'old boy' was not alright. The joint assembly of Masai elders from the southern clans had summoned him to make rain. He did not have the Okiuka.

Under the towering thorn tree used for important ceremonies close to the Counsellor's village a large colourful gathering of warriors in full dress and women adorned with grass pinned around their skirts were chanting and wailing quietly as though waiting for a solo singer. Elders wore ceremonial skins and patterned blankets and sat on stools surrounding their Laibon within his own small circle of dung next to an everlasting fire. This fire had been kept burning day and night regardless of weather and had been burning since the day he had become of age fifty years ago.

Olekowlish, father of rainmakers, much-revered Laibon, Chief Counsellor, spiritual head of the Ilaiser clan and of all Masai, on his stool, dipped his hand into a calabash and extracted age-old green and white rainstones and spread them onto a flat slab of rock. Against the dull grey they shone in the midday sun. He stared at them intently for some minutes then lifted his eyes to the north where, on the horizon Ol Doinyo Lengai, the immense, sacred volcano, 'Mountain of God', was just seen through the heat haze.

The elders were unquiet in their thoughts because the Laibon was without his symbol of power. The Okiuka was not in his hands. Now he was an Archbishop without a Crosier; a diviner without a rod; a Prospero with drowned book and no staff. Without it Olekowlish had to rely on his innate cunning and exceptional experience to maintain spiritual leadership and authority. Although he commanded the respect of his clan and of all the tribe, he was now vulnerable and had been put to the ultimate test.

Such was the will of NGAI that rain had failed for three years. The moon, strangely tinged with red when full, had waxed and waned too many times since rain had fallen. The land lay barren.

Boreholes and watercourses long ago had given up their water. Even the lion and elephant had gone looking for distant, greener pastures. Olekowlish's reputation was at stake and this was to be his final chance. If he could not make rain, and soon, he would be dishonoured and pegged out alive for the hyenas. He would be forced to be the first of tens of thousands of men, women, children and animals about to perish for the want of water. Such was the will of NGAI.

As a secondary measure he had improvised a baton made from seven tubular stems of grass. These tubes, bound and plugged at both ends, carried tiny seeds from acacia pods. To complete the power of this makeshift Okiuka he had inserted thorns at intervals through the walls of the tubes.

He rose and stepped forward. The chanting and ululating ceased. In silence, slowly, at arms' length, bending and twisting his wrist, he caused the seeds to run bouncing along the tubes to make the sound of rain. In the face of each elder in turn he twirled the staff and stamped his feet to a fast rhythm to make the sound of thunder. With flailing arm and juddering feet raising dust he went clockwise around the full circle, then, standing in his own circle he began to chant. Two of the elders rose, went to where a sacred black goat was tethered and brought it protesting into the circle. At a particular point in the chant Olekowlish nodded and the goat was knelt upon. A spear blade sliced through its throat to the vertebrae and bowls caught the warm blood. When no more blood flowed and the goat lay still the same hand deftly excised its full stomach that was placed in front of Olekowlish. Another signal brought his eldest wife with a dish of simsin oil to place alongside the rainstones.

Olekowlish raised a bowl of blood high then drank a mouthful. The bowl was handed around the circle, from which each elder drank. The Laibon then sat and concentrated on the rainstones, smearing them with oil, placing and replacing them many times in pre-determined patterns with the white and green of the stones sparkling in the dappled sunlight that filtered through a stratus of incense hanging in yellow branches from smouldering *Oseki* leaves.

The circle of warriors and women then began the rain dance with men leaping with stiff knees and women swaying and ululating.

Some of the men, seemingly out of time, grunted in unison on alternate footfalls while others made up a complex and compelling rhythm with the accent on every seventh beat. Headdresses and disc necklaces bobbed and flashed in a high sun. This eerie anthem continued to build in intensity until suddenly the old man leaped to his feet with arms extended in the direction of the distant sacred volcano. This was a signal for all to leave the arena.

The warriors formed a line and loped off with a massive grunt on each fourth step with the women following. The men went to the manyatta, their voices gradually dying with their footfalls. Here they gathered in established ages and retired to a longhut. The women went straight to the village to tend to cauldrons of honey beer that had been maturing to be ready for the ever-thirsty elders who now rose and left the circle carrying their stools. They retired to the longhut in the manyatta where they sat inside against its walls to talk and drink.

Olekowlish now alone, barely visible in a hovering cloud of dust in silence waited minutes for it to settle. Then with the improvised Okiuka, he scraped a large, perfect circle in the dust around his stool and ever-burning fire. He fanned up more white smoke and from under well-worn skins he produced a bag containing familiars of which only he knew the significance. These he emptied onto the slab and arranged around the glistening green and white patterns. Once more he faced Ol Doinyo Lengai and called to NGAI to be merciful and to accept his humble offerings. He slashed the goat's stomach with a spear blade and emptied the warm contents on to the rainstones smearing them with the half-digested mess until the green and white colours disappeared. From the encircling paraphernalia he took various pieces and passed them over the stones then placed them to form a spiral on the slab. As the last item was placed he spat into the centre and leaped to his feet. Taking a tobacco tin from his bag, he opened it and with a sweep of his arm flung finely ground powder into the air, which, so fine, and with rising heat, hovered among the branches of the thorn without falling to earth. The heavens had accepted his offerings. Then with the agility of a young athlete, belying his age, he went through a series of spell-making gyrations. He kept this up for a long time until, foaming at the mouth, he fell face down with arms and legs outstretched. He was now in a deep trance. While in that state his earthly spirit leaped from his body and flew instantly to the summit of Ol Doinyo Lengai where NGAI sat impassively. From the Laibon's foaming mouth a disembodied voice intoned a prayer:

"NGAI, my Lord I beseech thee guard us
NGAI, my God I implore thee save us.
Do I not approach thee morning and evening?
Have I not sacrificed the sacred goat?
Are not the stones in their rightful order?
Have I not fasted these three hungry days?
Spirit of our ancestors cover the cattle
Spirit of the elders look to our children.
O let loose the water of life from the heavens
O unyoke the thunder from mountains and hills.
O cover the sun with darkness and power
O veil the plains with weeping and joy."

He waited. Birds stopped singing. Leaves stopped rustling. A strange silence surrounded the area. He spoke again in the strained voice.

"NGAI, my Lord, my God, is it not true that for many years of remembered time you have listened to the pleas of your humble servant? . . . My duty and joy it has been to put to you, my lord, the prospering and torments of your sons, the Masai. . . . Do not now remain silent . . .?"

NGAI was not moved.

Receiving no reply to his entreaty, Olekowlish's spirit flung itself two hundred and fifty miles to the north to the crater of Menengai where four of the lesser gods roamed. They said they would have nothing to do with a mere mortal who dared demand rain – "For had he not a short memory? Was it not true that the clan still had to pay the full price to atone for the massacre of long ago? Was he not aware that we, the four Gods, were relegated to this invidious position for the actions of you mere mortals? Was he not aware that NGAI, and only NGAI could decide these things?" Then south and east his spirit soared to the snow-clad summit of Batian, the highest frozen peak of Mount Kenya where, since the original upheaval and creation of this vast mound when the Rift Valley was formed, the Masai Gods had lodged and governed the whole of the known earth. No respite was there here, for now the Kikuyu had claimed the whole of the Kirinyaga massif to install their Gods. Now the three Masai brother peaks of Batian, Nelion and Lenana housed the Kikuyu spirit of Mwininyaga – the possessor of whiteness – whom long since had condemned the Masai to roam the Valley for as long as time permitted.

Without the Okiuka Olekowlish's spirit was ineffectual in the face of the Kikuyu Deity, and now was very weak and near to expiring. It flew southwards another two hundred miles to the stately snows of Kilimanjaro, to Kibo, the loftiest peak in all Africa and nearest to heaven, known to all Masai as NgajiNgai – the house of the white-bearded father. NGAI was absent from this cold, barren dwelling. Only traces of his spirit remained. The glaciers and towering rocks, time frozen after having spewed from the venerable crater were coldly aloof from their dealings with man. Black volcanic glass and stalagmites of permanent ice echoed rejection of Olekowlish's spirit. Sheets of hard snow and unyielding rock threw back the weakening whispers of the old man's pleas. Lung-rasping thin air bore the crushing message from the absent NGAI to Olekowlish that:

"Time only can solve man's problems.

Time is the only arbiter.

Time is omnipotent."

Being thus repulsed the rainmaker's waning spirit then had no option but to take the final course from which a negative response could only mean the end. It appealed directly to Naiteru Kop – The Beginner of Things – Father of All.

The Beginner-Of-Things took no notice. He was busy looking down from his heavenly throne trying to placate a world in turmoil. But then he sensed an honest man without personal ambition in an act of appealing for others. He showed mercy and replied. For a few moments he discarded the lofty, sonorous tones he adopted for putting his message across to the world's masses. He spoke as an earthly father.

"Yes, my son. I know that things are serious for the clans in the Great Rift. But are there not other clans and other tribes to consider at this moment? I am experiencing difficult times just now. There are other large clans desperately needing immediate attention. Some have banded together to throw hurtful things at their enemies at the ends of the earth. They have misused the knowledge I so generously gave them and are destroying themselves in unprecedented numbers along with some of the wonderful things that I, The-Beginner-Of-Things, did create with loving care. All is now being spoiled. It is a state of affairs I cannot tolerate."

Naiteru Kop looked down again at the Great Rift in which, aeons ago, he had created the Garden of Eden. The Cradle of Mankind. He saw it lying dry and fallow.

"I have only one pair of hands . . . Everyone must take their turn . . ."

The Beginner-Of-Things then focused finely on Olekowlish. He saw a lone prostrate figure, now but a spec in the vast and near derelict sun-seared valley. He saw a man who was probably the last of the true diviners. One who appealed for all. One who was able to communicate direct with Naiteru Kop. One who dared go over the head of Ngai without fear.

"Hmmm," he thought. "When this appeal has been resolved I shall remind Ngai not to be so grudging in his dealings with this Laibon who has only a little more earthly time and spiritual power left within him before joining the elders on the summit of Ol Doinyo Lengai. The least I can do is listen."

Naiteru Kop, from his lofty height, cupped a hand to his good ear. He listened to Olekowlish with more concentration than ever he had used when listening to an army of prelates bedecked in their pompous finery, to whom, sometimes, he would turn his deaf ear. But now he pondered and after a while he spoke with considered gravity. Sonorous tones crept into his voice.

"You realise, my son, that what you ask is more than what is due? . . . You do realise that the scheme of things is already set? . . . You must realise that to do what you ask can be no mere gesture of goodwill? . . . Without your proper mark of authority you are seriously disadvantaged . . . No makeshift talisman such as seven stems of grass can replace that which you have not!" Naiteru Kop pondered some more. "To do what you ask requires the balance to be adjusted."

Olekowlish's spirit made obeisance. There was a long silence.

"Very well, my revered son. In our infinite wisdom I shall make you an offer which you cannot refuse . . . Listen . . ." Olekowlish's spirit summoned more strength from the prone body and listened.

*

Hours later the sun lowered its crimson mass to sit momentarily with a bulging bottom on the distant line of the western escarpment, then slipped inexorably and silently below the horizon. The spirit of Olekowlish rejoined the place in his head. His stiff body began to relax and loosen. When full awareness returned he took from a pouch a bundle of herb that he began chewing. He wiped sweat from his eyes, sat at the stone slab and drank from the special water before gathering rainstones into the calabash that became murky and where they were to be washed and remain until some future time when needed. He replaced the paraphernalia in the leather bag, scattered water from the gourd over the flat stone and rubbed it dry with the corner of his blanket. He stood tall to face Ol Doinyo Lengai, held aloft the makeshift Okiuka, broke it and was showered with acacia seeds. He dropped the two halves into the fire and watched blue flames and white smoke spurting along the tubes then picked up his stool and the gourd and with a sandalled foot scattered the circle of dung. With a sly twinkle in his ancient eye he picked up his stool, turned on his heel and strode stiffly to the manyatta to join the elders in the long hut. As soon as he sat in his appointed place he was handed a bowl full to the brim with warm, delicious honey beer.

Through the entrance to the hut where a skin was thrown back he looked out to see the sun's last defiant afterglow being hounded out of the sky by the swift progress of the night's cold stars. Darkness fell.

Shortly afterwards the warriors with all the villagers and elders congregated in the manyatta where those of a certain age and seniority went to a communal hut where young women served them a mixture of blood and milk. The very young went to their respective huts to fulfil their austere and chaste duties.

The clan settled down to the cauldrons of beer and as it took hold a few began beating shields with clubs. Dancers leaped to their feet and circled the central fire. Foot stamping and leaping with stiff knees came spontaneously. Dancing, ululating and drinking gathered momentum through the night's passage of a completely white full moon. Resonant, urgent beating of shields spread across the plains faster than a prairie fire. Dancers built up power within circles of thorn in the Masai engangs and manyattas spread along the many hundreds of miles of the Great Rift from Singida in the south to Marsabit in the north. Dancing reached a frenzied pace and what normally would have been many days of conjuring rain was concentrated into this one night. Every village throughout Masailand rang with furious drumming on shields accompanied with strange ritual and primitive dancing with tens of thousands of leaping Masai grunting and chanting. Corralled cattle lowed and fretted the night through. The black, all-enveloping sky full of pulsating stars and a touchable moon echoed the pleas for rain and willingly passed on the frantic entreaties from the plains to the heavens.

As the night began to wane along the Great Rift, every soul encircled by thorn sang to welcome the morning star.

\*

A golden dawn broke over a noisy village at Wemberi side. Those still standing were singing hoarsely and staggering to broken rhythms beaten on shields. Women ululated with tired throats. Eventually, in the middle of the scorching day, exhausted elders, warriors, dancers, drummers, women and children throughout Masailand retired to their dung huts. As the sun crept to its highest point in a vibrant sky the children's' voices slid down the scale and became quiet. Goats and dogs without shadows lay comatose with tongues lolling in the dust. Unremitting, merciless heat pervaded the valley and huts became ovens. Earth shimmered and made lakes of dust and stone. Tops of mountains disappeared and became upside-down reflections in a sea of boiling desert.

The whole of the inhabitants of Masailand, now still and in utter silence, bludgeoned by the intense heat, some with confidence in their Laibon, others in fear, lay, waiting for rain.

# 11.

## LEGEND

*A giant sauntering along the plains heard that a small mountain could make a louder noise than he could. "I'll flatten this pimple of a mountain with one blow of my club!"*

*He approached the mountain and as his club was raised the mountain blew its top with molten larva and ash full in his face. He fell backwards with such force he split the earth for countless miles to cause the Great Rift Valley. He raised his hand to grasp the top of the cliff he had made but he succumbed. As years went by his body and fist became covered in earth. The Masai named the giant's knuckles NGONG hills. Even today the giant wiggles a toe that causes more steam to escape from fissures in the crater of Longanot.*

\*

Now feeling better, having had Masai treatment for his fever, Peter drove along a stony track followed by a pall of dust that drifted into tall, dry as tinder grass. He was without Njoroge who, not fond of the Masai, he considered would get in his hair when confronting Sekento.

On reaching his objective, the legendary Ngong hills, he pointed his nose upwards to follow a track in the grass that took him to the top. He parked under an acacia and walked to where a broken outcrop fell four thousand feet into the Rift. Here he had an uninterrupted outlook north and south along the valley and clear across. He was sure that out there somewhere, according to what Steve Harris had told him, away from any recognised route, Sekento would be with an entourage heading north to seek his brother. Where Sianka was, Peter thought, was anybody's guess.

His view should have been almost limitless, but three years without rain, more than a lifetime for some, had caused dust to be held in the atmosphere. The sun took advantage of this and used the dust not as a filter but as a lens to focus its fierceness on those below. Ol Doinyo Lengai in the south and Mau Summit in the north were barely visible through a purple haze. The Aberdare range surmounting the eastern scarp and backed by Mount Kenya were intermittently discernible through burgeoning clouds.

The sun on Peter's back grew hotter by each quarter hour of his systematic search of the valley, first with binoculars, and then, if he saw something needing ultra magnification, with the range finder. After two hours of quartering and staring through glass he took a rest.

He considered the plains could not take much more of this intense parching without something dire happening. He knew the Masai had burnt off dry stubble to encourage new growth in their grazing grounds in the first year of the drought. The sun had finished the job the second year. Now anything left was tinder dry and waiting for a spark.

A wind sprang up and noticeably chilled his sweating back. In the north Mount Kenya was building up massive clouds. At the highest point of the Aberdare range a cloud, shrouding the rocks of the Dragon's Teeth, stood out horizontally. Each afternoon for the past week this had happened but the cloud usually lingered and selfishly withheld its moisture, eventually to disappear. Something in the air though, and a change of light gave Peter a nudge. The Aberdare cloud then joined forces with that from Mount Kenya and began to tumble down towards the escarpment. Here it met rising air that held it while it developed into a massive thundercloud that spread across to the western limits. Peter marvelled at the size of the cloud and the speed of its making.

Picking up the binoculars once more he continued searching for signs of movement north of Suswa. In a desolate part of the valley emerging from behind a kopje he saw dust being raised. His pocket compass gave him a bearing which he laid in the rangefinder and focussed many miles away on moving dots that he guessed was a group of Masai warriors loping at a steady pace northwards with something following he could not recognise. This group, if it was Sekento's, must have come from below the border, from Wemberi, and had covered a hundred and twenty miles in a matter of a few days. He never ceased to be astonished at the unflagging stamina and endurance of the Masai. Now he saw more dust in front of the warriors. Dots scattered as another group appeared, but as quickly as it had started, it finished. He saw no more movement.

\*

Seven warriors ran in battle array. Short, hard aprons covered vital parts while blankets were rolled and tightly bound over a shoulder. Headdresses of plumed black lion mane and ostrich feathers waved in rhythm with their loping run. Circlets of feathers decorated the piston levers of arms and legs as they moved untiringly across the wilderness. Each carried a spear and rungu with a simi at their waist. Decorated buffalo hide battle shields were beaten in time with the running. Sweat streaked their bodies and face paint while lungs breathed rhythmically as sandalled feet pounded rock-hard earth. Muscles shone in sunlight and eyes gleamed with the light of battle.

Anyone observing this picturesque primeval image would have their belief shattered by the incongruous sight of Sekento, dressed as all were, following them, not running, but driving a Jeep with Pat O'Brien's .577 elephant gun across his knees and a bandolier of steel-jackets slung across a shoulder.

Without warning they were confronted by a motley band of warriors, some dressed in skins, others in khaki, and armed severally with spears and clubs. One had a crude gun made from household conduit piping. There was no challenge, just a sudden launching of spears and sticks and a gunshot followed by two more.

The skirmish lasted but a few moments. The swiftly moving moran from the south did not stop and cower. The runners ran more swiftly to make difficult targets. Sekento was the only one to stop, and in a flash, had the gun at his shoulder while standing on the Jeep's seat and loosed off each barrel at enemies. Reloading, he sent the Jeep rocketing forward again. Sianka, with his companions who had laid the ambush, were not prepared for such stratagem. After the first flight of spears they found themselves being attacked and routed by superior tactics. Sekento and Sianka remained at the rear of their parties, both for different reasons. One so that he could martial his force to good advantage, the other, because he feared the gun his brother carried.

In the clash Sekento's warriors took good account but two of them fell. Two of Sianka's more courageous attackers were speared through and the one who fired his makeshift gun had no time even to be surprised, for the primitive wire-bound breach exploded in his face and he lost most of his head. His right arm went spinning and now lay some distance from his twitching body. A fourth of Sianka's men was clubbed down and Sekento despatched two more with the big gun.

Sianka was clever enough to turn tail. His few remaining followers scattered and fled. Now alone and deserted he sped northwards. He was fresh and knew he could outdistance the Jeep on this terrain by choosing the worst ground, leaping from rock to donga, knowing it would be folly for his brother to attempt to follow closely. He was out of gun range and headed for Longanot, now hidden by a black cloud.

\*

From where he lay, Peter saw no more movement. He had no idea how many might have fallen in the mêlée and wondered if the Okiuka was with the dead, for, knowing Sekento, dead there would be. He checked the range and bearing, stuffed his gear into the bag and headed for the truck while making a mental calculation.

The truck started at a touch and he swung it along the contour of the hills down to a track and sped southwards. Crossing a storm ditch he nosed on to an escarpment track. Tortuous turns along the stone-strewn dirt road with, here and there, a fall-away of earth and rock where boulders had been split by extremes of daytime heat and night-time cold, were a test for anyone's nerve and driving skill. He was seldom a reckless driver and had survived without a scratch on the paintwork on what were reckoned to be the world's worst roads. He did not look up at the majestic sights of escarpment cliffs on both sides of the Rift, and pulling a choker over his nose as dust swirled he drifted rear wheels on tight bends to avoid three-point turns. Dust floated down from zigzag tracks to meet him on the opposite tack, and more than a few times at narrow stretches the tyres gripped an uncertain dirt edge. His knuckles were white at the wheel and his feet see-sawed when pumping accelerator, brake and clutch to make rapid gear changes.

He rounded a rock-fall, negotiated a tight hairpin bend with a worrying overhang and sped down the last wide stretch where the track flattened out. Bumping across a storm ditch he headed out across the valley floor where it was ten degrees hotter than the hills he had left. Reading the compass on the dash he pointed his nose into the wilderness towards circling vultures.

Good time was made across the scrub avoiding dry cracks in tortured earth to where he could see the vultures descending. He stopped on a rise of weathered stone and leaped out of the cab. Ten yards in front of him was the severed arm of the unlucky attacker and it did not take long to find the remaining bodies now surrounded by scores of dancing vultures gnawing, squabbling and tearing at the warm flesh.

Snatching a shotgun from the cab he lashed out at the birds with the butt scaring off the main body and looked around for the Okiuka. He found nothing but two spent .577 shells twenty yards from two bodies with smashed sternum and great holes in their backs. Among all the bodies there he found a few specific clan markings and guessed that Sekento and Sianka, and maybe others, were still alive and heading north. He took photographs of the bodies and any clan markings he could see. And all the while the vultures were closing with tentative hops, wings half extended and with necks resembling the u-bends of drains thrusting murderous beaks forward to attack Peter. He rewarded them with swift kicks and the butt of his gun. He had no time to bury the dead but covered the corpses as best he could with brush. That did not deter the vultures that hopped and fought their ungainly way back to the feast before hyena; hoards of ants, flies and insects would pick the bones clean.

"Good God!" Peter exclaimed. "This is where Della arrived and I lost Bili over by that kopje!"

He found the spoor of sandals and winding tyre tracks and followed them northwards for half a mile towards the massive cloud while guessing the men were headed past Longanot, through Hell's Gate and the lakes of Naivasha and Elmenteita towards Nakuru, Sianka's home. Darkness was due in an hour or so and it made sense for him to return to the truck.

As he turned to go he glanced up and saw the anvil of the cloud lit by a low sun from over the western wall of the Rift, and rainbow rays angled down from the high ice. The whole cloud then became alive with electricity and began to rumble and roar. In the rapidly failing light, for the sun was now hidden, he saw the base of the cloud lift while the wind behind him increased to whip up dust. A twister picked up a bush and headed towards the cloud that now resembled a gigantic, battered, upturned pewter pot reaching across the whole valley. The cloud then began to walk forward on many stabs of lightning as though a group of stilt-walkers were approaching on rickety legs. The devil then took a hand and orchestrated the storm's overture with percussion the chief instrument.

The cloud marched towards Peter now mesmerised by its power. As it roared with sheet and forked lightning it hurled huge quantities of water earthwards. For some moments, deafened by thunder, he stood in a trance, then, as a particularly brilliant flash brought him to his senses he shook his head, hurriedly took off his shirt and trousers, wrapped the gun and camera in the legs of his trousers and ran the half-mile back to the truck.

He had two hundred yards to go when the wall of the storm hit him with cold rain and hail nearly bowling him over. Momentarily he was blinded by a flash and stumbled on the edge of a donga. Thunder crashed and earth crumbled as he fell into what was fast becoming a torrent. Unbalanced by his efforts to keep gun and camera above water he was swept a hundred yards along a fast filling depression. Determined to keep his arms above the surface he bounced off rocks while swirling among debris. Then an exposed root caught his legs and held him fast. His body swung in the current and his choker caught on another root that held him down as water rose above his head. Still struggling to keep the camera and gun above water he let air out of his lungs to sink and with the other hand loosened the choker. Although he was nearly blacking out he somehow freed his legs and hauled himself upright and staggered out of the donga.

A stab of lightning exploding a tree fifty yards from him lit up the shape of the truck outlined by a haze of rain and mist from the hot metal. His way to the truck was lit by an uninterrupted dance of electric light, and for the last few yards he flung up his head and sang out a few bars of Schiller's 'Ode to Joy' at the top of his voice.

Tossing soaking clothes into the back of the truck with camera and gun he leaped up and removed his boots that spilled mud.

After soaping and rinsing himself in the rain and drying under a canopy extended over the tailboard, he dabbed grazes with an antiseptic. Then dressing in dry clothes he cleaned his gun and camera and put them away. He knew now he was marooned until the next day. The escarpment track he had used from the Ngong hills, he guessed would be washed out, and the only way back would be to go north to the main Nairobi/Nakuru road.

He prepared for a night's stay. Not being able to light a fire he set up his father's old 'volcano' boiler that he filled with rainwater and stuffed the conical space underneath with two screwed-up pages of newspaper that he lit. He put ground coffee into a jug and seventy-five seconds later he poured water having boiled into the jug and let it infuse for a few minutes while unwrapping a strip of biltong. After filtering coffee into a mug, he selected from a collection of shellac discs he always carried a recording of Beethoven's Coriolan overture, put it on a jury-rigged portable player working off the truck's battery and turned the volume up to full. He sat on the tailboard with the canopy shielding him from the onslaught of the storm, sipped coffee, and with the strip of biltong in the other hand, conducted the whole of the overture while loudly la-la-ing the melodies in a passable baritone in defiance of the noise and in celebration of the coming of rain.

The storm, the first the valley had seen for a little more than three years, was sufficiently fierce even to beat Beethoven into submission at the end of the overture.

That night, lying in a sleeping bag, he woke to an eerie silence and in a half-awake state he was sure he heard the grumbling of lion nearby. Moments later a buffeting wind sprang up. The truck took a pounding and was rocked, but after five minutes the rain came bouncing back. He heard more grumbling from lion while lightning and thunder renewed the chaos, and he pulled the bag flap over his head and went back to sleep.

In a perfectly clear morning he woke and looked out to see a bright, fresh landscape. Putting on clothes and boots he walked around the truck on drying rock. He climbed on to the roof and looked about to see nothing of the previous day's battle. Every vestige of the slain and spoor had been washed away and there were no Jeep tracks. As far as he could see everywhere was different. Gone was the dried-up, drab, miserable look of despair. Instead, bushes, scrub and even rocks took on an air of optimism and cleanliness. High parts of the savannah were drying already and the low-lying areas were soaking up the last of the millions of tons of water unleashed by the storm. A brilliant rising sun was burning layers of mist away. The smell of scrubbed stone was taking over that of the distinctive peppery Kenya dust, but it would take many weeks and months of a daily dowsing to redress the balance of three years without.

A mist hung over Longanot, and to the south, Ol Doinyo Lengai had thrust its head through a vast sheet of mist and had a triumphal air about it. Separated in mood from the surrounding peaks it gave the impression that the Masai Deity had been at work and now appeared smug and satisfied. Peter looked east and up. The knuckles of the Ngong hills showed crisp and clear against a classic Kenya blue sky without haze.

He was taken out of his reverie by the sudden appearance of a young male lion and his mate from under the truck. They had been sheltering under his bed for most of the night and Peter had walked around the vehicle not moments ago and had not even smelled them. He watched the cats walk to a place where bodies of yesterday's battle must have lain. Here they sat and purred and rolled in the damp earth. Peter slipped into the cab, retrieved his camera and took shots while wondering if they had come to mourn the passing of Masai. Finally they moved off.

In good spirits, despite the disappointments and bruises of yesterday he fastidiously cleaned his gun again and reloaded the camera before setting out to the north. He decided to go direct to Nakuru where he could breakfast at the Stag's Head hotel, the five star local of the Rift Valley settlers and known unflatteringly as the 'Nag's Bed', where, no doubt, he would find some of his fellow farmers celebrating. After years without, rain was salvation and the excuse for uninhibited festivities.

Concentrating on his driving he picked his way from rise to rise up the valley towards Nakuru following in his mind's eye the mirage of the heap of bacon and eggs, kedgeree, toast, honey and coffee that awaited him there.

\*

Sekento was annoyed. The skirmish had delayed him. Any attack on him he considered to be futile because in ordinary circumstances he thought of himself as invulnerable. Now, being the possessor of the Okiuka, he reckoned to be invincible. The moran with him during the fight he saw as a mere bodyguard for show rather than a necessity although they had acquitted themselves well against Sianka's so-called warriors and had put them to flight.

His one concern now was that Sianka still lived. He did not doubt his brother's prowess in conventional Masai warfare for, when in training Sianka had shown himself to be remarkable in the lore of the spear. He could throw it long distances with pinpoint accuracy; use it for stabbing, as proved by wounding his brother, and as a protective staff in close fighting. He could use the blade and stiletto to deadly effect better than any other of his age group. This he had proved convincingly when killing his first lion while remaining unscathed himself. Sekento looked at the scar on his arm and grunted with contempt.

He spent an uncomfortable night trying to sleep beside the bogged-down Jeep while two of his ardent followers, wanting to please the one they thought to be their future leader, went to a nearby European farm to steal fuel for the Jeep. But now Sekento tried to forget his brother for the time being and concentrated on the pressing engagement he had close to Nakuru. He carried in his head knowledge unknown to others and in his own special way was going to demonstrate his authority.

\*

Sianka had a problem. He was a loner, was often drunk and deeply resentful of Sekento's false claim to the succession. Being the firstborn of Olekowlish's second wife, Sianka had privileges denied to Sekento. He had been betrothed to Naiyolang, daughter of the

Laibon of a different clan. But that now had been denied him by her father. He knew his brother's premature claim to the succession was false and that although having been banished he should go back and surrender the Okiuka to Olekowlish.

After failing at the skirmish and escaping from the gun and the Jeep, Sianka continued going northwards through Hell's Gate that he knew would be difficult terrain for Sekento, especially in torrential rain that would hamper the progress of a modern mechanical implement. Masai legs could carry one anywhere and at any time whereas a European wheeled vehicle could not. He was adept at moving in the dark since his early training by Fire-Stick-Elders. His legs carried him through Hell's Gate and a rhinoceros trail to reach the lake of Naivasha. Knowing he could not get immediate revenge on Sekento and believing him to be bogged down while the rain continued he turned east towards a more forested area where he sheltered for the remainder of the night. There was no doubt now that his elder brother and he would have to settle their differences at the proper time and proper place. That meant going north to a specific location.

The following morning he had an inspired idea. He would get rid of his immediate frustrations on the interfering young white farmer who was poking his nose into Masai affairs that did not concern him. He set off to start climbing the eastern escarpment, get food from the forest, steal suitable weapons from a Kikuyu, and make tracks for a certain farm at Kinangop.

# 12.

## LEGEND

*A clan of Masai in the north raided a clan in the south and stole many cattle and women. The southern clan joined forces with another and went north to find the offenders at a war council high on the slopes of a volcano near its crater. The northern clan was no match for the southerners who fought and drove them to the edge of the crater and forced them over the rim to fall vertically nine hundred feet into the bowl of the crater to perish on the rocks below.*

*NGAI was not pleased. He detailed four of the lesser Gods to don the skins of animals, to patrol the crater and to keep the peace. The crater was named MN-ENG-AI – The place of four Gods*
    *(MENENGAI,crater is eight miles across its rim)*

\*

    Before dawn, before the night was to be burned away by the inevitable sun, Naiyolang woke. She rose from a bed of skins, gathered a blanket about her young shoulders and yawned. She moved to the entrance to her hut of bent sticks packed with mud and dung, pushed aside a cowhide and stepped out into the cold air. It was dark with no sign yet in the eastern sky of the day to come.

    The engang perched high on the slopes of Menengai crater lay quiet under stars with a descending moon moving slowly through fitful streaks of cloud.

    Outside the thorn perimeter a leopard coughed and stirred dozing cattle. It had just encircled the enclosure but had found no point low enough over which to leap and claim breakfast. A mighty specimen, Chui would, if ever seen in daylight, surprise even the most experienced hunter. Great muscles showed under a spectacularly rosetted coat, and a benign pussycat face disguised fearsome teeth. He could kill a fully-grown cow, and with it in his jaws, clear a six-foot thorn hedge. The women had done a good job by piling the thorn just high enough for safety.

Naiyolang took no notice of the leopard. She was too occupied with an unaccustomed queasiness that she had felt for the last few mornings that kept her yawning and shivering when going across to the central fire just glowing within a circle of stones. She put more kindling on the embers and fed thick branches to overlap in the middle.

The leopard coughed again as new flames leapt and crackled. His tail lashed in anger as he padded away to the dark edge of the volcano's lip. There, while prowling with frustration he came across the spoor of a male lion, a buffalo and an elephant, all leading to a copse of old acacia and mahogany cresting a ridge. He lowered his snout, curled back lips with whiskers forward and brushed impressions in the dust for recognised scents, raised his head, looked in the direction of the trees and made a kittenish whinnying noise. Through bared teeth he grinned into the darkness, then licking flecks of dust from his nose and sneezing mightily he made for the ridge.

Some yards away from Naiyolang, lit by the dancing light of the fire a small boy standing on one leg with the other foot resting above a straight knee, was leaning on a long stick, fast asleep. She could not help but smile at this cherub, no more than five years old, enveloped in an adult blanket, entrusted to guard the engang and to keep the fire going all night.

Now kneeling, Naiyolang sat on her heels and decided to let him sleep for the time being. Heat on her breast and cold on her back took away the sickness. While staring at the ever-changing colours in the heart of the fire she saw faces forming and reforming. One face that remained constant and looking straight at her was that of her great-uncle Olekowlish. She loved the old man and remembered the time when he had come to Kenya a year ago. There had been talk of land trouble with the Kikuyu people that had been resolved. Also at that time Olekowlish had sent for her to be told that now she had reached twelve years she was to be betrothed. He told her that being the youngest daughter of her clan's Laibon she was to assume the status of 'untouched' till her marriage. She was not to join other young girls in the long hut of warriors and she should meet her husband on her betrothal day and he was to have her unsullied and intact without knowledge of Masai manhood. Today was to be her day to meet her future husband.

The momentary sickness in the pit of her stomach she put down to the excitement to follow. She was too naively innocent to think otherwise. She had heard that she would have to suffer the pain of clitoridectomy but was determined not to respond. Mere existence was joy to her. At the back of her mind was the memory of her recent visit to the south and of the things that happened to her there. A curious feeling rose in her lower abdomen as she recalled the revulsion she felt for Sianka when he came to her in the dark hut to defile her and the compassion she felt for the white stranger when she was ordered to lie with him, to keep him warm and alive, although unconscious. This she had done but wondered if he had survived after being taken, perhaps near death, to be hidden in the bush.

Now, today, she was to be given to a Masai of a southern clan named Sekento the elder brother of Sianka who claimed his right to husband her. While confused she thought that the elders and her father, the Laibon of her clan, must have thought Sekento to be a stronger, future leader.

The sensation of sickness faded and she concentrated on the pictures in the fire and what they had to say. The old Laibon's face grew larger and commanded her attention as cold air wafted across glowing embers. Hypnotic eyes displayed a great love for her, but with a fresh puff of air they sank inwards and took on a look of pity and deep sadness bordering on despair. This and other images then faded to nothing. She rocked on her heels, stood and drew the blanket tightly about her slender shoulders.

The boy, who had not shifted his position but whose eyes were now wide open, smiled. She looked long at the Masai cub in the light of the sweet-smelling fire, his figure painted against dark shapes of cattle and darker thorn hedge with a morning mist as a backdrop. She felt she must cling to this image as being the last peaceful moment of her existence, for when the sun was up she would join the company of the clan, bear new scars and lose all she treasured in her present tiny world. She stood straight and dignified as a thoroughbred and drank in the last dregs of the peaceful scene. The boy blinked and through a beaming smile his eyes implored her to think he had been awake and alert all night, instead of snatching a few minutes sleep. She said nothing and returned the smile as if to say, 'Your secret is safe with me. Go back to your vigil and grow to be a brave warrior as tall as a mountain. Protect us with your fine spear and strong spirit.' She turned, walked back to her hut and took one last look around before entering its snug warmth and comfortable bed of skins for her final hour of sleep.

The boy in the circle of light lowered his resting leg, went forward to stir the fire and to walk among the grey statues of cattle. His head barely reached the breastbone of some of the greater beasts, but he knew his orders. He would look after the cattle and the whole family and defend his charges to the death if he had to. He walked with renewed determination around the inner wall of thorn and on reaching the starting point he drew from a pouch under his trailing blanket a small bundle of herb and chewed a leaf of it. He returned to his place near the fire where he put a foot on a knee, leaned on the long stick and stood listening to the comforting crackle of burning branches.

\*

Four miles east in a temporary manyatta a fire cast an eerie light and flickering shadows on the faces and near naked bodies of three hundred warriors. Ever resourceful, Sekento, undeterred by rain and circumstance, now with new-found groups of followers, bought with promises, sat on his heels and chatted. Young women were busy mixing various dyes to adorn the men's torsos. Each determined his own pattern but all had a vermilion triangle high on the breastbone. Markings accomplished, the group donned lion mane and ostrich feather headdresses, colourful blankets and skins worn as togas, and prepared for the march westward to a meeting ground.

Sekento marshalled his troops together in the light of the fire, detailed twenty to protect the women and cattle, and with the remaining two hundred and eighty armed men with elders he set off at a trot. On each fourth step the whole regiment grunted in unison with deep, resonant but whispering voices. No dust was raised as the cold volcanic earth was still damp with the night's frosty dew.

\*

Naiyolang was now dressed in a new skirt of soft lamb's hide held by a belt hung with trinkets. Copper bracelets entwined her ankles and arms and a spiral of copper wire interwoven with shells and beads bound into a flat disk around her neck crackled as it bounced on firm, young breasts. Her half-shaved head was adorned with bands of beads hung with coloured stones about her forehead and dark, stunning eyes. Ear lobes swung with clusters of shells and beaten metal shapes as she moved with sprightly steps to her betrothal. The small clan, all, with much ululating from the women, moved out eastwards with a sprinkling of moran chatting and laughing in a happy bunch leading their elders to follow the line of the crater's rim. All had happy faces for this was to be a day for celebration.

In the pre-dawn mist copper cow bells jangled as cattle was driven out by the piping voice and whistles of the five year old boy carrying a long peeled stave. With a flash of juvenile devilment he turned from his charges and went to follow the warriors and tripped over his large blanket. He picked himself up, hoisted the blanket above his knees and followed the group of warriors while aping their loping strides and imagining his stave to be a spear. He ran on spindly legs in desperate spurts in order not to fall behind.

\*

Sekento's recruits reached the meeting place first and were directed by him to line around the east and south of the clearing with a gap at the west-side with the volcano lip making the square. His stratagem was simple and effective. He knew that Naiyolang, her father and all their small clan could enter the clearing only from the west giving him advantage. A rising sun would be in the other clan's eyes. He was determined that on this special day he would show himself to be a worthy contender and be well placed for what was to come.

\*

From a copse of acacia and mahogany on a ridge overlooking the meeting place four pairs of eyes looked out. The eyes were those of an immense elephant swaying his trunk from side to side in rhythm with his front feet as though dancing on the spot; a rock-still buffalo wheezing through moist nostrils; a black-maned lion lying on his side with impressive head angled around a tuft of yellow grass; and a leopard crouching with head on fore-paws purring malevolently and swishing his tail. The four Gods, *MN-ENG-AI*, disguised as earthly beasts surveyed their domain, a large volcano's crater standing as an ancient sentinel by the eastern scarp of the Great Rift.

The leopard's tail stopped swishing and his eyes glowed red as the eastern line of the volcano's cliffs appeared in the faint light of the approaching dawn. The elephant swung his trunk lower and scooped up dust from the foot of the nearest tree and snorted it over his back to clear parasites. The lion yawned with unbelievably large jaws showing a pink tongue behind treacherous yellowing teeth. The yawn turned from a squeal into a roar that shook leaves from a nearby bush. He shook a black mane and kneaded hard earth with claws as large a billhooks. The buffalo pawed the ground sending up a shower of shale and blew out hot lungfulls of air that condensed to mist in the cold dying night. He raised a proud head that supported a spread of curved horn that would be the envy of any trophy hunter.

The four pairs of eyes looked down towards the clearing of grassed shale, with patches of bare earth, where a regiment of Masai warriors stood quietly waiting.

\*

Propelled by the hand of Ngai the sun shot up over the eastern ridge of the Menengai crater and light burst upon the clearing with a silver-gilt shaft of glory.

Long shadows of the regiment of tall men with taller spears fell along ankle-deep mist, while elders now grouped near the centre of the clearing were brightly lit with Sekento standing prominently on the bole of a fallen tree. A reflected shaft of light sprang from the black jewel in the Okiuka held in a leather belt at Sekento's waist. The contingent stood waiting, and with every inch of the rise of the sun they grew in ominous splendour.

Naiyolang with her clan, almost a hundred in all, came joyfully up to the clearing. The leading warrior, utterly fearless, went straight into the centre of the assembly, halted twenty paces from Sekento and called his greeting in a clear tenor. All Sekento's men answered him with a stupendous HOOO! A lesser man would have flinched from the power generated in two hundred and eighty throats but he stood his ground and beckoned his clan forward. They came trotting, dancing and jingling into the arena where the elders assembled in a semi-circle opposite their brothers and placed stools on which to sit in dignified attitudes.

Surrounded by women and hidden from view Naiyolang was taken to a grassy patch near the crater's rim while the remainder took up a position with backs to the crater's bowl to face Sekento's gathering. At the right of each group elders and orators sat on their heels fingering long talk staves.

Bundles of gifts were then brought forward and placed before the elders of Naiyolang's clan. The eight gifts making up the bride price were traditional and had been set for many generations. They consisted of two heifers; one steer; one black ram; one ewe; tobacco; a cache of honey and a pair of matching soft sheep hides. No one had to fear that the offerings were inadequate. At this level they were the best to be found anywhere. The nods of approval and eeeh's when the bride's mother was handed a brass ornament and when something unusual was added to complement this special betrothal were the signal for the negotiations to begin.

The first orator from Naiyolang's family got to his feet and the assembly settled down to listen. Meanwhile, Sekento's recruits silently closed the gap on the west side of the clearing. Naiyolang's people were now surrounded on three sides with armed warriors; the fourth, a sheer drop of nine hundred feet into the crater.

The speeches got under way and both sides presented cases and criticisms as to the content, size and quality of the bride price. Guided by elders the arguments were long and fierce with waving fists and rattling staves. Clapping and laughter greeted the finer points of the debate. Some orators, seizing the opportunity to be noticed, 'played to the gallery' as ham actors, drawing applause and adulation from the assembly.

After hours of wrangling, not comfortable under a rising sun without shade, and with gathering clouds and oppressive humidity, the price was finally agreed as had been done for many decades. Honey beer was brought forward by the women for the elders and orators to slake their thirst, after which the Laibon of each clan was called to set the seal on the arrangements.

Mbatia, Naiyolang's father rose from his stool, stepped forward and waited for his counterpart to show himself. Sekento leaped down from the tree and strode forward holding the Okiuka aloft. He held a spear casually. All fell silent while he strutted to and fro' displaying himself to advantage, then faced her father.

"I have no quarrel with the bride price," he said. "It has been set with the proper dealings between our clans and I trust that the honourable brother opposite thinks likewise." There was the slightest pause before the word 'honourable'. "But before I touch the hand of my revered brother and before we spit our agreement it is my wish to say things." The sky was darkening and distant thunder began to roll. He faced the visiting clan and spoke in a resonant bass voice amplified by a close horseshoe of two hundred and eighty warriors. His words rang clear on the rarefied air.

"Is it not true that my betrothed is the youngest daughter of Mbatia the Laibon of his clan?"

"Aiya" came the collective assent from the elders.

"Is it not true that she is a beautiful young Masai woman?"

"Eeeeh."

All throats in the clearing assented in unison with ululating from the women. Sekento held up the Okiuka to quieten them.

"Is it not true that this marriage will bring our clans together to give the Masai nation strength?"

"Eeeeh."

"Is it not true that the union of two pure souls will please the Gods?"

He accented the word 'pure'.

"Eeeeh."

"Is it not true that I, Sekento, new Counsellor and Laibon of my clan, have a fitting lineage for this union to Naiyolang?"

"Eeeeh!"

The assent grew each time and was sung out as a chorus to Sekento's rhythm. He was now becoming excited.

"Is it not true that I am the greatest lion slayer of the whole of the Masai in the Great Rift Valley?"

"Eeeeh!"

"Is it not true that I am to have the fairest bride of all?"

"Eeeeh!"

"Is it not true that my bride will bring joy to the Masai by producing many fine warriors?"

"Eeeeh!"

All the assembly went wild with shouting.

"Is it not true she is to come to me untouched?"

"EEEEH!"

Again there was abandoned shouting and ululating, but above all he was heard clearly and distinctly while holding up the Okiuka.

"Is it not true she – has – lain – with – a – man – A – WHITE – MAN?"

There was deathly silence.

Mbatia was stunned. Under a burgeoning black cloud he stammered.

"W – W – What is this you speak?"

"It is the truth." Sekento said firmly. He repeated the accusation and with a nod in their direction he sneered, "Ask your women."

Mbatia called for his eldest wife and from the group of women surrounding Naiyolang a tall woman shuffled into sight and stood trembling in the circle.

"Now, woman, what is this? What trouble is this?"

"My Lord, I know nothing of a white man. No such man has been here with our clan for many years."

Sekento shook the Okiuka at her and she cringed. Thunder rolled closer while the heat and humidity grew.

"I do not talk of a white man here! I talk of a white man in the south and I talk of that white man who went to my father's village and slept there. I talk of that white man who was there and lay with Naiyolang. I talk of the white Peter Grant. That is the place; and the time, and the man. He has defiled us!"

A movement of his arm silenced one or two mutterings.

"Is this true, old wife?" Mbatia asked.

"Yes, my Lord. It is true that at the time of some part of the present moon at the time when three ngombi dropped calves and two other old ngombi died of starvation, I and the other women of the elders went to the south taking Naiyolang with us . . ."

"Yes, yes, yes, we know that!" he said testily. "What happened there?"

"My Lord, it is true that some time past the great man Olekowlish spoke with Naiyolang and told her to prepare finally for her betrothal to Sianka as is the custom."

"She lies!" Sekento broke in. "The betrothal is mine!"

"Go on old wife," said Mbatia.

"Yes, my Lord. It is true the white man Peter Grant came on foot to the village and fell sick."

"Is it true, old wife, that she lay with him?"

She hesitated.

"Come, come! Speak true! Answer!"

"We were ordered to put her with him."

"Who gave this order?"

"The women and elders of that clan, my Lord. They gave the order that the white man must recover by warmth. That Naiyolang must give him warmth. That the white man must not die immediately."

"Did the white man agree?" Sekento asked menacingly.

"No, my Lord. He did not know of it. He was sick with fever and near to death. It was done so that the village went to search for the killer of another girl taken from the hut of Naiyolang. Afterwards the white man was put to the bush and left to die."

"But afterwards he did not die!" came Sekento's deep cry. "Afterwards he still lives! The whole tribe of Masai and all the white tribes know he still lives!"

Now incensed, with a sweep of his arm holding the Okiuka aloft, Sekento scattered the women from their protective shield around Naiyolang. She stood dignified and serene. He called to the women.

"Is it true that Naiyolang is broken?"

"Eeeeh," the women called in chorus while Mbatia protested loudly.

"What proof is there of this dreadful thing? This cannot happen to my fairest daughter. Come wife. Is there proof of this?"

"Yes my Lord. In the south her vaginal blood was seen on the white man's naked body." She drew a deep breath and said in a loud whisper for all to hear: "They shared the same blanket!"

Wailing from the women began and grew in intensity. Sekento turned to face Naiyolang and all fell silent.

Naiyolang did not understand why no one spoke of Sianka and what he – not the white man – had done to her and that it was he who had caused the death of her friend who had been suffocated. She knew she could say nothing. She had given her word and her breeding demanded she should keep it. Sianka was not here to admit his own guilt. She looked with imploring eyes at the women for them to say more and to speak the truth that it was Sianka who had taken her and broken the strict tradition of a highborn girl to remain untouched until marriage. The women, abashed, avoided her gaze and kept silent. She turned to face Sekento and stood still and proud. Sekento again called to the women.

"You say the white man knows nothing of this, and yet, has she taken seed?"

"Eeeeh," came the affirmative. "Her blood has ceased to flow and she has the sickness these last three dawns!"

The 'Eeeeh' that followed from the whole assembly was deafening and rang around the crater to echo the word 'Shame'!

Close thunder rumbled during the long dreadful silence that followed.

Sekento strode to where Naiyolang stood defiant without cowering, and looked at her, his face close to hers. Then quietly and slowly, containing his great anger, he hissed "Fisi!" His eyes burned. "The white Peter Grant who pretends to be brother to us is a fisi!" He was barely audible and veins stood out on his neck and face. "And now my bride." He took a deep breath then with a menacing whisper he repeated "And - now - my - bride - is - a –_fisi!_" There was a long silence, then he screamed: "You shall not be mother to a white FISI!" He stood tall and stepped back three paces. His honed spear came arcing down to split her from breast to pubis. Her little round belly gaped as the skirt and trinkets fell to the ground. She was stock still for a moment. As pain hit her and blood gushed she grasped her stomach as if to hold it in.

Naiyolang's proud face showed no trace of surprise. Her eyes widened to show her disdain, and to every one's amazement, instead of screaming in terror and falling to the ground, she smiled. Her smile then faded as she looked with half-closed eyes at Sekento. Then she spat which hit him full in the eyes – the ultimate shame a man could receive from a woman. Then she deliberately stepped backwards to the volcano's brink. There she paused before taking an extra step and launched herself outwards. To all staring it was as though the air cradled her for a fraction of time, but then she went from view and hurtled downwards with the cry of S-I-A-N-K-A! echoing and fading. The assembly stood, helpless and benumbed.

A full five seconds went by before one of Naiyolang's warriors leapt forward and grabbed the nearest of Sekento's cohorts, lifted him clear over his head, ran to the edge and flung him out into space. He turned and screamed a challenge to Sekento, but was met by a thrown rungu the hardwood knob of which hit him between the eyes, cracked open his skull and toppled him backwards over the edge. A close flash of lightning followed by a crash of thunder that shook the earth.

"SOBA HOOO! SOBA HOOOO! SOBA HOOOOOO!"

The battle cry filled two hundred and eighty throats. Two hundred and eighty right feet raised then came down with a resonant thud. Dust flew. Sekento's warriors closed in with a rhythmic beating of shields. In unison they raised spears, rungus and simis and attacked with stabbing, cutting and clubbing. The northern clan was caught utterly defenceless and screamed in fear, pain and defiance. Sekento's men screamed in elation, lust and the joy of war. They came on remorselessly. Their blood was up and no quarter was given. The battle yodels outdid the screams of their adversaries and the home clan was driven to the edge of the abyss and forced over. Those left lying dead or wounded were picked up and thrown to join their hapless kin. With the last of Naiyolang's clan having been swept over the volcano's rim, some over-excited attackers followed their quarry too closely and with surprised shrieks joined their brothers in oblivion, their shields and spears floating down after them to add to the carnage on the rocks far below.

During the battle Sekento stood high on the fallen tree trunk brandishing the Okiuka while screaming his encouragement to goad on his warriors. Then with the accompaniment of more thunder a great and prolonged shouting grew among the victorious regiment and they began to chant and leap on the spot. The noise of frenzied voices and thudding feet backed by thunder was deafening and it required more than superhuman effort from an equally excited Sekento to bring his men under control. He led them, still leaping and chanting, in the direction from which they came towards their makeshift manyatta where they were to celebrate with unabated drinking and carousing. Their excited voices receded quickly with them down the slopes and in less than a minute nothing more was heard. Thunder abated.

All that remained under a burgeoning black cloud bringing on darkness at the meeting place was the unique smell of the dust of Kenya mingled with the human smells of victory, blood and death. The clearing was left desolate and utterly quiet.

It was a full minute before the silence was broken with a flash and immediate crash of thunder that rolled around the crater.

\*

In a thicket on the skirts of the clearing the five-year-old boy crouched. He had been there watching since sun-up. Small tight knuckles gripped the large blanket about him. His eyes were wide with terror but he summoned the courage to come out into the open. As he did, scores of spread wings scudded above him to the edge of the cliff where the scavengers momentarily staggered upwards on a swirling thermal, then headed downwards, wings half-folded, spiralling against rising hot air. A sinister silence went with them as they dropped below the rim to descend and to peck out their gruesome existence.

The boy stood on the edge of the dreadful drop. Putting a foot on the brink he peered down. He suffered neither vertigo nor urge to hurl himself into the abyss as white people do. Seeing no movement but images of what he feared at that frightful vertical distance he turned and walked back over bloodstained earth finding he could not cry. Before reaching the surrounding bush he paused and looked across the empty place of slaughter. His whole family including parents, brothers, sisters and all the clan's manhood, women and children were now no more. A song came to his confused mind, a song his father had taught him that told of times long ago and of clan raiding clan, of failing rains and of clans dying. The song finished abruptly as he realised that with the loss of his family he was now a man. All five years of him strode purposefully away down the southern slopes of Menengai to look for his cattle, his overlarge blanket trailing in the dust.

*

Above, in the copse of acacia and mahogany, an angry rogue elephant began trumpeting and butting a thorn tree to loosen its roots. With a curl of trunk and grip of tusk he tore it clean out of the ground to vent his furious temper. A black-maned lion reared up on hind legs and danced in fury while roaring in contempt of what he had seen then bounded off to find a track leading to an easy descent into the crater. A buffalo snorted and honed massive horns on the bark of a mahogany tree. His beady eyes became luminous with rage as he scented human blood. Seeing no approaching figure he spun on the spot and went head up at a determined trot and blowing steam into the gloom of the copse. A leopard coughed and belched with hunger. He leaped up into the jagged branches of a fallen tree and draped himself loose-limbed along yellow bark. Surveying the clearing now stained here and there with dark patches he looked for signs of life and saw none. Then turning his head a full half-circle he looked out across the great valley where a lake, shimmering like a jewel in a shaft of sunlight between storm clouds, shone pink with a myriad flamingo. His stomach rumbled as he yawned while savouring the sweet smell of longhorn cattle on the rising wind. A stab of lightning and immediate thunder opened the heavens and heavy drops of rain began to darken his coat.

# 13.

A stampede does not happen while all is well.
*(There is no smoke without fire)*

Della was pleased with herself. She had driven well and fast enough to have sight of the two vehicles well ahead on a rise while going out of wooded country onto the El Barta plains., The map she kept on her lap showed only this road up to Baragoi but beyond that there were one or two pencilled-in tracks going eastwards towards a range of mountains where, when she looked up could see heavy clouds massing. Six miles beyond Baragoi she stopped on a rise and looked through the binoculars just in time to see tell-tale dust turning off eastwards onto the second marked track.

Driving on she now had the feeling that the air was getting sticky and close with the light fading from a black cloud overhead while thinking it made a pleasant change from a burning sun. She continued up to the point where she had seen the vehicles turn. There she stopped off the road under a leafless tree, got out, stretched and had a cup of water.

On going across to check the tyre marks on a soft sandy patch of the track she bit her lip with pleasure for she could see the marks left by the cuts in the carrier's tyres. As she turned to go back to the pickup she was nearly blinded by an electric flash followed by a deafening clap of thunder that shook the ground, and rain as though someone had dowsed her with a bathful of cold water. The rain came down with such force as to bounce up a yard. She dashed for the cab door and jumped in but was soaked through. Winding up the window she saw a torrent of water running across the track. That was as far as she could see. A wall of rain limited her vision to about ten yards. She had not experienced anything like this since she was caught on the edge of a hurricane swirling in from the Caribbean to devastate the Louisiana coast.

\*

Peter sat at a dining room table of the Stag's Head hotel in Nakuru savouring a full breakfast. Other acquaintances now crowded the room with smiles replacing the anxious looks that had been on faces for a long time. Celebration without flagging was in their minds.

Rift Valley farmers, some with wives; some without; grass widows; unattached sons, daughters and itinerants all came in ex-army Land Rovers, Bedfords, Jeeps, Chevvies, GM trucks, vintage Rolls', old Fords, on horseback and on bicycles. Groups of settlers hearing of the shindig came down in droves and Nakuru became alive with music and dancing. Extra beds were put in the now jam-packed rooms, in corridors and on covered verandas. The space under bar tables was reserved for those who would sleep off the effects off their own celebrations.

The owners and managers of farms in the Rift, the White Highlands and the Kikuyu uplands were shedding themselves of three years of worry, frustration and financial struggle. Kikuyu farm workers were in the villages scattered about the tribal homelands getting drunk on banana beer and giving thanks to Muungu. Masai herdsmen up and down the Rift were out with their cattle gorging on water while standing in raging rivers where twenty-four hours before had been a sorry mess of dust and scorching rock.

Peter did not go to the ever-open bar to greet other revellers but decided to go back to his farm and start organising the schedules. He now considered the business of the Okiuka would have to wait for a while. He drove out of Nakuru for some miles and took an unfamiliar road between Menengai and the wooded slopes of the eastern escarpment to avoid the usual route that he learned was flooded. As he turned one of the sharp bends in the ascending scrub he came to a halt in front of a large herd of cattle stuck in mud. Rain had swept down the slopes and collected in a depression that had become a shallow lake into which the herd had wandered and turned it into a quagmire many feet deep. He switched off the engine, got out and looked for the herdsmen but all he could see was a boy of about five years wrapped in a sodden blanket sitting on the back of a large bull stuck fast up to his breast.

"Where are the herdsmen?" he called in Olmaa.

"Gone. All gone." Peter could see he was not happy.

"Come. Talk and eat."

The boy danced across the backs of the heaving and lowing beasts deftly missing the points of waving horns until reaching a shallow patch where he jumped down and came to Peter. Together they sorted out a free-standing cow and hobbled her while putting a leather thong about her neck and tightening it with a stick till a vein stood out. With a small bow the boy shot a stem of hollow grass with an angled point into the vein and Peter filled a mug with the blood that flowed. The boy finished it quickly and had another half mug topped up with milk taken from the cow. The beast's wound was sealed with mud and the tourniquet with hobbles removed. A rope was put around the horns of the stuck bull to winch it out and they drove the cattle to higher ground.

"You have a name boy?" he asked in the boy's tongue.

"I have two," he said proudly. "Saichella ole Tepidongoi."

"Where is your engang?" The boy looked north and jutted out his chin. Peter understood that to be a mile or so and they both began to drive the cattle. Peter used the truck to drive the main herd while the boy gathered stragglers. After half a mile up the slope of the Menengai crater they passed a copse of mahogany and acacia and after a further mile they came to an enclosure with most of the surround and huts washed away.

"Where are your people?" He sensed there was something very wrong.

"All are gone. All. There," he said pointing with his stick.

They secured the cattle inside the enclosure that they built up in weak places. Peter loaded a shotgun and slung binoculars over a shoulder. They walked quickly to the clearing at the crater's edge and the boy went to the rim and pointed down into the bowl. Peter came to the brink of the legendary cliffs and drew a sharp breath. He stepped back then lay on the edge and looked down through glasses. He looked up with a grave face.

"I see fisi – vultures – dogs. Little else except . . ." He broke off not wanting to upset Saichella who was on the verge of tears. He knelt and held the boy's hands. "How many kinsmen?"

"Many . . . many . . . all families . . . all."

"Who did this?"

"I saw. He was from the south with many moran."

"He has a name?"

"It is Sekento."

Peter shook his head. At that moment it started to rain again and they returned to the engang where a fire was built.

"We shall have a two hour watch tonight. If there is even small trouble during your watch you are to wake me. I shall make two beds in the truck. We shall make hot food then sleep for two hours. Do you read a watch?" he asked pointing to his wrist.

"No."

"You know two hours?"

"Yes."

Once or twice during the night a leopard coughed but caused no concern and they had a quiet night with the boy being good at judging two hours. The following morning they had breakfast in cool mist that took an hour to clear.

Peter knew he could not leave Saichella alone to look after his cattle in case of animals and raiders, and he decided to get him and the cattle back to the farm for safety. He learned from the boy that while at the clearing he overheard a moran say that Sekento was to go north to get more support from the Njemps and Kamasia clans.

The drive back to his farm along the western face of the Aberdares was not the easiest. They had to steer clear of settler's land and go through thick scrub that spooked the cattle on more than one occasion. Saichella, a bundle of energy, wielded his stick and whistled expertly to keep the herd moving while Peter drove behind them. Eventually, before sundown they reached the approaches to the farm. The cattle were guided through to a field with new grass sprouting. The chief dairyman came running thinking they had been invaded. The dairyman was put straight as to whom the cattle belonged and he was to look after and house Saichella until further notice and the cattle were to be counted and not mixed with the home herd and a vet was to be sent for.

He drove to the garage from where he walked up the path through trees to the house. He rounded a large bush of azalea and stopped short.

"What the hell . . .?"

A corner of the house had smoke billowing and drifting into the forest above. Racing ahead he found the northeast corner of his house ablaze while his African staff were doing what they could with buckets and a standpipe. He went straight to a store near the swimming pool where he got out a motorised pump and hose. In double-quick time he had a good jet of water, and to help him it began to rain heavily. A portable lighting generator was used as darkness fell and with the fire out he was able to dowse the hot spots. Fortunately only the northeast corner with a cloakroom and sparsely furnished spare room took the damage. The main hall was not touched.

The farm manager, having seen the smoke from the lower reaches of the farm arrived to help and he was told of the Masai cattle. He said he would camp out at the farm to help arrange things such as documenting and vetting the stock.

When things had quietened down Peter called all the principal house and farm staff to one of the sheds where, by lanterns and the rattle of heavy rain on the iron roof, first thanked them for their loyalty then questioned them. Most of them knew nothing but Kinyanjui said that while he was speaking to a gardener two hours before Peter had arrived he had seen a Masai come from the trees and use fire arrows which broke a window then run into the forest below and beyond the waterfall.

"A Masai use fire arrows? Are you sure? That is not a Masai trick. That is the work of a forest man and not one from the plains. A Masai fires his grass – not houses."

"But bwana," insisted Kinyanjui "it was a Masai with Kenya markings. Not a man I have seen before. He was not Burrgo. I think he is Leikipia."

"Leikipia? Damn!" Peter was sure it must have been Sianka who was now showing his hand. Knowing that Sekento was on is way north guessed that the younger brother, after an unsubtle show of anger, would now also be heading north for another confrontation with Sekento.

Peter thanked his staff again for attempting to put out the fire, dismissed them and went to the farm office to write letters. He was very angry. His parents had lavished love and effort on a home in which to bring up a boy. Sianka had now spoiled it. Also, Sekento had been instrumental in the massacre of a whole clan of his own kind. The brothers were now at the top of his list. Revenge was uppermost in his mind and he swore there and then to continue the search and recover the Okiuka, whatever the conditions.

As dawn came with no rain but a clinging damp mist he replenished the truck with stores, water, fuel, new tyres and additional spares from stock knowing that he may have to travel in uncharted country. Before leaving he surveyed the scene with his manager, cleared the debris from the two rooms that had been damaged and secured that part of the house. They made notes of what had to be done while Peter explained that he had to go out on urgent business and would be gone for a few days.

He drove out via Kinangop where he found Steve Harris to be out on a safari and left there without leaving a message, and posted the letters. While driving down to Kiambu to pick up Njoroge he thought that Sekento must be hard up for followers if he had to go as far north as Baringo for support from the Njemps clan. He doubted if the elder brother would get much change there because the Njemps on the south east of the lake were no longer warlike and were degenerating into domesticity. Also, the Kamasia people of Nilotic descent from the early Nile dwellers who lived in the hills in the west were not likely to countenance Hamitic people such as Sekento and his kind for whom they had a fair measure of contempt. Peter doubted the wisdom or even the success of Sekento's mission. Dwindling support must be galling him and no doubt he would be dangerous if cornered, as would Sianka. But, he vowed they must be followed and found.

It was raining heavily when he picked up Njoroge and they slithered down dirt roads to the main Nakuru road. On reaching the Stag's Head hotel he had the truck hosed with a jet underneath to clear thick mud that had coagulated under the wheel arches nearly to the point of jamming the steering. The hotel being full he found and paid for an African lodging house with food for the night for Njoroge, while he himself decided to bed down in the truck and dine on tinned meat and spinach.

Early next day they took the main dirt road north. Guessing Sekento would have had no luck with the Njemps and gone further north he went along the western shore of the Baringo lake and around to the northeast where they camped.

Some way ahead Peter saw a group of Masai loping southwards raising dust that hovered behind them as though attached. They appeared to be unreal and vignetted in space and time without getting nearer but suddenly they were within hailing distance. He drove over to them and passed the time of day. They settled under a stunted thorn tree on which were hanging clusters of weavers' nests.

The Masai had the markings of the Njemps clan and Peter gave them salt in exchange for news and learned that Sekento had been this way the day before heading north driving the 'motok' that had acquired dents and scratches. They said that Sekento had tried to exert his influence upon the locals but had been refused help and sent packing. They said he was now alone. His followers at Nakuru had become uncontrollably drunk and disorganised and had gone off in separate parties to raid the Burrgo cattlemen. Some had been rounded up by the authorities but not before Sekento had escaped. Having no remorse for his actions at Menengai he had gone blundering northwards in the Jeep.

Despite their knowledge of Sekento and his goings on most clans had closed ranks and kept quiet about him. They disliked the White Authorities while tolerating them and told them as little as possible. Over the years Peter's close association with the Masai had become respected and he and only a few other white Kenyans were privy to what went on in the clans.

The gathering of men got up to go about their business and left the shade of the tree. Now, barely fifty yards away, undressed sandals and callused heels were sending up spurts of dust that accumulated and almost hid them as they strode away into another century.

## 14.

A log in the store laughs at the one in the fire.
*(Today might be your day. But what of tomorrow?)*

If anyone should think they were in a different century then it would be Della. She was crouching behind a log with a camera looking out to a stretch of undulating savannah with one isolated tree throwing long early shadows while watching a cheetah stalking a herd of impala.

The previous night while she was marooned in the pickup mosquitoes had plagued her even after the rain abated in the early hours. And when daylight came she started along the now slippery track where she supposed the two vehicles had gone. After a mile or so, on rounding a rocky corner where the track started to rise into the northern approaches of the Ndoto Hills she saw a truck and a tent next to trees that opened out to savannah.

There she met two Norwegian couples making breakfast over a fire. Introductions made, they offered her breakfast and volunteered that if she was to go to a fallen tree about three hundred yards away she might have sight of a cheetah they had seen that morning. Her breakfast would be ready when she returned and her clothes of yesterday dried.

On reaching the fallen tree she looked out south and east across a savannah that went on for ever with just one tree. There was not a bush, not a kopje, just endless space, mostly new grass with here and there a bare patch of blood-red earth shimmering with heat. Here Della was beginning to get the true feeling of East Africa. Space unlimited. Tops of mountains showing as shadows beyond the horizon. She though that Texas had space but she had not seen anything there to compare with the Rift Valley. Feasting her eyes she then saw the cheetah and knelt behind the bole of the tree.

The cheetah was stalking a scattering of impala and tensing for the run. Della raised her camera with her elbows on the tree. When the chase came she experienced a tightening of the lower abdomen that she tried to ignore while she exposed frame after frame. The spasm in her womb was a purely feminine reaction because she could see the inevitable end of the chase. It was a pregnant female that had been selected. Lacking the speed and agility due to her pregnancy, a swerving chase and the swipe of a paw to catch the impala in mid leap were enough. The final shot, the last on the roll, captured both animals defying gravity with the cheetah's paw on a back leg of the impala and surrounded with flying clods of earth. When both crashed to earth a jaw clamped on a throat to stop blood to the head and air to the lungs that brought on immediate unconsciousness and unfeeling death to the victim. Della's natural feelings had not got in the way of the professional actions in recording the kill.

Afterwards what went through her mind was the fact that the female animal, of which she was one, was on this earth for the purpose of being hounded by the male and producing young for the continuance of the species. This she had shunned for the sake of her profession. Now, nothing was as rewarding and exciting as her current job.

She sealed, marked and stored away the exposed roll of film and loaded another while thinking that the tooth-and-claw world she had just witnessed was as uncompromising as her own profession. She recalled times when, while fighting for her own position among men and women in her line of work, she had been ambitious to the point of climbing over less tenacious backs by sheer personality and not by sleeping around. She might still have been typing in an office but her time at Radcliffe and in the Air Force she knew had helped. Now she could not envisage anything better than what she was doing at that moment – relishing space, the elements, freedom, fascinating animals and people.

Peter and Bili sprang to mind. After the first disastrous meeting he had shown that he was generous and had a quick turn of humour; was good fun and romantic when dancing at the Equator Club, then at the Commissioner's house party he was playful and attentive, but he seemed to have something on his mind and wanting to dash about doing something. What, she wondered? She was confused. On the one hand, until this visit to Kenya she had kept men at arm's length, but now on meeting Peter was affected in ways she had not experienced before. She constantly struggled to dismiss him from her mind.

While walking back to the camp she yawned expansively, thought of following poachers and took in the smell of sizzling bacon and eggs. Squatting on a log by the fire she volunteered she had seen the cheetah and had photographed it. "Did you by chance see a couple of trucks pass this way last evening?"

"We heard what could have been trucks but we were under cover from the rain. We have been to Marsabit in the north where there is no rain, but now we are on our way back to Nairobi. We leave here today. Are you on holiday?"

"Not exactly. I am writing a safari article for my newspaper."

"Then you must get further north if you can. Marsabit is wonderful. Not many people except for the Rendili and Boran. There is game there and lakes."

"I might well do that. I have time to look at the Ndoto hills first. I am told there are many animals in the forest there."

"Yes. We have heard there are a great number of elephants there. More coffee?"

"Yes please. Where does this road lead?"

"About twelve miles east from here it passes through Illaut and then Laisamia. From there it is about a hundred miles or so north to Marsabit or two hundred south to Mount Kenya. We came down that way but you need four-wheel drive on these roads."

"I suppose I am lucky to have good safari tyres."

She consulted her map to pinpoint her position and noticed that six miles from the Norwegian's camp was a track going south up the face of the Ndotos. At the junction Peter had marked 'Whistling Thorn' and along the track also was a mark '2m Camp'.

She stretched and stifled another yawn. "It has been very nice of you to have me stay for breakfast, and I have some pictures of the cheetah. I must get on. I have a deadline to meet. If ever you come to America in your travels look me up and I'll show you around." She wrote the name of her newspaper and her own on a paper tissue that was folded and put in a pocket. "Goodbye all and thanks again."

She drove east and had a cautious ride to where she thought the track up to the camp was. There was no sign of a turn off and all she could see twenty yards ahead was an enormous untidy bush with many nasty looking thorns and galls. She went over to it and discovered under one side was a dip with a muddy bottom large enough for a substantial vehicle, then a good track through trees. In the mud were tracks of tyres. On closer inspection the impression of cuts in the carrier's tyres were plain to see. She clenched her fists and said "YES!"

Back in the pickup she knew she had to make a controlled lunge to cross the dip. She engaged second gear instead of first so as not to put on too much power and took a steady run at the least muddy part. The tread gripped well with a slight slip she went up the other side on to the track.

After two miles she guessed she must be near the camp but did not want to blunder into it in case the two trucks were there. A hundred yards further and off the track to her right she saw a cul-de-sac clearing with bush at its end leaving a gap where the pickup could be hidden. She got out and tested the ground and found it firm. Following a habit she had of backing and filling with a hot engine she backed into the gap. Not only was this economical but her job had taught her to be ready to make a quick exit from trouble. She stopped the engine and put her mind to what she should do now. Picking up the binoculars she climbed on to the cab roof where she could see above the undergrowth through the trees. Her pulse quickened when she found the open camping place to be no more than fifty yards away. Beyond that was just bush rising into forest.

She let down the tailgate and found ex-military boxes, a comprehensive tool box and spares, highlift jacks, a blow torch, fire extinguisher, a full can of paraffin and portable burner, a rolled tent, two blankets and a sealed cardboard box marked 'Field use only. WD'. This intrigued her. On opening the seal, to her delight she found military food packs, water purifiers and a first aid pack. Yawning again she decided to make herself comfortable and set-to and covered the pickup front end first with the camouflage net then with fallen branches with foliage which she adjusted to look natural so that anyone passing would see nothing unusual. The tarpaulin she draped from the cab top to the tail to run off rain and made a comfortable nest in the rear.

The food packs were of the self-heating kind when opened. First she boiled water to make coffee then tackled a corned beef hash tin. It worked well even after a few years of storage and she thought it tasted good. The college pudding came next but the mixture dried quickly and tasted of cardboard.

Jumping down she filled the fuel tank from a jerrican and checked the oil and water in a cool engine then cleared everything away, buried the empty food cans, and flannel washed using the remainder of the hot water.

Settling under the tarpaulin with a flashlight she attempted to catch up on her notes but fell asleep. During her sleep she dreamed she heard gunfire from far off that lasted for some time, then was woken by a sudden rumble of thunder and immediate heavy rain. She went back to her notes, but tiredness and being lulled by the relentless noise of rain she slipped into a deep sleep

*

Gunfire and dawn woke her. The shots were close. She slipped from under cover, picked up binoculars and climbed to the cab roof. "Good God!" she said through her teeth and bit her lip.

Six elephants were running from the gloom of the high forest into the light of the open scrub to be met by a line of four Africans with raised rifles. She saw the beasts crumple to the ground as tiny bursts of smoke came from the guns with echoing shots following. Five lay dead while one screamed and ran at one of the Africans who, although still firing, was picked up in a trunk, swung against points of tusks, dashed to the ground then knelt upon. Other rifles continued to shoot until the elephant toppled. Even then it tried to rise until another half a dozen shots were fired.

Della was transfixed. Another two Africans appeared and began to hack at the base of what tusks could be found on the dead elephants and carried them to the Bedford truck that came into view. The carrier appeared behind it and she recognised Smith and an African who she guessed must be Chief Thukuru sitting in front. They got out and supervised the loading of tusks into the Bedford that appeared to be almost full. The chief then pointed down to the campsite to her left where another nine elephants had appeared.

Although shocked at what she had seen, she got down from the cab, grabbed the camera and made her way quickly and as quietly as possible through the trees towards the open site and found a place on its edge where she was hidden by the fat trunk of a tree and bush.

The Africans swiftly left the truck and while reloading the ex-service S.M.L.E.303s, inadequate in all but expert hands, made their way to the campsite dodging from cover to cover. The lead female elephant, sensing danger, trumpeted and charged an African who showed himself and fired. Four shots followed from others and the elephant dropped. She had photographed the African aiming and the elephant falling. The other elephants ran forward to help the dead beast as seven Africans began emptying their rifles into them.

She exposed frame after frame of the carnage and executioners and had to stop herself from screaming with anger, particularly when capturing on film the strewn carcases lying in running blood with some of the Africans standing on them and hacking tusks from bodies, some not yet dead.

The carrier and Bedford were now driven down to the site to begin loading. The Bedford soon had a bulging canvass cover and was down on the springs. Della took a shot of the stacked tusks before the auditor and chief Thukuru, unaware they were being observed could now be heard talking with voices that carried with a flat echo in the morning air.

"A good load this time, chief. I counted two hundred and twenty five tusks. I estimate they average about fifty pounds in weight a tusk. That's . . . let me see . . . eleven thousand two hundred and fifty pounds, just about five tons."

The chief looked pleased. "Our contact has promised ten dollars a pound. How much is that in total?"

" . . . A little more than a hundred thousand dollars."

"How does that cut up into shares – now we have one less boy to pay?"

"Two hundred dollars each for the boys; fuel – tyres – rations. That leaves about a hundred thousand between us."

"Yes," came another voice close to where Della was hidden. "Yes. Between us three."

Chief Inspector Andrews stepped into view with his burly African sergeant while she nearly dropped her camera with the shock. In the excitement and noise she had not heard the police Land Rover drive along the track up to the campsite. She could not see it from her tree.

"You are both fools. Keep your voices down in front of the boys."

"Ah, Andrews," said the over-confident Smith. "We were just discussing . . ."

"Yes, I heard you. Voices carry to sharp ears. Is it a good haul this time? I see the Bedford's loaded. Did you have to leave this mess so close to the road?"

"Yes." Thukuru was not happy at being called a fool. "We did not have time to drive them up. The best herd was shot yesterday up in the forest. These nine were too good to miss and there are another six up there before the trees."

Andrews went over to the Bedford and looked at the haul not yet hidden by canvas still rolled up at the rear. "Hmmm. Not bad. You reckon on thirty thou' or so each?"

"That's right. Thereabouts."

"Then my work in keeping this place clear of people for this operation is finished. I had the road closed with a felled tree behind me as I drove up. I had better have my cut now. Drop the back canvass down and I shall escort you to Laisamia where my jurisdiction ends. You know the way across towards Wajir and the rendezvous."

So that the shooters would not see the money handed over the chief ordered the seven riflemen get aboard the carrier that was now covered against rain. Della craned around the tree and got two good shots of the transfer from an open briefcase to the auditor. She thought she could do better when the chief was about to hand over a wad of notes to Andrews. She shifted her feet on to a root of the tree and leant against the bark to steady her arm. The shutter in her Leica whispered three times to get perfect images. On winding on again her foot slipped on the damp root and she went sprawling on her face out into the open in full view of the group.

The three men froze for a second then came to life as one. Thukuru shut the case with a snap; Smith threw up his hands in horror; and Andrews ran across to her while drawing his revolver. He hoisted her to her feet.

"You Yankee bitch! Caught up with you at last. That's the last picture you'll ever take. Hand over that camera!"

She held it behind her back. Still holding her arm he clicked back the hammer of the revolver and held it to her head.

"Shall I take it from a dead girl?" His lip curled but it was not a smile. She was about to hand the camera to him when Smith shouted "Leave her to me Andrews. Leave her to me!" He pulled a Luger pistol from the inside pocket of a neat jacket and cocked the trigger.

"No!" Andrews said quickly and calmly. "No Herbert. Do not have a girl's death on your conscience. Let the police handle this. We can cover our tracks. Put that gun away."

"I'll do as I please, Andrews. She called me a son of a bitch. I'll not stand for that from a descendant of European steerage trash and I'll not have her leave here to report what she has seen."

He raised the pistol to level it at her. As he took a step forward there was a snap and twang as a poacher's snare noose tightened around his foot and whipped him off balance. An overhanging branch of a tree snapped upwards and swept him off the ground to hang by a leg. The pistol dropped and he bounced once in the air before he knew what had happened; then he screamed. He could not have known it was vanity that was his undoing. The snare, cleverly constructed and hidden by a lone poacher weeks before, was hooked just around the welt of his small hand-made shoe. If he had worn proper boots for the terrain he would have survived, for the boot would have gripped his ankle and not come away, but the slip wire was tight and the weight of a bouncing body took the shoe off his foot and he fell eight feet on to his head. All there heard the crack as his neck was broken. But Della, after having the luger pointed at her, her fingers went into action. In that fraction of a second when it seemed that all were locked in slow motion, and although her upper arm was tightly gripped, Della's journalist's reflexes came into play and exposed two frames from the waist of his hanging there and of the fall on to his head.

"Sergeant! Hold this girl!" She felt from behind the grip of strong hands on her upper arms as Andrews left her and went over to the crumpled body. "Stupid idiot!" Andrews never swore. His control over people came from cold eyes and a measured voice. He displayed no sympathy whatever for Smith whose body finally shuddered and lay still. The auditor's death had caused the policeman's quick brain to think of a brilliant idea.

"What do we do now?" asked Chief Thukuru, "put his body with the *ndovu*?"

"We do not do that sort of thing with our people. I shall arrange to have him taken back to Nairobi for identification." He took the wad of notes from Smith's pocket, put some back, gave Thukuru roughly half and pocketed the other.

His policeman's logic told him he would return the body and proudly claim that Herbert Smith was the ringleader of the poaching ring he had been trailing. He would explain that he and just one sergeant were not enough to contain a whole group of armed poachers, who, on seeing their leader dead had fled. All he had to do was to get together a force and track down them down. This would aid his quest for career advancement. Also, to keep his own hands clean, he now knew what to do with the girl. The sergeant would have to take care of that.

"Sergeant. Take this American girl out of my sight." He spoke slowly and pointedly. "She is not to be seen by anyone – ever – again. Not – ever. Do you understand?" The sergeant nodded with a grin. "Also destroy that camera."

"Yes sah! I know what to do." He understood fully and his bloodshot eyes lit up with the prospect. Andrews' lip curled again.

"So, Miss Mitchell. You came here to see Africa? Well now, you shall see what Africa can do for you. Do it sergeant!" He turned to the chief to discuss the next move.

With rifle over a shoulder on a loose sling the sergeant marched her unceremoniously gripping her elbows behind her to where the track started down out of the clearing and marched her the twenty yards to the parked Land Rover. He was savouring the prospect of raping a white girl before killing her. He turned her and changed his grip to her shoulders and went to push her to the ground. With trained precision from her service days she fell backwards with a foot in his stomach, used his momentum and straightened her leg. He was only aware of flying upside down when he hit the ground awkwardly on his head and shoulder that gave a loud crack as the collarbone snapped. The brass butt of the rifle flayed open his cheek and smashed the bone, a sliver of which jabbed his eye as he momentarily lost consciousness. Her training took over. She grabbed both his hands behind his back, twisted the rifle sling tightly around his wrists while forcing his feet up to wedge his boots in the gap between sling and trigger guard. She slipped out the cartridge holder and threw it into the bushes then pulled his jersey up from his big stomach to stretch it over his head. Then, picking up the undamaged camera, she took two quick shots of him lying there with the Land Rover number plate in view and sped the fifty yards through the bushes back to the pickup, heaved the branches aside, hauled the net from the front and bundled it under the tarpaulin.

 The pickup started at a touch and lurched forward bouncing over the branches. She pointed the nose at the track and sped forward just as a cloudburst hit the forest. When she reached the hollow under the whistling thorn she saw more water than mud and rushed at it steering herself around the rim of the depression. The spinning wheels with deep treads tore her out of the hollow and she bounced on to the road where she stopped with foot down on clutch with her other heel on the brake and toe on accelerator with engine racing. Under the whistling thorn tension now gripped her. Trembling, stomach muscles taught, hands grasping the wheel, freely perspiring and with tears of shock streaming she looked up into the rain. Sickened by dying elephants, home and security half a world away, alone, frightened, having looked death in the face, she cried as never before. "Peter!" she screamed in panic, "Where the hell are you when I want you? You ornery S.O.B. Help me! What the hell way do I go now?!"

 With continuous lightning the cloud lit up and she swore she saw through the screen wipers the image of a Masai warrior appear in the cloud pointing the way with a spear. She let in the clutch and turned the wheel.

# 15.

Stop a flood at a distance.
*(Do not let evil come too close)*

Andrews was elated to have found a way of using Smith's death to his advantage. Right now he was not worried about Della. He knew that the sergeant would deal with that problem quietly, hide her dead body, and be waiting at the Land Rover with a smashed camera and roll of film exposed.

"I shall escort you to Illaut" Andrews said to Thukuru, "not Laisamia as originally planned. You go by the chosen route to the rendezvous. I shall go to the police post in Illaut to do what has to be done with Smith's body and make a report that will keep us in the clear. My jurisdiction ends here now. Get a couple of the boys to wrap him up in something and carry his body to the Land Rover. I'll lead the way out of this place. He picked up a cape from a hook in the cab and walked in the rain past scores of winged scavengers squabbling and tearing noisily at the elephants' bodies. On reaching the Land Rover he was dumbstruck when he found his trussed-up sergeant making strange noises at the base of a tree.

"How . . . did a chit of a girl do this to you and where is she?"

The sergeant did not answer the rhetorical question but screamed and swore vehemently in the Jaluo tongue as the jersey was pulled from his head and the rifle sling cut to release his hands and feet. Andrews saw the sergeant's arm was useless and blood from his face ran down his neck and chest. The rain and blood-sodden jersey when removed uncovered a broken collarbone sticking up through skin.

Smith's body arrived and was put in the back of the Land Rover. The sergeant was ordered to get in with the body without help. Andrews did not want to have his uniform contaminated with someone else's blood. Now he would have to dispose of the injured sergeant to avoid him telling anyone what had happened and decided he would take him to the desert believing he could not survive in his condition and would save him the job of actually killing him. Out of sight of anyone he took the fat bundle of notes from his pocket, opened the box between the seats where he carried a spare battery, lifted it out and put the money in a recently made compartment beneath. He returned the battery, checked the fuel level and led the way down the track.

In four-wheel drive the three vehicles negotiated the waterlogged dip that now covered the pickup's tracks. Andrews had a gut feeling she went east and north to Marsabit and would be easy to find with the pickup having Nairobi plates. The three vehicles turned right to head east. Before Illaut he stopped and let the two heavy vehicles go ahead on their way to the rendezvous. Then he turned off the road northwards and headed straight into the southern reaches of the Chalbi Desert, out of rain into a fierce climbing sun. Looking back into the rear he saw the sergeant in a bad way, holding first his shoulder then his face that was becoming unrecognisable as a face.

He drove for two dozen miles into a rainless, bleak, featureless area, where the ground was so hard it showed no tracks nor raised dust. Here, with nothing but an all-round thick purple haze obscuring the middle ground and beyond with the sun nearing its zenith, he stopped and told his sergeant to get out. He drew his revolver and aimed at the sergeant's genitals.

"N – No, please bwana!" he stammered stepping backwards.

Andrews lowered his hand. "You do not deserve even that indignity. You will find what it is like to be stupid enough to let an American bitch get the better of you and upset me. You shall suffer for your misdemeanours." With a sadistic streak he pistol-whipped the sergeant across his injured face that drew a spurt of blood and a scream of pain.

"Sit!"

The sergeant remained on his feet. Andrews' swagger cane came smartly down on the broken shoulder and he sank to his knees. The cane came down again on the shoulder. He sat and almost passed out with pain. Andrews' lip curled, this time into a broad toothy grin and his pale eyes watered. A knife was drawn, laces were cut and boots were flung in different directions.

"There. Now you are bare-footed. All stupid sergeants should try waking in bare feet." The sergeant howled again as Andrews put a foot on his knees and with masochistic pleasure caned the soles of his feet in rhythm with his own words. "But I do not think you will get very far. There are two things on this earth I cannot abide, sergeant. One is the female of the species. The other is a stupid sergeant." He caned the loyal African's feet again and again until blood came. "I see you are bleeding well. Good. Die slowly as a stupid sergeant should."

He wiped his soiled cane on the sergeant's shorts and stepped back to leave him lying bare-chested, bare-footed, bleeding freely and moaning, without shade, without water, under the hottest sun the sergeant would ever know.

Now looking up Andrews saw vultures circling hungrily in a hot, white sky marking the place of red-blooded life in jeopardy. "I shall leave you now, sergeant. I would like to have seen what those vultures could make of you, but I haven't the time." The sergeant rolled onto his knees and good arm but collapsed crying.

Andrews turned the vehicle to face south and mopped the first sweat his face had shown in twenty years. While driving he thought he would have the rear of the Land Rover hosed down, ostensibly to remove the smell of the auditor's body. This would eliminate any trace of the sergeant.

\*

A train of six camels led by a trader and his family travelling across the southern reaches of the desert from Marsabit to South Horr was just beyond the influence of the heat haze obscuring the sergeant. They were getting short of food and the sharp-eyed son of the trader saw fleeting glimpses of vultures gathering. Because they did not descend it was obvious that the creature below was moving and not yet dead. The boy persuaded the father to deviate a little and see if the victim was worth eating. The trader turned south and came across the sergeant crawling on one arm and knees with puttees dragging around bruised and bleeding feet before finally collapsing. The trader was in half a mind to shoot him to put him out of his misery, but when the sergeant haltingly disclosed his rank in the police force, the trader thought there must be some kind of bounty payable for his return. They gave him precious water and fixed a sling cot on one of the camels for him and decided to keep going south to Illaut, it being nearer than South Horr. The trader knew there was an American mission and clinic a mile or two east of Illaut where he would take the sergeant. He would be worth nothing dead.

The camels' pace was not that of the Land Rover and Andrews reached Illaut police post in torrential rain the early afternoon. He handed over the auditor's body, made his report, and had the interior back of the Land Rover hosed down. He asked the African sergeant there if anything out of the ordinary had passed that way, or if a dark green pickup had been seen. The reply was negative on both counts because the sergeant said he was in a back office doing his paperwork and the two constables were at the village looking into a disturbance among some road labourers who were off work due to the rain.

Andrews still had Della to contend with. He considered driving immediately to Marsabit but the storm drains were overflowing, and knew conditions were against him. He went to a small hotel outside Illaut where he became agitated and had a sleepless night thinking of her camera and what it would contain.

\*

The trader had camped overnight ten miles outside Illaut, made an early start before dawn and went directly to the mission clinic with the injured sergeant. The doctor, an American woman, was called from her breakfast and she transfused blood into a very weak sergeant, operated on his face and shoulder with an African dentist as anaesthetist. She said there was no such thing as a bounty for anyone including a police sergeant. The trader, disgruntled, beat his son soundly and stayed long enough to replenish some of his stores.

Hurrying breakfast Andrews saw that his tank and jerricans were filled, drove east and passed the mission station and noticed a group of six camels outside the clinic. It meant nothing to him except that if it were trouble the station sergeant would sort it out. He drove on to Laisamia and turned north on to a surface that belied its status of a major route and put his foot down to get to Marsabit quickly. For the first time in his life he began to be worried.

"Damned stupid sergeant" he muttered. "Now I shall have to do the job myself when I find her. There is a way I know that is not in the book."

# 16.

Catastrophies cannot be predicted.
*(Badness comes unnoticed)*

"Would you like to see some volcanoes Njoroge?" Peter asked his bearer.

"I am not happy with volcanoes, bwana. But the land under them I think should be as it is at Kiambu."

"That is a possibility Njoroge." He closed his eyes and his mind's eye saw Kiambu and other places among the dark, mist-shrouded forests around the white cap of Mount Kenya. He could see rambling villages of round, mud and grass thatched huts surrounded by two-acre shambas growing banana and maize; red roads that had been cut through forests; eroded hillsides crowded with buses; bicycles; flourishing beer halls; and where old women carried heavy loads on their backs held with straps around misshapen heads while others carried children on their backs in swaddles of coloured cloth with exposed heads lolling. He opened his eyes and saw around him a great semi-desert dotted here and there with vast lakes, forests, towering mountains, stark volcanoes and endless grasslands teeming with wildlife on hoof, paw and wing and occasional tall people driving large herds of Boran and Masai cattle.

"Who knows, Njoroge, who knows?" he said with feeling. "Come, let's away. We have tyre tracks to find."

When letting in the gears to go north they left the group of Njemps disappearing southwards into their own dust mingled with heat haze. Peter had a hunch that Sekento would head for a pocket of Samburu up in the remote mountains of that name if he wanted to try for support, or perhaps go east of there to the heart of the wilderness under the northern escarpments from where the true speakers of OlMaa commenced populating the Rift Valley, and traditionally where all private feuds were to be settled while being unobserved.

Having filled the truck's 150-gallon tanks and jerricans with fuel at the farm he now had the best part of a thousand miles to play with, and pressing on for an hour or more they found traces of the Jeep's tyres turning east off the old Kolossia road. Peter was immediately confident for he saw that three were bald with another showing the metal binding. He knew now that Sekento could not go too far on wheels. It was obvious he had, at times, driven too incompetently on such terrain.

Peter followed the tracks north-eastwards into an ever-increasing wasteland. Sometimes they had to dismount and look for tracks that had been obliterated by wind, then guess at Sekento's direction in a terrain that was a mass of flat-topped cones that once, aeons ago, had been a vast field of erupting lava as though the earth had developed a nasty case of smallpox. There were no distinct features to guide him in this uncharted territory to get a precise compass bearing. He looked up into the hot sky without a vestige of cloud and reckoned that Ngai had forgotten this part of the Rift, or more than likely had chosen to do nothing with it. Or perhaps had shifted hell into this place to keep an eye on it. For all that, to Peter's eye, it had a primitive grandeur. Volcanoes, some with perfect symmetry, others misshapen as badly thrown lumps of pottery, had burnished surfaces honed by wind, dust, and rare freak hailstorms, with colours ranging from jet black to aching white. The further north they went, following Sekento, the deeper they went into the southern edge of the *Kharif,* a northeast wind that scoured everything in its path. Starkly breathtaking, the place was without benevolence and without mercy. Here the land was in agony. The true *Nyika*. The wasteland. The wilderness.

After one overnight stop they continued carefully through the day until the jeep's tracks in the dust now showed a shredded tyre and wheel rim. Further they found a miracle of bush growing in a *kloof.* It gave sufficient shelter for them to make camp. Wind was continuous and dust was everywhere, in the crevices of their teeth, hair and food. Every cup of Njoroge's tea contained a skin of floating dust.

"Well, Njoroge, what do you think of it so far?"

The answer was spoken in Kikuyu, and for a mission-schooled person, very rude.

\*

In completely opposite weather Della, far from relaxed, furiously drove the pickup in torrential rain slithering and sliding on a glutinous track. On leaving the scene of the shooting and her own near death she had turned left and west out of the dip under the whistling thorn to follow the guiding spear of the apparition of the Masai warrior. Without mishap, she reached the winding track among the rocks near where she had camped with the Norwegians. Then drove more carefully in the middle of the slippery track and chanced plunging into a stream running across her path. Here she negotiated a newly felled tree now washed half across the road with little room to pass, and with the fan belt screeching and engine coughing she just made it across and kept running in gear before the engine picked up again.

Turning south onto the wider road she went faster but about twenty miles from Maralal she saw the Norwegians off the road with the engine bonnet up and felt obliged to stop and ask if she could do anything.

"We have lost water and I am replacing the top hose."

"Are you alright for spare water?" she asked, causing laughter. Rain was filling saucepans to top up the radiator and running off their waterproof coats.

"There is something that you could do for us. We were giving this African a lift to Losiolo that is just down the road but we have been delayed with this problem. It is not more than a mile or so. It seems he got a lift but missed the road on the way up. We have to be in Nairobi soon to hand back this hired vehicle. Would you give him a lift?"

Under a nearby tree a Masai sat wrapped in a blanket with rain running off his bowed, ochred head. "Well I'd like to oblige, but I too am in a hurry. I have more than one deadline to meet. But . . ." She looked again at the African who was, in her mind, a sorry sight. He saw her looking, stood and came across to her. She was struck by the sudden change in him. He strode with an easy, dignified, graceful walk casually carrying a spear, shield and rungu. She did a double take. This Masai was the exact manifestation of the fantasy image pointing the way she had seen in the rain at the whistling thorn. He stood some paces apart from the group and looked straight at her then went directly to the pickup, let down the tailgate, loosened the tarpaulin and draped it around himself.

Surprised by the natural assumption that she would give him a lift she felt the power of his presence mingling with the image of the spectre in her head. She thought that perhaps this was a prophetic meeting. The American Indians back in Texas constantly talked of solving problems with uncanny primitive foresight. This then must be an instance of the bush telegraph that Peter spoke of and not just a trick of the light. Perhaps it meant salvation from her present plight. "Er, yes" she said climbing into the driving seat. "Make yourself at home." While drawing away the Masai in the back took a drink from a leather pouch and put it back under his blanket where he carried a parcel.

The turn off to the west appeared and he motioned to her through the cab's back window to turn and go on. Some distance along a slight incline she came out of rain into sunshine and dryness. The storm drain here was dry. After another mile Della was getting worried as to how far the African wanted to go, and perhaps hold her up, but just as she reached a rise he banged on the cab roof. She slowed and stopped just on the top of the rise where the continuing road dropped sharply and she opened her eyes in wonder. The view she now had was electrifying.

They were on the very edge of the Losiolo escarpment two thousand feet sheer above a fantastic moonscape part of the Rift Valley. Below, scores of comparatively small, extinct and senile volcanoes lay scarring the valley. The sun was past its zenith and give-away shadows showed the western escarpments through a vague purple haze.

Here was the most primitive sight she was ever to see, and walked down to just beyond a bush in the storm ditch to stand on the edge of the frightening precipice where the road turned sharply to the right. She stepped back from the sheer drop with a gasp and returned to the pickup to see the Masai standing on the back gazing down into the abyss. He raised his spear and pointed down. Della heard him speak some words in Masai, then, presumably for her benefit, in a basic English:

"Sianka goes back to the place where the beginnings of the Masai were seeded, before the time of the great ascent!"

He got down and stood for a moment then without a word turned to the tailgate to retrieve his spear. What he had said meant nothing to her and under her breath she said, 'hitch-hikers in the States usually say thanks' – but put it down to African behaviour. She shrugged her shoulders and gave him a theatrical wave and got into the cab. Sianka saw the wave out of the corner of his eye and misinterpreted it. He came around to the nearside, wrenched open the door, leered, made a clumsy move towards her and lifted his blanket.

"You sassy son of a bitch!" she said and pushed him away.

He had never been used to immediate rejection and made a serious lunge at her. She lifted a leg from under the steering wheel and pushed him on the chest with a boot. This incensed him and unbalanced her. She fell out of the open door and her hat went flying. In falling her boot caught the retaining lever on the handbrake and the pickup started to roll forward but a wheel came up against a stone and stopped it. Getting up she stood, only to find he had swiftly come around to her. He grasped her arm. Instinctively the close combat technique she had learned came into play and he went spinning and to roll finishing close to the edge of the precipice. She dashed for the open cab door and turned to see him, still prone, pick up a large round stone and throw it. His throw was so swift and accurate her arm came to her face for her forearm to deflect the stone to catch her a glancing blow on the head where the bandanna was tied. Stunned and dazed with head ringing, she sank to her knees. Sianka, recovered, picked her up, dumped her on the tailboard and with a leather thong from his waist he hog-tied her hands and feet behind her back and pulled the bandanna down and stuck it in her mouth. He was not going to let a girl get the better of him, especially a white one. His dander was up and he thought it would be a novel and first time experience of possessing a white girl and wondered if she would be different from the many Masai girls he had lain with. Before parting her knees he grasped at the waistband of her trousers and pulled. Nothing happened and he gave it more force splitting a seam to expose her underwear. In doing so his thighs pushed against the tailboard causing the wheel to ride over the stone. With the handbrake off the pickup began to roll down the slope and although he held her he could not stop the vehicle moving faster. He decided that his spear and shield were more important than a white girl and he just managed to snatch his precious things as the vehicle moved away from him gathering speed and heading straight towards the acute right turn where the road's edge dropped sheer down two thousand feet into the wilderness. Sianka watched the receding pickup for no more than a second and dismissed from his mind what he knew would happen and now did not care.

Della was only vaguely aware of what was happening. Her head was spinning and a dull ache behind her eyes made her think she was dreaming. She was aware of movement and could only manage a muffled cry owing to the tightness of the bandanna in her mouth.

He turned abruptly, leaped the storm ditch, took from a bush a pliable frond that he tied around his waist in place of the leather thong and found a precipitous path leading down the escarpment.

Before he tackled the path he undid a string around his neck that carried a parcel. From it he took small leather containers of various dies that he used on his legs and face, and then tied bands of feathers his legs and arms. His pride and joy came next, a magnificent lion-mane and monkey fur headdress that he combed with his fingers before tying it to stand proud on his ochred head. He then drank the remainder of the contents of the leather pouch and threw it out into space for it to fall a long, long way. Now he went to the path not fearing the rugged, and in places vertical, descent, for he could feel under his sandals the tread of his ancestors who, eons before had climbed out of the cauldron to enable a continuing life for the tribe. This gave him heart. He had an appointment down there that he was determined to keep.

\*

While the pickup was rolling Della felt a bump as a front wheel hit a rock in the dry road and she rolled as it lurched to the nearside causing it to plunge into the storm ditch and come to an abrupt stop with the front end digging into a thick bush which grew out from under a rock on the very edge of the precipice. She shot from the tailboard to the cab and her head crunched against the steel toolbox. Lightening flashes occurred in her brain and she sank into oblivion.

# 17.

Kumaisha Kugumu – Kufa Kurahisi.
[*Swahili*]
*(To live is hard – To die is easy)*

It was a bad night in the kloof with the wind trying to tear away the awning attached to the truck, but both Peter and Njoroge were relieved when, the next morning, they were left with just a slight breeze.

After a makeshift breakfast Peter told Njoroge to stay put and gave him precise details of the directions and distances he was to undertake while quartering the wilderness. With a loaded shotgun, more cartridges in a pocket and shoulder bag containing a camera, water bottle and dried fruit he set out. As the sun rose it warmed the Rift Valley, and where Peter was the temperature seemed to rise a degree a minute. He used a compass and watch to go out in increasing squares losing sight of the kloof and the truck in a growing haze. After three squares he felt like giving up in the unbearable heat but he persisted in temperatures well above 45°c. He rested with a gulp of water and wondered if he was going mad or stupid to seek a ferocious Masai who carried a large calibre gun and was used to these conditions.

Before the end of the first leg of the fourth square a flash of light hit his eyes. Making for it he discovered Pat's Jeep half buried in soda dust. The sun had reflected from a shattered windscreen. It was beyond recovery and in a few days it would be covered completely. He saw no footprints for the wind had done its work. He calculated the distance and bearing to the Jeep from the kloof and decided to continue squaring. He photographed the Jeep before stepping out again.

Now the wind had stopped altogether and the ground under his boots became hotter at every step. While on the second leg of the square the ground dipped into what Peter could just discern was a huge shallow pan of white caustic earth where the sun was reflected fiercely upwards. He put on dark glasses and going into the pan he was surrounded by shimmering images in thick haze, but doggedly he followed his compass in insufferable heat. Now, although wearing dark glasses he was half-blinded by the whiteness and baked by the heat. He chewed on dried fruit and a gulp of water.

In the inferno Sekento materialised out of the haze as though by magic. He stood sandal-footed on the searing earth with O'Brien's gun across his shoulders; hands draped over barrel and butt and a faded patterned blanket belted low about the waist. Disdainfully he seemed to ignore Peter. Unblinking, unshielded eyes were concentrating on more worthy prey beyond the wall of haze.

Stopping ten yards away and wary of any move that might be made Peter kept his eyes on him while slipping the bag off his shoulder, and with shotgun at the port spoke a Masai greeting through a parched throat and dry lips. As Sekento turned to acknowledge the compliment, breeding demanding that courtesy, the polished Okiuka in his belt shone in the harsh light.

Now Peter could see what time and circumstance had done to the elder son of Olekowlish. He had thought of what he would say to Sekento should they meet, but he was tongue-tied with the heat. All he could say was "Sekento." The Masai responded with "Peter!" They faced each other with guns that twenty years ago had been smiles.

Sekento turned his head to where he had been looking, and a blob began to manifest itself in the haze. The blob was moving without direction and behaving as though made with partly set jelly. Then the shape assumed tallness with disconnected legs propelling the object nearer. Moments later, Sianka came striding out of the haze and took up a position completing a triangle. Both seemed scornful of Peter's intrusion.

They were perhaps the most adept at surviving in the desert wastes of East Africa. Here in the centre of this fearful wilderness, no doubt one of the hottest and driest places to be found anywhere in Africa, their ancestors had passed through from the north many hundreds of years before, had lived, survived, and for many generations had issued their progeny as though to defy the worst that nature could fling in man's way.

Peter's brain, dulled by the intense heat, searched for the next move. The brothers nodded grimly without speaking, seemingly passing identical thoughts while Peter stood his ground. He knew no words were to be spoken in his hearing and that some action would be taken to eliminate him from the proceedings in order not to be observed, but now that he had come this far to get possession of the Okiuka he was going to stay put. Sekento, standing arrogantly confident with the big gun, need only swing it in one movement and fire. Sianka, now sober, graceful and poised, could give any Masai a lesson in deadliness with the razor-sharp spear he held with perfect balance. Peter knew the unaccustomed heat would dull his own reactions and he shifted his thumb to the safety catch of the shotgun and took comfort in the two barrels while mentally placing his bets.

Without a breath of wind, in stillness and throbbing silence the three tall men stood, each with a strong heritage flowing in full-blooded veins, and each knowing it was a matter of chance as to the outcome while waiting for the slightest move. They were aware of nothing but each other and the crucible in which they stood. There was no horizon. No shadows. Just a merging of earth and air as though they were enclosed in a white-hot box. Somewhere overhead the brilliance increased but that was the only sign of the source of the sensational heat.

Peter flung himself forward and was halfway to the ground as Sekento's first bullet scored a groove in the flesh on his shoulder blade. Sianka's rungu missed his head by inches and went on to smash the heel off one of his boots. He hit the ground face down as Sekento's second bullet found its mark high in the throat of his brother, but Sianka's spear was on its way. Just as Sekento had swung the ·577 to fire the second barrel Sianka had launched his spear. Having been struck by the heel of the hand to give it true flight the long blade vibrated and sang its way to Sekento catching him dead centre in the chest to cut its way through bone and heart, to slice through the backbone and come to a halt with the blade sticking out between his shoulders. The singing stopped but the air still rang with the two shots and Sekento's cry of FISI! FISI!

The two men died where they stood; both with proud defiant faces carving shapes in the desert air and accepting death as quickly as it had come. Then both, from the impact of bullet and spear fell backwards and lay still. Peter lay holding the shotgun pointing at Sekento but had not yet put a finger on the trigger. Suddenly he was aware of his elbows and knees being scorched. He went over to Sekento and stared at the blood spreading quickly and soaking into the earth. Going to Sianka he saw the bullet's dark entry hole in his throat. A colourless liquid streaked with blood oozed from the back of a shattered skull.

He retrieved his camera but when back by the bodies he sank to his knees with a stab of pain in his shoulder and felt blood trickling down to his waist. Steeling himself and hoping the film emulsion had not run in the heat he took what shots he felt were necessary. Then with difficulty he withdrew the spear, now bent, from Sekento's body and straightened it under his foot before taking it over to Sianka to lay it beside his body. He turned the warrior's head to face east to greet the rising sun. Sekento had no spear but his head lolled towards the east and Peter left the body as it was. He took the Okiuka from the elder brother's waist and picked up O'Brien's gun by the barrel to avoid leaving fingerprints on the stock. With his belt he tied the wooden baton along the barrels with the jewel not evident. His camera bag was too small to carry it.

No grave could be dug in the unyielding earth and both Masai stared sightlessly into the blazing sky. He knew that Africa would take care of its dead, for within minutes there would be nothing but scattered bones. Even in this wilderness other creatures would devour nourishing protein from the bodies, and if dust did not cover the bones the next rare rainstorm would wash them into a donga to be swallowed by volcanic debris to disappear for ever, or to be discovered in millennia to come. He turned quietly to salute the two warriors who lay without shadows. Both had died as they had lived, striving for what they believed was theirs.

Now Peter put his mind to getting back to the kloof. He took a long drink before calculating the direction in which he should go to make a beeline for his haven. He did not want to linger in this place, for already vultures were circling with eager beaks.

Starting out with compass in hand but now carrying both guns by the barrels over a shoulder with the camera bag, he walked only a dozen paces before feeling weak. The wind had sprung up again and it tried to take the shirt off his back. He tied his choker over his hat and under his chin to secure it and clutched his left arm to his stomach. Vultures were now landing and starting to tear flesh from the bodies. He turned to shout at them. "Go on you bloody scavengers! Eat all you can. You'll never again get better or more aristocratic flesh in your guts. That might teach you a few table manners. I hope those two men choke the lot of you!" A few of them looked up at the sound of his voice, then, having lost their places turned and fought back into the mêlée.

Peter plodded on for some minutes before feeling exhausted. He found a rock from which a sorry-looking bush sprang and sat under it. He raised the water bottle to his lips but found it empty. He flung it to the ground in disgust and passed out.

\*

Flamingo wings beat his face and he choked on water being poured into his mouth. His senses struggled through partial oblivion into light and Njoroge's face appeared. "Bwana Peter . . . Bwana Peter . . . You must not lie here, bwana. Drink this water. I put in your mix." He had used Peter's mixture of glucose and salt.

"That's bright of you. Thanks. How did you get here?"

"I hear shooting and fearing for you I came to where the sound told me to come. What man did this?" he asked seeing the blood-soaked shirt.

"I think you would not wish to know him. He will not fire another gun."

"I hear two shots bwana."

"Yes both from his gun. Have no fear. I did not kill anyone. My gun remains unfired."

"But . . ."

"No buts my friend. Not your business. You found your way here, now find your way back to the ghari. Let's get the hell out of here. I am beginning to dislike this place," he said with gross understatement.

The journey back with Njoroge using his memory of reversed features and Peter using his watch and compass was slow and painful. Njoroge carried the shoulder bag and shotgun while Peter carried the ·577. He guessed that his bearer knew nothing of the Okiuka or its provenance for he did not ask why a piece of wood was strapped to an elephant gun.

With hunters' knowledge they reached the kloof where Peter removed his shirt to let Njoroge wash and clean the wound.

"Sit here bwana. First I boil water then I go for things."

He went to the first aid box but not before rummaging around a bush at the back of the kloof. When he had finished lengthy and painful work on Peter's shoulder he fixed his arm to his stomach with a bandage.

"You must keep the arm still bwana until we reach a place where you must rest."

Then he stirred the fire to a blaze and made hot food for them both with a can of his infamous tea. After eating they sat at the fire as darkness came without wind while stars spread in a black sky with a waning moon.

"My shoulder is comfortable now, Njoroge. How did you fix it?"

"It is something I learn when leaving mission school. I went to your box and found the white powder you put on wounds, then I used needle and cotton, the web of the spider, and the *siafu* that stay there till dead."

For a moment Peter was speechless. Layers of web, being one of his late mother's remedies he understood. Antibiotic powder he expected, but soldier ant pincers that would cling until dead and needle and cotton he thought rather primitive.

"But I boiled the needle and cotton first" said his faithful bearer.

"Thank you."

Njoroge kept the fire going and stayed awake all night that passed without incident except that Peter woke once in a cold sweat. He had been dreaming he was chased by two Masai warriors, one jabbing him in the shoulder with a spear while the other beat him with a flaming ebony stick. He drank water and slept again until he woke in the morning with a sore shoulder and cramp in his arm. The wound was washed and dressed again and the dead ants exchanged for live ones.

They ate stiff porridge and honey-laced coffee before Peter said he was fit enough to drive.

"We shall not go back the way we came. It is too arduous. I remember my father telling me there was a usable track at the north end of the eastern escarpment that leads to the top. That will be cooler. You may have to endure a few Samburu on the way. I cannot say they are any worse or better than the Masai, coming from the same ancestry."

"Anywhere away from this place bwana. I do not wish to die here. There may be beauty for the Masai and for your camera, but not for the Kikuyu. I smell death here."

"That is because you are tired. You may sleep as I drive."

They struck camp and headed north and kept under the cliffs of the dramatic escarpment that had appeared out of the wind driven dust. Peter kept a steady pace on bad volcanic terrain. The Kharif wind had died as they approached the north end of the scarp that had now lost its stark face and height. He took a zigzag course up and discovered a cattle run on which a group of Samburu were leading a large Boran herd. He spoke to them in OlMaa knowing their language had deviated during the hundreds of years of separation from the true Masai, but expected to be understood. They told him to continue up the run to a visible pile of rocks the other side of which he would find the track. He gave them salt for the information.

For the next twenty miles he drove on a tortuous track with sometimes barely enough room between a rock wall and a dangerous drop. Daytime heat and cold nights had done their worst and the track in places had no recognisable surface. Then, rising into cooler air the track ran wider on a steady incline. Above them clouds were developing in a white sky. He had nearly reached the top of the escarpment and he stopped and woke Njoroge to admire the view.

"Bwana, I do not believe we were down there in all that badness. I shall never again go to that place. I shall track and carry for you in all other places. Please bwana; do not make me go there again. You were hurt there. I should die there. It is a place without Muungu. It is a place of death."

"You may be right." He said when steadying his camera on a rolled-up jersey on the truck door sill. "But then again . . ."

He put the camera away, started up the rise and came to a place where the track was on the edge of the sheer drop of two thousand feet and where it rose to a sharp left turn. He changed to a lower gear to negotiate the turn when the sun came from behind a puffball cloud and he was startled by a brilliant flash from a bush that grew out from a rock on the edge of the drop.

"What the . . ."

"Bwana! That big stone . . ."

"Hell, Njoroge, that isn't a stone it's a hat," he said coming to a halt. He switched off, got out and picked it up. "Where have I seen this hat before? And what was that flash from the bush?" He went over to it and stopped short. "Bloody hell! That's my pickup!" The shattered wing mirror had a sliver of glass sticking out at an angle. He looked in the open cab door, saw the keys in the dash and caught his breath knowing that Della had been using it. "Jees! I hope she's not hurt. Njoroge, M'sabu Mitchell was driving this ghari. This is her hat. Go find her." As Njoroge went to the storm ditch Peter looked into the back. "Hey! She's here!" Della was lying half under the tarpaulin bunched up against the tool box. "Give me a hand." The first thing Peter did was to release the bandanna gag and feel for a pulse while Njoroge cut the thong about her hands and feet.

"Thank God. She's alive. Bring water."

He sat on the tailboard, supported her with an arm and emptied water onto her lips then soaked the bandanna and dabbed her face while noticing a purple and yellowing bruise just above the hairline. Putting the water bottle again to her lips he noticed her eyelids move. Gradually she began to take the water and blink. He vigorously rubbed her legs and arms while noticing a nasty bruise on her forearm.

"Where . . . where . . ."

"You are safe. Don't talk, drink."

"Legs . . . cramp . . ."

He continued rubbing through her trousers and noticed the tear down the side seam.

"I'd like to know who did this. I'll kill the bastard. Don't talk now. Get this down you."

While she drank slowly to avoid gagging Peter realised how much he cared for her. Yes, he was helping a girl in distress, but what a girl! He had had his moments in the past, but he found himself with feelings he had not had before. These feelings did not change even while he thought of her being wanted by the police having broken the law. He stroked her cheek and was rewarded with a wan smile and pursed lips in a kiss.

"Right, my darling, up with you," he said, saying the word he had used often without the sincerity it carried right now. Despite a sharp pain in his shoulder he carried her to the truck and laid her on a bedroll in the back. He made her drink a stiff dose of quinine and covered her with a blanket.

"Peter" she murmured. "Sorry . . . I . . . Head aches . . ."

"Don't say a word now. Relax." He kissed her on her forehead.

Her eyes blinked then with a smile they closed in natural sleep. He made sure she was comfortable. Njoroge called him and went up to where there were vague marks in the road and across the storm ditch.

"Here, bwana. Sandals. Many marks. Also small boots. Perhaps a struggle. *Ghari* then go down . . . see *mpira* mark on the stone. Also he go this way."

Across the ditch he showed Peter a sandal print in dust and tiny colour blots on a stone slab. Peter fingered the dry colours.

"These are Masai dies if I'm not mistaken."

They looked further and found sandal marks leading to and beginning to descend a precipitous path down the sheer face of the escarpment.

"That would take some climbing down. I should think at least a whole day. Possibly more. Brave chap whoever . . ." Peter's thoughts suddenly gelled into one. "Ye Gods! We were down there . . . It can't be!"

"Bwana?"

"I don't know. My imagination is getting the better of me. Let's get out of here. How long do you think the m'sabu was lying in the ghari?"

"I go look." He went down to the pickup and inspected where the metal had been damaged by the bush. Peter followed deep in thought.

"No rain here," said Njoroge. I think two days and nights."

"Njoroge, my lad, do you worship God?"

"But yes. For sure."

"The Christian God?"

"Not now. The mountain belonging to *Muungu* I can touch. The Christian God has nothing to touch."

"Then give Muungu thanks for m'sabu's deliverance as I shall give thanks to the great God Chance. It must have been . . ." he checked himself from saying 'the Okiuka' in front of Njoroge, "that flash of light which came from the heavens to show us where she was. It was his guidance that took us this way instead of going back by the lakes. You do not have to touch anything Njoroge to be a true believer." For a moment they looked at each other without saying anything. Peter saw in the young man an African whose twentieth century Mission schooling was wearing thin.

"That's enough evangelising for now. Let us pull this thing out. Get the rope."

When the pickup was hauled to the top of the rise Peter checked it over and found it had lost water from a leak in the radiator where the bush had damaged it. Apart from that and the wing mirror and a few scratches he could see nothing more to worry about. He got out the brazing kit, repaired the radiator and topped it up. The battery voltage was down from having the doors open and courtesy lights on. After cleaning condensation and dust from the distributor he applied jump leads from the truck for it to start at the second try. Nothing was missing from the back of the pickup and the fuel tank was three-quarters full.

"You drive this, Njoroge and follow me. I think this road will lead to a turn off for Maralal. I know some people there who may help."

"Your back is bleeding again, bwana. I look at it before we go."

He took a clean field dressing from the box and applied it over the wound where the cotton had snapped.

Peter checked that Della was comfortable and still asleep while sweating freely then drove at a moderate pace before coming to the junction where they turned south and went the twenty miles or so to Maralal. Before the town Peter turned off onto a concrete slab over a storm drain and then through trees to the front of the house belonging to his late father's hunting partner. A steward in a kanzu came out.

"Is the bwana Pretorius at home?" he asked getting down from the cab.

"At the sawmill."

"Tell him Peter Grant is here."

There was no need for him to go to the sawmill for Eghardt came from the back of the house on hearing the two vehicles.

"Why, it's that young scallywag Peter as I live and breathe! How are you m'boy?" Eghardt said as he pumped his hand.

"Well. Am I glad to see you."

"And how is Della?" he said going over to the pickup.

"You know Della? How is that?"

"She not here."

"She's in the truck. Has fever. She's been hurt."

Eghardt went to her. "Ah, my girl. You come to Pretty again. What have you been doing to get hurt? You come to the house." He carried her across to the veranda where Annie had come out to see what the commotion was. "Annie m'Frau, get this girl to bed. She sick."

In less than a few minutes her bed was turned down, a bath was drawn and her clothes were taken for washing. While Annie was bathing her she murmured "My bag . . . tell Peter . . . photographs . . . agent . . . important."

"Yes, my dear. We look after you. We know this fever. You be safe here. You come to bed now and have some of my soup and you be right as rain. What's this bruise? You been hit?"

"Yes" she said as Annie finally dried her and wrapped her in the towel.

"You say nothing now. Beauty will be at your beck and call. I bring you my special onion soup in five minutes and you see if you are not better then."

The truck and the pickup were put into the compound with the pickup battery on charge, while Eghardt said that they must stay until Della was better. The Somali steward took Njoroge to the servants' house.

"You must tell me what happened," said Eghardt. "Della came up here by herself driving that pickup and stayed for a night. You are nowhere to be seen for some years and you turn up with her injured and with fever and you have a bleeding back. What you been up to m'lad?"

"I'll tell you something of my side of things after you have seen to my shoulder. I don't know what she's been up to. The last time I saw her was at the manager's house at the farm." He said nothing about her being wanted by the police.

"She said something about photographs and agent. She also said important."

"I'll have a look in her bag and find out what she means. Perhaps she has some exposed film that needs processing for her agent. I have a few rolls too."

"First we look at your back. Then we go to my dark room and process the negatives."

When it came to fixing Peter's shoulder Eghardt whistled when he saw what Njoroge had done to close the wound. He opened a comprehensive medical kit carried by most hunters, snipped at the cotton, removed the remaining ants that were dead, cleaned and disinfected the wound and used sterile surgical clips.

"You know, while you are here you are our son and daughter. We your ma and pa. We speak nicely to you but sis! a steel-jacket does this. How come you be so stupid as to get shot?" he asked while giving Peter a tetanus booster.

"Do you mind if I tell you later what I have been up to? It is Della that worries me. How come she is knocked on the head, bound and gagged, trousers torn, and by a hair's breadth escapes going over a two thousand-foot drop? It just doesn't tie up. As far as I know she had nothing to do with the Masai, but I'm pretty certain it was a Masai that did this to her. Perhaps we'll get to know a bit more if we have a look at her photographs."

After soup Della was feeling better but still weak and asked for Peter. He came with an arm in a sling. "How's my glamorous girl?"

"Glamorous? With my hair not done, no make-up, red-eyed and wearing a borrowed flannel nightshirt?"

He laughed. "Most becoming. I'll fetch my camera."

"You dare!"

"Ah well. We've both been in the wars." Now serious, "How are you? Really."

"Oh, utterly superb. We Yanks can take it as well as you Limeys."

"Want to talk about it?"

"Right this minute, only to ask you to get my agent up here urgently. I want him to have some negatives for processing and I must talk to him."

"Give me the negs. Eghardt and I will do them in his dark room, and print them if you like. We'll get your agent to fly up here in the morning."

"That's good of you, but they are for his eyes only."

"Trust me? We shan't bandy them about. Exclusively yours whatever they turn out to be, Eghardt and I are souls of discretion. Promise. I'll show you some of mine too. Afterwards you can tell me what you have been up to – dashing about and getting into trouble."

She coloured, realising she would have to confess to breaking bail. "I. . ."

"Not now. Get better first. How did you get that bruise on your arm?"

"Oh, that? A stone."

He held her hand and kissed the bruise. "Better?"

"Much . . . thanks. . . Why is your arm in a sling?"

"Oh . . . mosquito bite I think."

"Now who's being cagey? Annie tells me it's serious."

"You know what these mosquitoes are."

"I think you are lying," she said with a smile.

"That's my girl. Back on form. Now where's your bag?"

The number of negatives to be processed surprised him.

"Contacts or prints?"

"Contacts and prints if you have the paper . . . er please. Can you manage half-plate?" She wrote down the number of her agent. "It is highly confidential."

"I'll burn it when we have contacted him. Now, there's some more of Annie's soup and another dose of quinine coming your way in a few minutes, then you get some sleep. I am off right now to have a three-quarter pound steak for supper."

"Oh, you pig!" she said laughing. "I hope it chokes you! . . . By the way . . . Peter?" She had become serious and a tear appeared in her eye that she blinked down her cheek. A hand moved involuntarily towards him.

"Thank you. You saved my life."

He sat on the bed and gently wiped the tear away with a little finger. Holding her hand in his he said, "Just get better quickly – you'll do that – for me?"

She nodded. Her eyes had an appealing look in them. He lifted her hand and kissed the palm then the bruise on her forearm again and looked into her eyes and smiled as though he'd discovered something. "Oh, yes," she breathed. "Just for you Peter." Their hands lingered together. He stood picked up the rolls of negatives and was gone.

She closed her eyes and held the hand he had kissed next to her heart. "Oh, Peter. I wish; how I wish . . ."

Beauty came through the door with a tray.

# 18.

A thorn in your foot does not cause a pain in mine.
*(A man feels his own shortcomings)*

Chief Inspector Andrews had a frustrating day on a bad road up to Marsabit. At the police post the station Inspector said that he knew the movement of every vehicle coming and going on and off the roads in his district and there was no dark green pickup with a Nairobi number plate anywhere in the area.

"I am damned sure she is up here somewhere!" said Andrews. "That girl is dangerous. I want a team out scouring every nook and cranny of the area, including the mountain to find an American girl without a passport who has broken every rule in the book. I want this girl, and I want her before she does another damned-fool thing."

"Sir," said the Inspector "I know this district like the back of my hand, and the conditions. It would be foolhardy to start out just before dark. We shall go first light tomorrow. Five a.m. I can rustle up four teams with radios. Two of my sergeants can look after two parties, I shall lead another and you, sir, lead the fourth. We should cover most of the ground in less than two days that way. I have Police Ordinance maps here and if you will look at the main wall map we can decide who shall go where. Meanwhile I shall put scouts out tonight to cover the road south in case."

While studying the map the Inspector asked Andrews if he had somewhere to stay the night. "I live at the police house which has spare rooms."

"Are you married Inspector?"

"Yes. My wife would be happy to make you comfortable with a meal a bed and a good breakfast."

"Thank you for the offer. I should not want to upset her arrangements," he said not caring for the obligatory social chat he would have to endure. "The Game Lodge will suit me fine."

At precisely five am next day all four teams set out, each with radio and binoculars. Two constables were left to man the station radio and watch the adjacent roads. The teams scoured the area until dark, all having drawn a blank.

Andrews' mood was dark when they arrived back at the post. The duty constable handed the Inspector a signal as he stepped into the Post.

*All stations. Inform C.I.Andrews pickup and safari truck belonging P.Grant seen entering residence of E.Pretorius, Maralal. Instruct soonest. Act. Ins. Abdul Malik. Maralal.*

The message was timed and dated late that afternoon and did nothing for Andrews' mood except to make it blacker. He hated to be made a fool by a chit of a girl in front of his inferiors.

"Send a reply Inspector. *Observe only. Do not act. Await arrival of C.I.Andrews.* That's all. I shall drive overnight."

"You had better take one of my drivers sir, to share the wheel. There has been rain and there are herds of wandering camels and wild animals on that route at night."

While he was saying this he was brought another message.

*All stations. Marsabit/Laisamia/Baragoi roads flooded. Impassable. Met. Dept. Illaut.*

This was the only route Andrews could take.

"Dammit, Inspector, surely I could get through in a Land Rover."

"I doubt it sir. If the Met people up here say impassable then nothing but a boat could make it."

Andrews went out and looked up at a clear night sky with stars but with clouds in the south and west being lit with lightning flashes. He went to the Game Lodge for another bad night thinking of Della's camera and what might be in it.

The morning brought news that the floods were subsiding and Andrews drove down to Laisamia. Had he let the borrowed driver who was used to these conditions take the wheel he would not, while angry, have slid off the road into a full storm ditch. This delayed him two hours before a passing big truck was able to haul him out.

In the afternoon and in the worst of spirits having passed the clinic at Illaut with no camels in evidence he stopped at the police post.

"Get me Maralal on the telephone, constable."

"The lines are down sah."

"Dammit constable, you have a radio?"

"Yes sah."

"The for God's sake get them on that!" he said barely controlling his ice-cold exterior. Send this."

*For Acting Inspector Malik MARALAL. C.I.Andrews E.T.A. P.M. today. Make no move other than observe. On arrival of C.I. report whereabouts female Mitchell and male Grant without fail.*

On receiving acknowledgement through heavy electrical interference he got back into his vehicle without the driver and started off immediately.

A short distance from the police post in the clinic the injured sergeant with shoulder and half his face bandaged with arm bound to his chest had heard the familiar whine of the vehicle he had driven for many months pass the room in which he was bedded. Although still dazed and wearing a hospital shift and just carpet slippers on his bandaged feet he left the clinic and limped painfully towards the police post hoping to find the Chief Inspector there to confront him. He was two hundred yards short of the post when he saw Andrews drive away. He shouted and waved with his good arm but Andrews did not see him while accelerating swiftly.

Then the sergeant heard the engines of vehicles coming through trees from the north. A Land Rover led the troop carrier and the Bedford with bulging canvas followed by a thirty-hundredweight caged truck. He went towards the carrier thinking they had returned from the border having sold the ivory. The vehicles stopped and Steve Harris dressed in combat clothes got down from the Land Rover. When asked what his business was the injured sergeant gave a halting story of his visit to the Ndotos with his Chief Inspector and of his being taken to the desert and beaten and left there to die.

"So, you are the sergeant who was driver for Chief Inspector Andrews?"

"Yes sah." He gave his full name, rank and service number.

"Then welcome sergeant" he said smiling broadly. "Come and join your friends. They too will make you welcome." He led the injured man to the back of the caged truck to sit with the manacled poachers.

They stopped at the police post where Harris went inside and came out almost immediately.

"We are getting warm, sergeant Gupta. He left five minutes ago. Get onto the blue frequency again and tell the post at Kisima that the Super is to meet us at rendezvous two without delay."

"Right, sir. Rendezvous two."

"We shall have to be careful driving. There's been rain here. Be sure the prisoners have water. We now have Andrews' driver. He's been badly beaten up but he'll live. He has to. He has a very interesting story to tell."

\*

In Eghardt's darkroom at Langlaagter after supper Peter and Eghardt worked till midnight. Both were very surprised when the prints of Della's negatives began to show in the developing trays, Eghardt scratched his head when he saw the Peter's photographs.

"So, you go around East Africa taking shots of dead Masai? And how did they die I have to ask? You are not getting yourself into trouble?"

"No."

"Ach. You youngsters. Always getting into scrapes. Now these other pictures of Della's are a different kettle of fish. She told me she was doing a holiday article for her newspaper. Some holiday!"

"I suppose you can guess that she was investigating the poaching racket here. Looks as though she stumbled on to something big. I've not seen such revealing pictures of elephants being shot before. They are brilliant!" Other prints were now beginning to show in the trays. "Ye Gods! That's Chief Inspector Andrews. I haven't seen that African before with the briefcase, and Herbie Smith from the treasury? Never! How in hell could he and Andrews be mixed up in this, and who is that hanging by the foot? It's Herbie! – look – he's fallen. Whatever the content of these pictures I sure raise my hat to her. And there's another thing, how did she come to be bound and gagged by a Masai? I feel sure it was one of the two I was following."

"This world is full of strange people doing strange things, but she's a nice girl for all that. How come you meet her?"

"She booked a safari which for many reasons hasn't happened yet and I have spoken to her a few times since. And yes, she is a nice girl! I reckon these photographs of hers are hot stuff and we had better get her agent up here first thing."

"And you had better get to bed now. You look all in. Did she say how we contact her agent?"

"She gave me this exclusive number."

"Just in case our telephone is tapped I will go across the airstrip to the hotel and telephone from there. I know the owner well. Give me the number. I shall go across with the dogs. I have a good lamp. You get to bed."

While clearing up the dark room Peter was deep in thought and made a decision. Nearly two hours later when going to his bed Eghardt returned and said that her agent answered the telephone from his bed and would fly up to the strip from Nairobi and be here shortly after sun up.

*

It was fresh in the morning and still dark when Eghardt with his dogs walked to the airstrip to wait for Della's agent. Della herself was feeling much better and came to sit on the front veranda when the sun came up. She was sipping coffee and being enthralled by the morning birdsong and watching a gardener burning hedge cuttings and scraps from the sawmill when Peter came down to join her.

"How are you? Shouldn't you be in bed?"

"Not on a glorious morning like this. I have been out here for half an hour and I shall be one hundred and one percent when I've had one of Annie's breakfasts. She should be a doctor."

"Want to see some pictures?"

He handed her an envelope with her name written on it and he poured coffee for himself.

It was some minutes before she looked up from them and turned to him.

"I guess you printed these?"

"And Eghardt."

"Then you must see that my agent has to have them urgently."

"He's due at the airstrip at any minute."

"Oh, thanks. I owe you a great deal. You are putting yourself out for me when in fact you should be scolding me for abusing your trust and dashing all over the country with your pickup and getting it damaged. I don't think the police think a lot of me either. I have to find one on my side pretty quickly, otherwise I am sunk – it's a long story and I haven't been quite truthful."

"I know an inspector at Kinangop who might help, and not to worry about the pickup. My mechanic will put things right. I'm not angry. I'm just curious. It was only a bush that scratched it – the one that saved you from going over the escarpment." She shuddered and he put a comforting arm around her. "I have only two questions I would like answers for right now" he said, "then you can tell me all if you want to answer, that is. I am curious to know where you took the pictures of the elephant shooting, and I want to know who hit and hog-tied you."

"I followed who I thought to be the poachers up to that spot on the map you marked 'whistling thorn' on the north side of the Ndoto mountains. The elephants were in the clearing you marked 'camp'."

"Good heavens! All that way? Up in the Ndoto Hills? I thought that I and only one or two others knew of that place. I was up there last year and photographed some baby tuskers. It's not only a crying shame, it's downright criminal. The culprits shall pay dearly."

"One already has," she said and looked up from the pictures. She took a deep breath as if to shut all that had happened from her mind and snuggled closer to him in the growing light. Both then looked deeply at each other and both experienced a similar feeling and found themselves hugging as if never to let go.

A low, orange sun angled through trees and lit veils of morning mist among the branches and painted the base of clouds. There was silence broken only by the magic of the Kenya dawn chorus. "It is so beautiful here," she said quietly. "One has only to have heard the birds at sunrise and one has heard everything in this country. Fascinating enough to write a whole article, but I wonder who would believe it. It begins to search your soul for something you did not know you had . . . and I love the smell of woodsmoke . . . I love it here . . . sitting here – with you. Oh Peter, I don't suppose the Garden of Eden could have been more lovely. The birds. The early morning smells. The trees. It is so peaceful."

They were sitting back in the lounger on the veranda gazing up into a sky with faces close looking at cumulus beginning to form.

"Oh, Peter," she breathed again as he traced her eyebrows, nose, jaw-line and lips with a soft finger . . . she was making little cooing noises . . . he lifted her chin but before their lips met the tranquillity was shattered by a Land Rover speeding along the path between the trees and skidding to a halt in front of the house. Four African armed police leaped from the back and formed a semi-circle with rifles at the port while Chief Inspector Andrews alighted from the front with Acting Inspector Malik.

Peter rose. "What the hell . . .?" Della remained seated.

"Ah!" said Andrews coming forward with swagger stick held under his arm as though on parade. "Two birds with one stone! Della Mitchell, you are under arrest firstly for jumping bail; secondly for resisting arrest; and thirdly for questioning regarding the deaths of Patrick O'Brien, White Hunter; Herbert Smith, Civil Servant, both of Nairobi; and police sergeant Guchiru of Mukuyu. Anything you say . . ."

"Come off it Andrews!" Peter cut in. "What nonsense. You know full well she's . . ."

"Chief Inspector to you, Mr. Grant! Furthermore, you are under arrest for aiding and abetting this woman. Go Malik. You are the arresting Officer. Read them their rights . . . Wait!" He had seen the bunch of photographs Della was holding. He stepped forward and went to snatch them from her. She resisted and a struggle ensued. Peter intervened.

"Let him have them. You cannot stop the law."

She stood, and turned on Peter.

"What?" she exclaimed, "who the heck's side are you on!"

The momentary lapse of concentration allowed Andrews to take all the prints and envelope from her hand.

"Don't you dare move Miss Mitchell. My men are armed."

She stood transfixed looking first at Andrews then at Peter who stood a pace away from her. There was a long pause while Andrews waked off the veranda with the prints and when in sunlight looked at them one by one. He saw the poachers shooting, elephants falling, poachers standing on dead beasts and hacking at tusks, and in some prints the vehicles and the syndicate of three in view. But more importantly, shots of Chief Thukuru handing wads of notes unmistakably to himself and Smith. He was surprised by the two pictures of the unfortunate auditor hanging and falling minus a shoe and visibly blanched at the pictures of his sergeant lying trussed with the rifle sling.

"So!" Andrews exclaimed as he walked over to the bonfire. He dropped the prints one by one into the flames and watched them curl while the damning pictures shrivelled and combusted. Stirring the ashes till nothing of them could be seen he tossed some more pruning onto flames to spit and crackle. He came back to the veranda.

Della was beside herself with rage – at the opposite end of her emotions from only minutes ago. She was appalled at what Peter had said.

"All we want now, Miss Mitchell are the negatives."

"I do not have them," she cried. "Don't you dare let him have them Peter."

"I am sorry Chief Inspector, but you can't have them. Nobody can. You are too late. I have destroyed them."

"You've done <u>what</u>?" she screamed.

"Destroyed them. Stuff like that is too hot to handle."

She was speechless with her mouth open and eyes wide.

"That was a stupid thing to do Mr.Grant." said Andrews.

"Yes I burned them on the drawing room fire last night." He stepped forward and spoke quietly close to Andrews' face – "I destroyed then so as not to compromise anybody if they went astray."

Andrews looked surprised and relieved. He got the message and realised Grant was not such a fool after all. Della heard every word.

"Traitor!" she shouted. "How could you! . . . You . . . bastard!" She swung a punch at his face but he ducked and she hit the side of his head near an eye. He grasped her wrist. Then she used words learned from her two years in the US Air Force and while pummelling his chest with her free fist she said, "those negatives were my only proof! I ought to have known - you too are one of the damned poachers! What the hell have you gotten me into?!" She was hysterical. Peter moved to put an arm around her but she screamed "Keep away from me, you detestable stinker!" Annie came out to see what the commotion was. She looked surprised to see armed police.

"Ah, Mrs. Pretorius," said Andrews. "I am arresting wanted criminals. Where's your husband?"

"He out."

"Out where?"

"Out." She had sized up the situation quickly realising the Della and Peter were in trouble. "He gone out for the day. He has work to do."

"Then send your boy to fetch him. We shall wait. Meanwhile, it is thirsty work out here. I fancy a cup of tea. Perhaps you would be so kind . . .?"

"Make tea for police?" she said angrily, but suddenly smiled. "Best you find I do not put something in it."

"You'll take the first cup Mrs. Pretorius."

"My joke. I go and put on the kettle." Annie glanced at Della in tears. Not knowing what to say she went in shaking her head. After putting the kettle on the hob, went through the house to the sawmill and signalled to Eghardt with Della's contact from the Embassy coming to the wire. They went quietly to the sawmill office where Annie told them quickly of the situation. The two men stayed there while Annie went back to the house.

Andrews told Malik to arrest Della and handcuff her and read the rights. Now looking his bland self with the inner feeling of great relief that all evidence of his part in the affair had been destroyed, the Chief Inspector took a step towards the entrance to the house.

"Drop those guns!" A clear voice rang out and a European with six African police, all in combat gear, camouflaged faces and automatic weapons came out from the trees covering Andrew's police who, seeing they were outnumbered hurriedly dropped their rifles. The European stepped forward.

"Chief Inspector Andrews, sir, will you please give me your revolver."

"What the blazes? Who are you?"

"Inspector Harris, Kinangop."

"Harris! What do you mean coming here dressed for combat? I have just arrested these two on various charges and you come barging in unannounced and armed. I'll see you charged for this. Get back to your own patch Inspector and call off your men."

"No sir."

"I order you!"

"I order you, sir. I have six guns pointing at you, sir."

"Get out! Do you hear me? Get out! Report to me in Nairobi!"

While he was saying this a Land Rover, the troop carrier, the Bedford, still loaded with tusks, and the caged truck drove into sight with an official Humber car following. All lined up behind Andrews' Land Rover. A high-ranking police officer came from the car.

"Chief Inspector, sir," said Harris, "you know Superintendent Morrissy."

Andrews stood stiffly and uncertain.

"Sir?"

"Andrews. We have something urgent to talk about. Give Harris your revolver and swagger stick. Is there somewhere here private?"

Just then Annie came from the house.

"The tea . . . Oh, I didn't expect . . ."

"Madam," said Morrissy, "I am sorry to disturb you. It would be kind if you had a room undisturbed? We shall not keep it for long."

"If you will come to the library," she said more puzzled than before.

Harris told Malik to release the cuffs from Della and to stay by her and Peter. He then went to Andrews' vehicle with Gupta the Eurasian sergeant and began a search. The rifles were taken from Andrews' constables, ordered to sit apart in a circle facing outwards and were left with a guard over them. As the senior police were led into the library the Africans in the caged truck began to sing a dirge.

On hearing the Africans singing, curiosity got the better of Annie's servant Beauty, and she stopped what she was doing in the house and went out to the front. One of the singers called her name and banged the cage with chained wrists. She ran across to the truck to discover the boy who had promised marriage, a prisoner. She went down on her knees and wailed a Xhosa lament through tears. The dirge for the condition in which the five poachers and the injured sergeant found themselves, and the girl's thin descant pleading for her lover in another language with the Xhosa click did not mix too happily, but gave the clearing in front of the Pretorius' house an evocative veil of pathos. All the African policemen there affected to take no notice.

Inspector Harris came from Andrews' vehicle with a grin on his face and a cotton bag containing bundles of high denomination dollar notes. He went to the veranda where Malik was standing next to Della and Peter both sitting either end of the lounger not speaking. Her face was dark with anger and desperation. Peter's face was blank.

"Miss Mitchell, Peter, bear with me for a bit. Just a couple of things to do and I'll be with you."

He went with his sergeant Gupta to the carrier and helped a handcuffed Chief Thukuru down from the back, and while guarded was taken to the library. Gupta went back to his men, while in the library all sat and Harris spoke.

"Chief Inspector Andrews sir, and Chief Thukuru sir, I have to inform you that we know you two and Herbert Smith of the treasury to be ringleaders of a syndicate of poachers. We confirm the death of Mr.Smith. The consignment of ivory in the Bedford outside and five men with unlicensed ex service rifles you had kill the elephants are now in our custody. They tell us that another met his death when shooting. The Somali Consignees escaped back across the border denying us capture but one of their senior men carrying the case of money for this illegal consignment was shot in the crossfire and buried at that place. That money is now in our possession. Chief Thukuru, what have you to say?"

He said nothing.

"Against this known evidence do you still stick to your story you told us on capture?"

"I do," he said. "The man who is responsible for this debacle is the man here, this Chief Inspector. I was only delivering the ivory because he said it was a Government consignment to the Somali Nation and I was to take him the money which he was to hand over to the Legislative Council."

"That is outrageous and easily checked."

"I did not collect any tusks. I met him at Illaut where he handed over the vehicles. I was to be paid nothing. That money does not belong to me. I have been wrongly accused and the Council of Chiefs shall know of this. Andrews here, is the one who collects the money. If this is not above board then he is the culprit."

"That is not what we understand," retorted Harris who pulled from a bag the Chief's briefcase and another, both of which he opened. They were full with dollar banknotes. "Chief. This other case with what was topped up in yours, are payment for the tusks. The notes shall be checked for fingerprints. Furthermore we have copies of bank statements of deposits and transfers to the Channel Isles, the Isle of Man and Switzerland, although numbered, bear your details. They were traced through bankers here in Nairobi, and one of the under-managers is in custody. These accounts have been under scrutiny for six months now."

The chief was silent for some minutes.

"I want my lawyer present before I say another word."

Harris picked up the bag of notes recovered from the Land Rover.

"Chief Inspector, sir, this was discovered under the spare battery compartment in your vehicle."

"Battery compartment? That's for the mechanics. I would not soil my hands. I know nothing of dollars. They have been planted. Thukuru is lying through his teeth. I was in that area looking for him and Smith to arrest them for poaching. You are out of your area here, Harris. This is my *shauri*."

Superintendent Morrissy leaned forward.

"I gave Inspector Harris special dispensation eight months ago to look into this affair, Andrews. You seem to have covered your tracks pretty well until Harris was given this brief. What were those banknotes doing in your vehicle?"

"I protest. This is a farce. That money was planted. There is absolutely no evidence against me. I have been close to arresting the Chief for weeks now."

"Then what are you doing here?"

"I came here pro tem to arrest Miss Mitchell and Mr Grant on other charges that have a bearing on this case. Mitchell has jumped bail and has other more serious charges to face and I knew her to be here."

"Where is your sergeant driver?"

It was a split second before Andrews replied.

"That is one of the charges she faces, that of wounding him severely enough for him to go wandering and is now presumed dead. That charge is now attempted murder."

"Oh? Would it surprise you to know that your sergeant is at the moment outside, and although has an injury or two, is recovering well? He has made a statement that makes interesting reading." There was a long pause and Andrews looked a little pale and blinked for the first time in years. With a nod to Harris Morrissey said, "I think we will see Miss Mitchell and Mr. Grant now. Harris went to the veranda.

"Come this way please, both of you."

"Steve," Peter said, "there is something urgent I must get. It will be in the sawmill and will take no more than a minute. It's important."

"Alright. You can't run far. Go with him, Malik." Harris turned to Della who looked daggers at him. The Africans in the caged truck and Beauty were still singing but she had too much on her mind to take any notice.

"Aren't you going to arrest Peter? He is one of the syndicate, I know. He destroyed the evidence I had on the poachers and put me in a rotten fix."

"I am here to do my job, Miss. I make no comments until you have seen the Superintendent. I see you have a bruise on your head. Did the sergeant do that?"

"No." She turned away not wanting to remember the incident.

Peter returned with Malik and while they went to the library she turned on Peter.

"Let go of my arm you damned traitor. You've dropped me right in it, you – you – detestable stinker!" and she flounced into the room followed by Peter and Harris.

"Please sit Miss" Morrissy said. "Name is Mitchell, isn't it? I hear you came to this country to write a holiday article. I look forward to reading it."

"There's another article you would like to read if I had my way. This . . . this . . ." she curbed her tongue. "This policeman here deserves all he gets for burning my photographs."

"What photographs are these?"

"All of them – a couple of dozen – including him and his sidekicks shooting elephants – poor creatures – and money changing hands – and that Mr.Smith hanging there and falling on his head – and those elephants crying and not dying until they were shot a dozen times and that African policeman who tried to kill me . . . and . . . and . . ." Tears were beginning to show.

An aircraft was heard flying overhead.

"What is that you say? Photographs? Shooting elephants? Policeman tried to kill you? Where are these photographs?"

"I told you he threw them on the fire. He burned them all!"

"Sir, I protest" cut in Andrews. "I know nothing about photographs. She's talking out of the back of her head. She's hysterical because she's been arrested for crimes committed here."

"That's not true! You burned the evidence there was against you. She turned on Peter. "And you! You let him take them. You destroyed the negatives! You stupid idiot! Why did you do this?" A tear ran down her cheek. Peter put his hand on her arm but she shrugged it away.

"Excuse me Superintendent" Peter said. "I have something to show you. First I have to apologise to Miss Mitchell." She sniffed. "Please listen Della. I took it upon myself, much against your wish, to have three sets of prints made. That aircraft you heard a minute ago is an aide from your Embassy flying back to Nairobi with a complete set of all your pictures. He will meet you back at Nairobi."

Della looked at him open-mouthed. He turned to the Superintendent. "This," he said, taking from under his shirt a large envelope, "is the third complete set of relevant prints and negatives which will verify them, taken with Miss Mitchell's camera that I can vouch for because there are others taken of which I have the prints, not relevant here. You will see all the negatives are there."

Andrews shot him a dirty look. Morrissy spread the photographs on the library desk while Della, with tearful face and open mouth looked at Peter unable to say a word. Eventually she whispered "You

"... You ... You louse ... oh, I don't know! Why did you embarrass me so?"

"I had to. We'll talk later."

Morrissy looked up from the prints and negatives he had been studying against the light from a window. "All these photographs are sensitive material. I shall contact the American embassy immediately on my return. Meanwhile, Andrews, if what Miss Mitchell says is true then you will know the contents of these prints."

"I deny any part of this."

"Can you deny this is you being handed money by Chief Thukuru?"

"Obviously a fake."

"Not according to the negatives. How much ivory was there, Harris?"

"Estimated five tons sir."

"I see ... I happen to know the going rate. That is a lot of money. In my reckoning, five tons, if the beasts carried anything like fifty pounds a side, constitutes at least a hundred elephants. Am I right, Harris?"

"Yes sir. Some of the tusks are smaller. Immature. Many were shot not carrying tusks. It could be significantly more than a hundred."

"Do you deny Andrews that you were responsible along with the Chief and Smith for having more than a hundred elephants unlawfully shot?"

"My report of the incident was sent from Illaut when I left Smith's body there."

The superintendent slowly shook his head. "You disgust me! This evidence contradicts every word of it. Harris, take these photographs and add them to your file along with the revolver and swagger stick for the Forensic people. Wait outside Miss Mitchell and Mr. Grant. I'll call you."

Outside on the veranda she grasped his arms.

"Oh Peter! Why, oh why, did you frighten me like that?"

"I had to. I wanted Andrews to believe the negatives had been destroyed and you put up such a good show he believed it."

"It wasn't a show. I was serious. I was sure you had destroyed them and because you have been out and about and not saying what you were doing I honestly thought you were one of syndicate."

"I am sorry if you were deceived."

"Oh Peter, I am so sorry," she said, now crying freely. "Your poor eye. Please forgive me hitting you and for swearing at you."

He smiled and kissed away a tear. "You were very impressive. I've learnt a new word or two – and you pack quite a punch!"

"Does it hurt?"

"Only when I laugh."

"Please don't joke. What made you print <u>three</u> copies?"

"I don't know. Perhaps at the back of my mind was that both your newspaper and the Embassy would want a copy, then you would surely want a copy for yourself – photographer's instinct I guess."

She kissed him. Not just a 'thank you' peck, but a lingering kiss that came with love. The kiss was returned with fervour. Now she knew that kissing Peter meant more to her than she had realised before. "Hold me tight, Peter. I have been in Hell for the last few days. I don't want ever to be there again."

"As long as I am here I won't let it happen to you," he said sincerely. Her arms were around his neck and she cried deeply. "Hey, what's all this?" He said gently.

"Didn't you know that sometimes a girl cries with happiness?"

"I usually laugh."

In the library the Superintendent sat back and addressed the two men.

"Chief Inspector Andrews, Chief Thukuru. The evidence we have against you is overwhelming. I am left with no other course but to have you both arrested and pass this matter to the D.P.P. The law must take its course. Chief, you must realise that you have narrowly escaped the bullet. If it had not been for Inspector Harris wanting the capture rather than more extreme allowable measures, you and your men may well have perished. You may both engage counsel when in Nairobi but you will face injunctions regarding the press. You, Chief and you, Andrews will travel to Nairobi under guard." They both began to protest but Morrissy cut in. "Read them their rights, Harris, arrest them and have them guarded in separate vehicles, then send in Mitchell and Grant."

A knock came at the door and Annie stepped in.

"Would you want tea in here?" She asked.

"We shall be only a few minutes," said Morrissey. "Later, if we may?"

Annie nodded and left.

Della and Peter came in and Morrissy looked at them seriously, then grinned.

"Now, what am I to do with you two vagabonds? I see you have injured your shoulder Mr Grant."

"Yes."

"Want to say how it was done?"

"It was an accident. I fell."

"Very clumsy of you. Be more careful in future. Now, Miss Mitchell, I have to admonish you for your actions and yet in the same breath thank you for these photographs. But I shall have to confiscate these prints and negatives."

"I should like the negatives returned if you please. That copyright remains with my newspaper and the private ones with me as you should know."

"And you should know, Miss, they are too sensitive to release. You shall have our receipt for them. Furthermore you will have to submit all of your negatives with pictures taken this visit to see if they contain any other forbidden or sensitive subjects. That is the law here, especially for foreign journalists. As your Embassy has a set of prints regarding this business we shall discuss with them the question of copyright and what prints are to be released to your newspaper." He paused for a moment. "You sail very close to the wind, Miss Mitchell."

"It is my job to investigate and report on such matters as my editor decides."

"It is not your job to take police matters into your own hands in a foreign country and to jump bail. That has got you into trouble."

"If I had not done so you would not have had this conclusive evidence. And the person who bailed me was one of the syndicate and protecting himself."

"But until his arrest an active policeman. I take your point, Miss Mitchell, but do not forget you entered this country on a false premise and until we find the culprit you are to be more fully questioned regarding O'Brien's death. The police here are not fools. We have the crucial evidence of the haul of tusks, the monies concerned, the main suspects and the shooters. Your photographic evidence, although seemingly vital, has yet to be verified."

Once more she was disconsolate and showed it. "So what will happen to me?"

"I shall need a full statement of your movements since you were bailed and I shall arrange with your embassy to get you legal representation should that become necessary. You are to travel with me back to Nairobi and when there you will stick rigidly to the bail conditions until the preliminaries of this poaching business are finalised, and while the more pressing matter of O'Brien's death is properly investigated. Another matter. Sergeant Guchiru has turned King's evidence in the hope of being exonerated for his part in being a willing participant in the whole affair. Also he has admitted Attempted Actual Harm upon an American woman without saying how he received his injuries. Can you enlighten me?"

"I plead self defence."

He looked at her lack of weight and muscle with incredulity. "Self defence?"

"Yes. I did not use a weapon. The sergeant had orders to kill me. He was about to rape me first. He fell awkwardly." Morrissey looked at her wanting more of an explanation. "I did an unarmed combat course with the American Military during the war. My life was threatened. I had to defend myself."

"Hmmm." After a pause he turned to Peter. "Mr.Grant, I find in Chief Inspector Andrew's report that you are listed as an accessory to Miss Mitchell's absconding. Can you explain why and how a Kinangop farmer is found in Maralal with a person who jumped bail in Nairobi?"

"I gave Miss Mitchell the use of my farm manager's house and the pickup to catch up on her writing and to see some of the country. I heard that she had gone to the north. I know the dangers of travelling alone in this country and I became concerned for her safety and I followed. Eventually I found her up near Losiolo and brought her here to a family friend to help quell a fever."

"A Kinangop farmer travelling all that way from his work on the off chance of finding someone in all that space?"

Peter spoke with spirit. "Can't a fellow can take a bit of time off now and then? I have a good farm manager to look after things. I know most areas like the back of my hand. I can recognise my own vehicle and Miss Mitchell knows that the pickup is not an off-road vehicle and will stick to known routes, and I have a tongue in my head."

Della knew his plausible answer was far from the truth and that he did not want to reveal his movements. But lending the pickup and house was true. "I admit I broke rules," she said, "but I honestly think I did the right thing. If I had managed to get back to my Embassy in Nairobi from the Ndoto mountains you'd have had these photographs without all this fuss."

"Fuss it happens to be! Jumping bail in this country is a serious offence. And why did you not go straight back to Nairobi?"

Not wanting the superintendent to know she was foolish enough to give a lift to someone while alone she said she had skidded into a ditch and knocked her head and some time later Peter had found her.

"That comes of travelling alone," Morrissey said.

Peter was surprised and yet relieved she had said nothing of being trussed up in the pickup. That would have started another line of questioning leading to his own movements.

"Mr.Grant, were you aware that Miss Mitchell is also being questioned about the death of Patrick O'Brien?"

"Yes, but can you imagine her wanting to kill anyone – and with a spear?"

"Miss Mitchell did severely injure a fifteen stone armed police sergeant."

"Unarmed combat training can help the lightest of people with technique and surprise. I held a commission in the Kenya Regiment, and I have had the same training."

Morrissy paused then picked up his cap. "Miss Mitchell, will you take me to Mrs.Pretorius. I have to thank her for her hospitality. You will travel with me while the Chief Inspector and Chief Thukuru travel with Harris under guard. Mr.Grant, I need to ask you further questions. I shall speak to you in Nairobi. There is another matter I shall want to discuss."

"But of course. I shall be staying in my Nairobi apartment for a day or so to see a consultant about my shoulder. Then I shall be going back to Kinangop."

On going out onto the veranda Morrissey drew Harris aside. "I want you to put a tail on Mr.Grant. I strongly believe he is up to something. We have nothing on him now, but he is likely to reveal his hand before long."

Annie Pretorius had gathered up Beauty from the truck where she was keening through her Xhosa song. They all went to the house where Annie served tea and scones with ginger preserve and cream. Peter assured Annie and Eghardt that neither he nor Della had done anything illegal. "It's all down to the CI and what he and others have done. Thanks for the use of the darkroom; I'll send up a batch of paper to cover all we used."

"Come back soon and stay," said Eghardt as he shook Peter's hand while Annie gave Della a hug.

Before she went out to the vehicles Peter drew Della aside and held her hands.

"I'm so sorry you have all this to cope with. Had it worked out differently I could have taken you down to the coast for a spell to relax instead of being confined to Nairobi."

"I wish!" . . . Then with brittle bravado, "C'est la vie! Apart from a report or two I'll have to write I can play the field at the Norfolk hotel lunching on poached trout and clicking my fingers for the odd drink and work up a tan by the pool," repeating some of his words.

"With those oil salesmen? It's a good thing I know you have better taste. I shall be with you in spirit and in person. There will be a way."

"Thanks Peter," she said with a wan smile and a lingering look. Both knew there was something deeper than just friendship between them. Their eyes did not leave each other until their hands slowly parted. But before she turned to walk away he held her head in his hands and kissed her lingeringly on the lips. After murmuring and opening her eyes they parted slowly for her to join Superintendent

Morrissy to sit with him in the leading police Humber. Her back showed the wrench she felt on parting.

Peter stared in her direction. "Hell! Why should it end like this? She's got what it takes, has Della. I love that girl. I can't let her just go. So what if she did break a few rules. I've broken a few here and there – and upset some people in my time. There must be a way to sort this out!" He called Njoroge and told him to drive the pickup back to the farm. "Here's your month's wages plus extra for a month's leave. Bosco will take you to Kiambu and I'll pick you up from there when I need you."

"Thank you bwana."

Of the money he had collected from Arap Kamau for the portrait, and from cashing the cheque Herbert Smith had written for the photographs at El Molo Bay, he still had half, but now the rains were here he knew the bank would support him. He went to his truck, switched on and let in the clutch.

The convoy started up, turned a half circle in line astern while the prisoners continued their dirge. Then Harris' policemen struck up a happier song in contrast and the mixture of songs in different rhythms struck a dissonant note before fading as they all went through the trees towards the road.

Before Peter or any of the convoy reached Nairobi the rain fell upon the Rift with suddenness as though clouds held their moisture like balloons filled with water until they could stretch no more and burst.

# 19.

Do not let a nose lead blindly.
*(Things can happen without warning)*

At his apartment the following day Peter contacted his doctor who arranged an appointment with a consultant surgeon that afternoon. On leaving the hospital two hours later his shoulder was more comfortable with an expert's attention and he had been told to rest for six weeks, not to drive and not to use his arm for that time.

Back in his apartment where his steward had made a meal he dined on a casserole of goat while considering what to do. "I think I had better get the Okiuka down to Olekowlish first thing tomorrow before I tell Steve all I know – better still, I shall take it tonight. Nobody would think that I would travel with my arm in a sling, or in this weather. I'd rather get it out of my hands before the Governor finds that he hasn't the real thing. I'll see Della when I get back. It was dark as he drove out of Jeevanjee Gardens.

\*

Morrissey and Harris had gone through Della's statements at length all day and through a sandwich lunch with her. When it had become dark they had word from the forensic laboratory with the return of her camera that her photographs were authentic and from that camera.

"Miss Mitchell," Morrissey said, "It is now more than likely we shall use these prints as evidence, in which case we thank you for them. Here is a receipt for them, all listed with descriptions. Your *Chargé d Affaires* is being sent your dissertation for your newspaper on both the holiday article, your photographs and the accompanying photographs and negatives regarding the court case and release date. But as far as jumping bail is concerned I'm afraid we cannot let you off the hook. The law states quite clearly that any misdemeanour of this sort by a foreign journalist cannot be tolerated in any circumstance, especially as your visa was issued under a false declaration of intent." Della went to object but Morrissey continued.

"Accordingly you are to be deported and travel with one of your Embassy's officials from Nairobi airport."

"Have I no redress?"

"None."

"Not even having given you the best piece of evidence about one of the major poaching syndicates you'll ever likely to get a conviction for?"

"We cannot turn a blind eye on your unlawful actions. They are too well documented. I have spoken to a high authority on the law and raised the question of redress. But with the current political circumstances here, foreign journalists come high on the list of unwanted persons. An appeal would be rejected. We are sorry. I am sorry. Now, stay at your hotel and do not move out of it until you are picked up from there. If you do not comply it will mean jail." As he was saying this his telephone rang. He picked it up and his face changed. "Yes, Sir. Immediately." He replaced the receiver with a frown. "Harris, you know where Peter Grant is; bring him in. The Commissioner has told me that Sir Rupert is back from Dar-es-Salaam and is hopping mad about something to do with Mr.Grant and wants to speak to him urgently."

"Yes, sir. I'll drop Miss Mitchell at the Norfolk and pick him up myself."

"Now, Miss Mitchell, Let us go over the details once more of your sworn deposition. I want to be very sure that your evidence has no loopholes that Andrews can slip through."

\*

It was eight o'clock in the evening, dark and humid with wet roads glistening under a few street lights. Harris with Della in the passenger seat was pulling away from the police station after the lengthy interview. He was about to accelerate when an African came running into the headlights of the Land Rover and waved it down. The 'tail' who had been put on Peter came to Harris' open window.

"Inspector sir, the bwana Grant has driven away from Nairobi an hour ago. I followed him expecting him to go to Thika and the Kinangop road but he turned on to the road south. I followed but my radio is not getting through. He turned off the Mombasa road to go on the Tanganyika road. It was there my vehicle broke a spring and I lost him. I came back here to tell you. My radio is still not working."

"That was the right thing to do Joseph. Go to the desk and get them to radio the border post with the vehicle number and hold him; then get word to Superintendent Morrissey. Tell him I'm after Mr.Grant . . . Dammit! What does he think he's playing at!" He let in the clutch and with headlights flashing weaved through heavy traffic out to the main road and turned south. "I'm sorry, Miss Mitchell, but there is no time to lose. I don't have time to drop you off. Your hotel is the other end of town. Too much traffic so you'll have to bear with me. I have to stop him before he gets too far. Tanganyika is out of our jurisdiction and he knows that. I'll radio the border post when we're in range if we haven't caught him before then. God knows what he is up to. I have fuel, rations and water aboard. We'll catch him."

Although Della was in deep dudgeon with having two misdemeanours on record and to be suspected killing Pat she was intrigued with the situation. Expecting to go to the comparative comfort of Nairobi's premier hotel, suddenly she was being whisked away at speed down to Tanganyika in a black night under storm clouds on a bad road having suffered the onslaught of three years' pent up rain. She mused that Peter and Steve Harris, both about the same age and stamp, seemingly good friends, were on opposite sides of the official fence.

"So why is Peter dashing all over the country like this? I thought he was a farmer."

"He is. And a damned good one. And a damned good hunter. And damned good with a gun. And a damned good photographer. About the best we have. And damned good at anything else I could think of. He should stick to what he does best. But he's likely to be out of his league at present and he's getting in our hair."

"Why is that?"

"I can't tell you. He has been a little too devious for my liking and pushing our friendship too far. And now, to scoot off like this when he's wanted is asking for trouble. The top brass are after his hide."

Della was now more intrigued than ever but she kept quiet while Steve concentrated on his driving. They had left the tarmac and were on the road approaching the turn to go south where in parts the murram surface had been virtually washed away with the unprecedented force and quantity of the rain. His headlights cut into pitch-blackness while both were perspiring and feeling warm damp air through the half open windows.

\*

Peter was not enjoying his drive. The consultant surgeon of yesterday had spent an hour joining skin over damaged flesh and had finely stitched the wound with artistry and covered it with a special constricting dressing. Now, while driving, having discarded the sling his arm movement was freer but limited.

Unaware that he was being followed he was driving carefully and more slowly than usual, but had an hour's advantage over the Land Rover that did not have the same clearance that forced Harris to be careful not to choke the exhaust while driving through water that sometimes reached over the axle. Peter's safari truck had a high clearance, a high mounted carburettor on the engine and an extended vertical exhaust above the roof, especially designed for negotiating such conditions.

In ordinary circumstances in daylight Peter would have covered the distance to the border in no more than two hours. But it was nearing midnight as he dropped down from a plateau to the next steppe two thirds of the way to the border to approach what had been a minor stream running alongside the road on his right. He could see in the headlights that the stream was up and running across the road. It was at a negotiable depth and he drove between two lines of ripples indicating the storm drains either side of him. While he was doing this he heard thunder. When clear of the stream the way was lit by lightning flashes behind him accompanied with heavy thunder that he guessed to be on the descent he had just made. Adjusting the mirror to dim the flashes in his eyes he thought he saw a pair of distant headlights that he dismissed as fanciful in this weather.

\*

Lulled by the constant engine noise Della was dozing with head back and hat pulled down over her eyes. Harris, according to his estimation, had made good time and had progressed two thirds of the way to the border, without having had sight of Peter's vehicle, and had reached the top of the descent without mishap. Then carefully picking his way down the dark road he peered into the night and swore he saw rear lights through the black night. "Aha! Got you, Peter old friend!" he said and increased speed. Now sweating he mopped his brow and dropped his uniform cap behind his seat.

\*

Under black clouds Peter drove carefully along a straight section where the surface was almost non existent and with rocks showing through. He had some miles to go before reaching the border. He stopped and got out to stretch his legs and ease his arm and shoulder that was getting stiff and uncomfortable. He had a mouthful of coffee and chewed s few nuts and fruit, stamped about and got back into the truck to drive slowly on towards the border.

\*

Steve was half-way down the descent when the storm broke suddenly with more flashes, thunder and torrential rain. Now with windscreen wipers barely cleaning the glass and demister working he drove with skill, slithering and sliding around curves, avoiding the now overflowing storm drains while keeping the vehicle in the middle of the road.

When approaching the swollen stream at the bottom of the descent there was a roar louder than the rainfall and they were hit in the rear with a four-foot wave of muddy water pouring down the slope taking everything in its path. The Land Rover was carried forward for a hundred yards then was hit again on the driver's side by a bore of water coming down the 'stream' and across the road. The vehicle was knocked sideways into the storm drain then rolled completely over by the surge of water, miraculously to stand upright beyond the drain with a rushing torrent over the axles.

Della was dreaming of swimming in the pool at the Norfolk hotel when someone from a diving board landed on top of her to send her spinning and gasping under the surface. She struggled and half came to her senses while spitting out mud with Harris lying awkwardly across her. Although conscious but bemused in the pitch darkness and noise of the storm she thought she was still in her nightmare and fought valiantly to get free of the body smothering her. When Harris moaned it was as if her dream was real, and panicking, with a final heave she pushed him back into his seat. She sat with an ache in her forehead and realised that something had happened. They were sitting, soaked through, with water swilling seat high and gradually spilling out of a crushed door on her side. "Dear Christ! What is happening?!" she called. Then with gasping breath called again, "Peter, oh Peter, where are you Peter?" Then she sobbed but pulled herself together when something touched her knee.

She picked up a floating torch with a rubber casing. Switching it on she saw that the door windows were broken with rain pouring in and windscreen cracked. Still bemused and with head spinning, she shone the torch on Harris who was now slumped across the wheel. His head was gashed and blood ran down the side of his face. He did not stir. She came to her senses, kicked open the door and stepped into harsh rain and the torrent of water up to her knees, went around to Harris' door, took the key from the dash and not ever knowing how she did it, lifted him out over her shoulder, went to the rear of the Land Rover and put him as gently as possible through the open door above water level. Climbing in she pulled him further in and put a rolled blanket under his head. He was breathing and had a pulse and with the torch propped up she staunched the blood from his head and made a compress with a dressing from a first aid box and bound it tightly around his head. Feeling her own head where it ached she found no abrasion and thanked her lucky stars that she had been wearing a hat. "Stars?" she said, "With all this going on shall I ever see a star again?!"

*

It was in the early hours and black with clouds when Peter reached the border post. It was not lit. He stopped and with a flashlight went to the office door that he opened to a dark interior. When knocking on the high counter he sniffed and smelled scorching, and he called without response.

"Huh! they're probably asleep," he said He did not investigate further but went to the wattle pole barrier and found the padlock open. "Now that's curious. No border guards? Padlock open? It's always locked from six to six." He shrugged his shoulders and lifted the barrier on the counterweight, drove through, stopped, replaced the barrier, hooked the padlock in the hasp without closing it and carried on driving. Now feeling tired he decided that as soon as it became light he would find a place to park and have forty winks before going on to the plains, thence to the engangs and manyattas he knew so well.

The clouds here were dispersing and a few stars were showing. When the moon, now beginning to wane beyond full, showed itself briefly he found a rise, stopped, switched off, and dozed.

He woke at sunrise, poured coffee from a flask, started up and drove off the road and took to the plains in four-wheel drive to steer by compass noting landmarks and eventually, recognising the set of trees and a kopje, found the rise he was looking for and picked up his binoculars.

*

Della searched among the safari gear in a box in the back of the Land Rover and found rations and water; tried to get Harris to take water but he was still unconscious. She thought the only thing to do was to drive down to the border post for help but unable to get a response from the car's battery she had to give it up. Then she took stock and knew that they had to stay there until a passing vehicle could help. But she doubted if anyone in their right mind would be travelling in this weather. She rummaged around and found two more blankets, one of which she draped over Harris and the other she wrapped around herself after removing her trousers and shirt wringing them out. She switched off the torch to conserve the batteries and sat and drew the blanket tightly around herself. The shock of what had happened now took over. She put her head on her knees and began to tremble.

# 20.

A man's destiny is ordained.
*(No one dies until his day comes)*

Now Peter was thinking everything was all right with the world while sitting on the cab roof of his truck scanning the plains. He always felt good after rain had come to replenish life.

All around him was green. Leaves and fresh thorns were sprouting. Bushes pushing up eager branches into clean air were sending down new roots to siphon up rain from the red earth while new grass and flowers, now sporting un-polarized colours, sought the spotlight of a sun now near its zenith that played dodgems with burgeoning cumulus clouds.

Where he had driven he left tyre impressions in yielding earth, and had raised no dust. Behind him a kopje of tumbled rocks played host to carmine bee-eaters feeding merrily on wasps and the spawning inhabitants of rock-pools. A lizard with rounded fingertips clutched a smooth rock until a flying predator brushed a shadow of wings across alert eyes. Four legs and a tail flailed a speedy way to a crack in the rock. The bird missed a feast, but the lizard blundered straight into the jaws of a striking snake.

In the distance Peter could see huge swathes of dark moving patches on the now green plains of the Serengeti. Hordes of wildebeest, zebra and antelope were gorging themselves on sweet grass. Here and there bold, overfed lion, cheetah, hyena, hunting dog and jackal followed the herds. There was hardly a tree without vultures and marabou storks waiting to alight and squabble over the next meal for which cat and dog would have fought fiercely for possession. Seemingly aloof from nature's food chain herds of humped boran and longhorn cattle, without attendant predators, but with elegant Masai among them, were savouring the seasonal giver of life. Three years without rain had been a long time.

He saw what he was looking for, took a bearing, jumped down and drove the truck on a course avoiding flooded dongas. On coming to a small rise he looked down to the engang of Olekowlish. He stopped where bushes grew and cut clumps to put between the wheels not wanting a predator to hide there waiting for his return. He walked the half-mile to the enclosure and called the Swahili "Hodi?" And heard "Karibu!" to welcome him. He was met by and elder, an upright slender man wearing a grey blanket rolled under his arms around an ample chest. Children looked wide-eyed at the stranger as they played among goats and dogs. Some hid behind mothers' legs while some more adventurous, followed, copying the strides of the two men. His guide turned and scattered the followers with a look. They ran laughing.

"You will find Olekowlish in his hut, there." They brushed hands and the elder turned on his heel.

Peter walked to the hut, called the Laibon's name and entered where it was dark after the brilliance of the sun. He caught his breath against the strong smell of cow dung, goats' urine, rotting skins, human sweat and woodsmoke. Regaining his breath he greeted Olekowlish in the Arabic way reserved for a revered senior.

"*Shikamuu!*"

In answer to the lesser man's 'I kiss your feet' Olekowlish's "*Marahaba!*" from a dark recess led Peter to his side where the pleasantries of formal greeting went easily between them. Peter sat on his heels.

"I have news for you, old gentleman."

"Eeeeh."

"Shall we go outside?"

"Eeeeh" said the old man. "Give me your arm."

As Peter helped him to his feet he felt the frail frame carrying ageing flesh. They went into sunlight and across to the shade of an old thorn where they sat on their heels. The Laibon called out "Wife. Bring beer!" A pretty girl barely out of her 'teens materialised from nowhere carrying a gourd and two bowls. She gave Peter a ravishing smile and disappeared as quietly as she had come.

"I see your taste in wives is as good as ever, Mzee," he said as he sipped the fermented honey, and added, "Your beer is as *khali* as ever!" They emptied the dishes and before they were refilled Peter tempted the old man to some whisky.

"Mix it for me" he said with eyes glinting. Peter gave him a mixture while putting only a dash of whisky in his own bowl.

"Your beer will be the death of me, old friend. It puts hyenas in my stomach and sends me to my home without legs."

"You are but a toto, my son. You are no warrior if you cannot drink my beer. Call yourself a slayer of lion? Dare you call yourself a man among men? Your spear will not run true if you have no honey in your veins!"

The good-natured banter, full of innuendo, went on for some minutes and Olekowlish seemed his old self again as the spirit eased his tongue and limbs. His laughing eyes lit up his long, lined face and dignity returned to the set of his head.

"Peter Grant, I hear you have been on a long safari away from the evils of Nairobi and the Kikuyu." They both laughed then suddenly the old man was serious. "Tell me, and tell me true. I wish to know how my sons died."

"News travels faster than my safari truck! Your sons died as Masai warriors."

"Do not lie! I know that Sekento was a thief, a liar and a murderer. I know that Sianka was a rapist and a drunkard."

Peter was quick to answer. "These things you say about your sons are true. Neither Sekento nor Sianka could be trusted to live as you wished. That is the folly of separation and blind ambition. Although their lives were ordained, both wanted power. Both wanted the same wife. Both were prepared to kill for the fulfilment of their desires. But, I say truly my father; your sons died as proud warriors. Neither feared death. They met it as it came, without surprise. Both were true moran. Each killed the other and died with their faces looking for the rising sun as befits true believers in Ngai."

"Did both carry a spear?"

"Sianka only carried a spear. It ran true. Truer than any spear your warriors are ever likely to see."

"What of Sekento?"

"He carried a White Hunter's gun."

Olekowlish shook his head slowly.

"What of their bones?"

"Where they were, in a fearful place, perhaps that endured by the whole tribe before the Great Ascent, they could not be buried. No thorns could cover them. Their bodies may nurture other creatures of this earth but their spirits remain."

The old man's face did not move but his eyes were deep with the tragedy of needless loss of life. "It is the way of things," he murmured. "Aiya."

Thunder rolled in from the north where clouds were now massing and an angry sun lit distant columns of rain. Moist air made an oppressive silence between the rumbles.

Peter topped up the Laibon's dish with more of the comforting mix and asked of the affairs of the clan.

"The affairs of the clan go on as before." He looked Peter in the eye. "Tell me Peter Grant, how are affairs with you? Why are you here? Have you still no m'sabu making you welcome at the place where you dig the earth?"

"You know very well the one with whom I might have married did so with another."

"You white people have strange habits. We Masai have more than one wife to produce children. Do not grow old before the delights of marriage pass you by."

He paused and reflected. "There is nothing for old men to do now. The young are looking after things. I cannot enjoy what they do and I cannot stop them from doing it, but whatever they do I pray they are young enough to learn and to put right their mistakes."

"Oh, come, my friend. Are you giving up your strength already? You, the number one Counsellor and Laibon of all Masai? One small word from you and great deeds are done."

"I am without my power!" Olekowlish's eyes burned. "No longer can I command things to happen."

"You brought rain! No other man in the whole tribe could have done that. You still have control."

"No, my son. I am without proper control. That is certain. Just one thing on this earth has power for me but I have it not!"

Thunder rumbled closer.

"Mzee," Peter said quietly "it is best I say why I am here to your full council." He looked up to judge the time when rain would reach them. "Be in the place where the elders meet at two hours before sunset." He then held both hands of the old man. "Go well and in peace Mzee."

He rose leaving Olekowlish sitting on his heels in the shade and walked with long, unsteady strides through the engang while thinking he must, in future, never mix fermented honey with whisky.

\*

Under a darkening turbulent sky beset with moisture, and at a few minutes before the appointed time Peter arrived at the old spreading thorn outside the engang and approached the circle of elders. Their usual numbers had increased by a gathering of new elders just become of age. All wore ceremonial blankets, but against normal peaceful procedures, most of the young were armed with spears, rungus and *simis*.

Olekowlish arrived dressed in his finery looking younger and sprightly with his face and legs decorated with grease, ochre and zigzagged blue dye.

As one they sat on stools, Olekowlish on his next to the ever-burning fire. The ring of elders thrust spears into the soft earth, blades uppermost. Peter approached and in the vernacular asked to enter the circle. The assent came readily. He addressed them while the Laibon stood.

"Elders. Brothers. True friends. I have been on a long safari and return bearing the fruits and scars of my quest. But first, is it not true that this man who stands before you is your Counsellor and Laibon?"

"Eeeeh."

"Is it not true he has served and led you well and faithfully for many years through the good times and the bad?"

"Eeeeh."

"Does he not reach a great age?"

"Eeeeh."

"Does not this great age bring wisdom?"

"Eeeeh."

"The wisdom of a Laibon is sacred and unsurpassed. Is this not true?"

"Eeeeh."

"Then why do you use the tongues of children to say your Laibon has no power?" There was no answer. "Olekowlish has not failed you. He used his powers and brought rain."

"Eeeeh."

"In doing this he has saved the lives of many clans of Masai. Also he has saved your cattle." At this mention of cattle the "Eeeeh" was enthusiastic.

"Moran are happy now that the lion is returning to the plains."

"Eeeeh!"

"Many children now shall live and look to your cattle. The cattle shall increase in untold numbers." This was greeted with prolonged eeeehs and hand clapping. "For this action Olekowlish has to account to Ngai. Now he is closer to Ngai than any of you can imagine. Working for the good of the clan has cost him dear!" The resulting Eeeeh had the intonation of 'shame!' "Even more than all his cattle!" The Eeeeh rose to a high pitch. "Then why do you sit about and talk as hyenas and say this man is not fit for office?" There was an embarrassed silence.

One of the new young elders stood and held up his talk stave for all to see.

"It is time for me to speak."

"For whom do you speak?"

"I speak for myself and for the new elders who have no voice against the prattling of old men. The old men do not listen. They have a good ear and a deaf ear. They choose to turn the bad one to us new elders."

"Then what is it you have to say that is not heard by your brothers?"

The young man strutted and brandished his stave. "It is time for changes. The old order does nothing. It is impotent. I and others are ready to do things."

"What are these 'things'?" spat a senior elder from his stool.

"There is a question of land settlement. There is a question of the age of marriage. There is a question of the price of cattle. There is . . ."

The elder from his place cut in. "Settlement of land was discussed and agreed with the English during the time of the Masai's former great Counsellors. Your forebears set the time when a man takes his first wife. It is the only way to control the family and numbers. Consorting and marriage before manhood is of age will bring us ill. The price of cattle remains open for bargaining. It always has been so and always shall be so." He then spoke to test the younger man's mettle. "You raise these questions because you usually have the worst of a bargain. You have yet to learn, if you ever could, how to bargain properly. It is not your new-found talk stave that works for you; it is your mouth and what comes out of it. You could not talk your way out of an unstoppered gourd!"

This rejoinder was met with gusts of laughter from the assembly and was not lost on the embarrassed young elder. The older man continued.

"Do you want to change our way of life? For what reason? For the sake of change alone? These things were discussed and agreed before you came onto this earth. They shall remain as they are for many generations to come. You have nothing new to say."

He stopped speaking waiting to hear a convincing argument but the younger man lost his nerve and blustered.

"B . . . But the old man who calls himself Counsellor has . . . no . . . strength."

The older man got up from his stool and looked at him with contempt.

"Can you kill two lions together with but one spear? This, your Counsellor has done. This 'old man' in his lifetime has killed forty!" The elders applauded while some younger men gasped 'eeeeh!' "We wait with bated breath till you have the courage to go out and kill your first!" All laughed derisively.

"But the old man has no power!"

"Can you bring rain? Can you make the medicine for ridding cattle of sickness? Can you mix the herbs to make a barren wife fertile? Can you speak as an equal with the great Princes of other countries when they come for lion safaris? No! You can do nothing. This 'old man' has done all these things and more so that you may live. Although you have the talk stave of an elder you are still a whinging toto!" He spat copiously and expertly into the fire that sizzled and raised a puff of smoke, then sat with a contemptuous smile.

Humiliated, the young man became incensed and shouted. "But the old man has no power for himself. The old man is without control. The old man consorts with white men and tries to convince us he still has authority! Authority does not come from this white man here. He is not one of us. Authority comes from Ngai!"

He turned, snatched up his spear, stepped a pace forward and flung it from high over his head for it to plunge upright in the earth a yard from Peter's feet. The greater part of the young elders in the circle rose from their stools, took up spears and, as one, launched spears for them to thud around Peter to encircle him. There was a short metallic hiss as simis were withdrawn from scabbards.

Now within the cage of spears Peter took the Okiuka from under his jacket and held it aloft. A surprised murmur surrounded him and a spear directly in front of him fell outwards as though the cage door had opened. Still holding the Okiuka over his head he ignored the threatening ring of warriors and walked through the gap up to the Laibon. Low angry sunlight reflected red from the black stone at the Okiuka's end.

"Here, Mzee. Here, Olekowlish. Here is your power."

The Chief Counsellor put out his hands and grasped the baton. Peter felt strength enter the old man's body. Olekowlish rose in stature and for a brief moment had the feeling he was once more the tall, elegant Masai leader he had been for fifty years.

Peter could not let go of the Okiuka. A curious feeling stole along his arm and down his body. His head buzzed and he had a vignetted vision of many elders sitting around the rim of the sacred Ol Doinyo Lengai. The image persisted for a few moments before it faded and normal feelings came back to him. He found himself relaxed and invigorated with hands at his side, with no pain from his shoulder. Olekowlish was facing the sacred volcano with the Okiuka above his head. The elders, in unison, intoned a prolonged "eeeeeh" then gently and slowly clapped their hands.

Feeling no more than eyes on his back Peter left the circle and walked into the engang and sat on his heels outside Olekowlish's hut.

The young wife came and put a bowl of a mixture of milk and blood at his feet. Again she gave him a melting smile and disappeared.

He sipped from the bowl and looked up at the sound of the beginning of close, prolonged thunder. Black clouds were now overhead with a line of red sky resting on the horizon in the west. Accompanying the thunder Peter could hear rhythmical grunting as the circle of Masai danced on sandalled feet with stiff knees.

\*

The last of the sun's rays made long shadows as Olekowlish came back to his hut. He motioned with his head for Peter to enter, once more to experience the cauldron of dung, urine, sweat, skins and woodsmoke. Now he could just see Olekowlish in the gloom lit by a small, recently refurbished fire in a ring of blackened stones.

Peter sat on a stool with his head just below a layer of smoke that filled the roof and kept flies away.

"My son," the Laibon began. "You brought me today that which has completed my life. I could not go to Ngai without the knowledge that it was safe. But I did not think it would come from a white bwana."

"My father, I am not your bwana. Your memory is fading. You forget I was born in Africa. It is no more than two day's journey for me to reach the place in the Great Rift Valley where I was conceived and born. I am an African."

"You have a white skin."

"You have red. The Kikuyu have black. People originating from parts of Asia have brown, and others yellow. Yes, I have a white skin. Skin that came from my father and mother as is given to every child on this earth whatever the colour. I did not ask for it and I do not complain about it. I do not consider myself a prisoner in it as others do. There may come a day when the white man, whether or not he was born here, may have to leave. When that day comes it will be my fervent wish the Masai shall continue to rule this great valley; that the elders of Ol Doinyo Lengai shall continue to be the Lords of the Rift."

"That talk is not unseemly, my son. It is sometimes strange why the colour of the skin determines what is in the head of some people."

"The Masai are revered for what is in theirs."

"Ah, yes. But the Masai are a fading family. There are so few now in the north. They became soft under the rule of the English. They came too close to your world, Peter Grant." He laughed inwardly with a sneer. "Do not forget that the Masai were here long before the Kikuyu and the White Man. When we overcame the rigours of ascending the escarpments of Endikir Ekerio and established our home in the Rift Valley we were not to know it would be a matter of countable years before invading men with pale skins, firearms and disease would reduce us to this!" His outstretched arms metaphorically encompassed the whole of Masailand. He kicked a brand in the fire and sparks rose to reveal blazing eyes. "Huh!" he exclaimed. "The Samburu and others approach even closer from the north. The Kikuyu grow greedy in their bellies and soft in their heads. Their numbers increase. They spread uncontrollably and will have trouble among themselves before many moons are out." He became thoughtful. "Tell me. Do the Kikuyu know the whereabouts of the Okiuka?"

"I think not. They believe they still have it, but all they have is a worthless copy I had made on a brown-skinned man's machine."

Olekowlish smiled. The smile broke into a small laugh then into a guffaw that turned into loud laughter.

"You are as devious as the Kikuyu, Peter Grant." As his laughter subsided he became serious once more. "Look to it, young man. In the south here, we cling fiercely to what we are. We did not join with your enemy in this place thirty and more years ago, or officially in the recent conflict. We shall not join with you in the future – unless you decide to fight the Kikuyu!" he added slyly and spat into the fire.

He looked out to the black, storm-swept sky and fast approaching sheets of rain, and listened to the growling thunder.

"I foresee the day when there will be so many different skins in the valley. Then the Masai will be able to do nothing but act as guides to the people who come to see what is left of our lions and us. "How strange," they will say. "How quaint! Why do they not wear safari suits as we do? They wear blankets and skins and paint their faces. They put feathers around their legs and arms and put mud on their heads! They no longer slay lions!" Olekowlish paused, kicked the fire again and said "Huh! These people with different skins will lift cameras from their necks and make pictures to show their timid memsa'bs how brave they are. Then, when they go to their safari beds they will lie at night quaking with fear lest a moran comes to spit them on his spear, or that a lion might come to drag them to the bushes and bite on their bones!"

He paused for a long time and took no notice of a close clap of thunder.

"You and I, my African friend, must hold on to what we are, here and now. We must make the most of Africa. We must make the most of time. One day, for sure, both of us will not be here." He looked out again and spoke tenderly. "My two sons are not here . . . Naiyolang is not here . . . Her family are not here."

"Then why am I still here?" Peter asked quietly with eyes full of woodsmoke. Olekowlish looked hard at him.

"Ngai put out his hand to you. The council considered that what you did came with thought only for the clan and not for yourself. What you accomplished, though, came too late. It brought argument, bloodshed and killing on a scale not seen for many years. A whole clan was lost." He shook his head in anguish. "We have learned the truth of the matter and I am forced to admit it fitting that my two sons were punished. The clan will be punished severely for what was done at Menengai. Ngai is wrathful. It is the way of things. He has punished you a little, but a small hurt is nothing. He will punish you more by having you live with the knowledge of your intervention in the affairs of the clan. Your close association with the Masai gives you no right to decide what to do outside the convention of elders. Had you consulted us before your precipitous act these matters would have been better resolved. It is a grievous fault and has to be put right."

"But I recovered the Okiuka for you. I did what I did in order that the Kikuyu were not aware of what was happening. Otherwise they would have guarded the Okiuka beyond reach."

Olekowlish stirred the fire with his foot.

"True, but nevertheless, the deed was done. The elders decided you are to be fined forty-nine cattle including your best bull."

"I say! That's a bit steep! Especially after having helped the clan."

"Two of my sons were murdered in your presence! You are fortunate the fine for one death covers both." He became gentle again. "It is evident you have acted without the approval of your elders. You have endangered your life for the sake of their indifference. In that regard you have been used. But Ngai, in his infinite wisdom put out his hand to you. If he had not done this, you too my son, before now, would be out there feeding the vultures."

He took a deep breath and looked at Peter with a steely eye.

"I have heard you call this great valley the Garden of Eden. I know of these things you worship. For too long, Peter Grant, your people have been gathering apples. You have bitten the apple, but you have ignored the serpent. Look to the serpent, my white warrior, he is always lurking. Look to the serpent!"

There followed some minutes with the two men deep in thought with the silence broken only by heavy thunder and large drops of rain beginning to drop and run off the cloud-coloured moisture-polished huts.

His eldest wife entered the open doorway bringing a bowl of milk and blood. She was not her usual smiling self and her old eyes were tear-stained. She wore no decorations and not one bead adorned her plain, soft lambskin cloak. She knelt in front of her Lord and touched his hands with hers. He took them and pressed them to his forehead and said nothing. In the next few brief moments they both experienced the time from when they first were married; she as a pretty twelve-year-old and he as a bloodied warrior passing into the council of elders, then through all of the eventful things that had happened up to the present moment. Peter felt he was an interloper and was embarrassed but they took no notice of him. She stood, ignored Peter as though she had not seen him and left the hut. Olekowlish drank from the bowl and put it down empty.

Rain came with a roar with flashes and more thunder.

"Peter Grant," he said, raising his voice. "I have no more time for this earth. The tasks laid out and accomplished have outwitted my body. I am to join the elders of Ol Doinyo Lengai . . . that time is here. When you were a toto you drank the milk and the blood of the

Masai and have enjoyed the privileges of the clan. Now you must do something to return that honour. Circumstances demand it."

"What have I to do? You have my word."

"Hold this Okiuka."

"Me?"

"Peter Grant it is you who must keep and guard with vigilance the staff of power until the next chosen Laibon appears."

"But surely this belongs to the Masai."

"There are those in the clans who cannot be trusted. It is a matter of who Ngai has chosen to inherit, not just of passing it on to those who falsely claim the honour. Three of us old elders of this clan know the ritual and without the presence of any others have agreed that it is to be passed on in due course to the rightful successor. Until the time when the new Laibon appears it has to be lodged safely without the knowledge of other clans. This is a spiritual matter that goes back very many years to when the Masai populated the Rift Valley and the first Laibon appeared. We have to obey that which Ngai ordains."

"But when will the new Laibon come?"

"He is present but it will be some time before he is ready."

"How shall I know it is he?"

"You will know. You shall know him well. It is he who is to take the Masai further into this changing world." Olekowlish was looking out into the distance to unseen mountains and vast, rain-swept plains. Slowly he shook his head and with a smile continued. "You know him now. Now, he is but five years old."

Peter suddenly realised it was to be the young boy he had picked up at Menengai and marvelled at the spiritual powers of Olekowlish. But then he remembered his father talking of the old legend of the five-year-old boy who, on reaching a certain age, became an elder and the first Laibon of Masai.

The old man held the Okiuka out to Peter who grasped it with both hands. From a pouch Olekowlish took familiars including a length of soft bark cloth that he laid over Peter's hands as a priest would when joining a couple in marriage. Over this he laid the limp entrails of a sacred black goat, a sprig or two of herbs and the tufted end of a lion's tail. He sprinkled Peter's wrists with fine powder pinched up from a dish and with a bunch of leleshwa leaves tapped his wrist seven times. Peter began to experience a religious feeling far deeper than he had ever felt when worshiping at any European designated church. Raising his voice above the noise of the storm Olekowlish began to chant a prayer.

"By the authority and powers invested in me
By my Lord Ngai and by my hand
I pass this wand.
It carries the potent art and the workings of mystery
It carries the love and the dread of Ngai.
It carries the blackness of thunder
It carries the light of living.
Never to be broken
Never to be buried.
It shall remain between the heavens and the earth."

With a smouldering stick from the fire he touched the powder that flared and scorched hair on Peter's wrists. Olekowlish then spat blessings on his hands. Thunder rattled the huts and rain roared as an express train in a tunnel.

The old man eased off ceremonial skins and headdress, placed all the paraphernalia to one side and fixed the red and grey blanket around his shoulders with a simple clasp. Over this he enveloped himself in another large plain red blanket. He moved to the door and stepped outside, made a final effort, inhaled deeply and stood tall. From a rack he took his spear and without looking back he walked out into the ferocious storm. Peter looked at the tall figure receding into the darkness towards the open gates of the engang.

With the startling sound of tearing silk a lance of lightning exploded into many scorched pieces the tree that for a hundred years had sheltered the gatherings of elders. Peter's skin felt the electricity in the air and he smelled the burn while a prolonged blue-white light lit the old Laibon's frail frame striding through the dancing rain. Peter called out over the storm's noise.

"*SERE NDAVO* OLEKOWLISH!"

An immediate darkness and deafening crack of thunder took the words from his mouth. It shook the ground and huts fell, and then went charging across the plains towards the distant sacred mountain,

Ol Doinyo Lengai. A lion in the grasses nearby added its penetrating roar to the din and others took up the lion's call and the growing clamour spread up the Rift Valley as quickly as the noise of the storm. The hair on Peter's neck tingled as the uproar from lions rose to be as deafening as the thunder. He gripped the Okiuka in tight fists, and quietly to himself, he mouthed "Farewell, old gentleman. Go well and with good fortune . . . Go well!"

# 21.

A holed calabash cannot be filled.
*(When things are finished they cannot be corrected)*

The storm lasted for another half an hour with the clouds dispersing quickly to reveal stars in their profusion and a brilliant moon. The temperature dropped to near freezing. There was not a male to be seen in the village but the women of the engang were wailing and ululating creating an air of pathos over the whole enclosure.

Peter was brought a bowl of blood and milk by the youngest wife with an unsmiling face who busied herself in collecting all of Olekowlish's paraphernalia into a bundle that she placed at Peter's feet. He drank the warming mixture and walked out of the hut with the Okiuka and bundle and made his way past a fallen hut to a large gap in the surrounding wattle and thorn. In moonlight he passed the smouldering remains of the shattered, once great spreading thorn tree, paused, looked back, shook his head slowly, then, in an eerie silence, walked to his truck.

It was not difficult in the moonlight for him to follow the tracks back the way he had come that morning. Where the tyre marks had been washed away he followed his compass until picking them up again all the way to the road on which he turned to the north.

In a short time the moon, yet again, was covered with cloud and it began to drizzle. Headlight beams cut into gloomy darkness. He drove slowly, only to find himself dozing. Shaking his head he stopped, got out and stamped about, did a few bending and stretching exercises and poured a cupful of coffee from a flask. He leant against the truck and thought of the young boy realising that the Masai male traditional coming of age for marriage and to be an elder was twenty-seven years. "My God," he thought, "officially it'll be twenty two years before Saichella comes of age! Whatever will happen during that time?" He decided not to think about it and drove on.

When reaching the border post he found it in the same state as before, let himself through, closed the barrier and continued now under clouds without rain.

Coming to within a mile of the bottom of the rise he noticed that the road was no longer waterlogged and that the drains were carrying less. The gloom was still deep and the temperature down.

On approaching the rise up to the next steppe he thought he saw a glimmer of a light, but brushed the thought aside. Then the light flashed again. This time it was a definite SOS signal. He approached and switched on his swivel lights. He saw a dented Land Rover with a blanket-wrapped figure on its crumpled roof. The figure waved the light about excitedly.

Peter stopped, kept the lights on the scene, hurriedly loaded the Springfield rifle in case it was an ambush and walked out of the light's beam up to the vehicle with rifle at the ready. He recognised it to be a police Land Rover and heard a weak "please help!" in a voice he knew that shocked him.

"Della?" he called.

"Is that Peter?"

"Yes."

"Thank God! Oh, thank God!"

He crossed the half full storm drain, propped up the rifle and helped her down. She hugged him tightly for a full minute and cried deeply then began shivering.

"My darling girl you've hardly any clothes on. What the hell has happened?"

"I'm not sure but I believe we were washed off the road in a storm."

"Looks as though you were rolled . . . We?"

"Yes. Steve Harris was driving. Trying to catch you before the border. He said you were being devious. Steve's in the back."

Peter climbed in and felt Steve's pulse. "He's alive but in a bad way. We'd better get him in my truck and find you some dry clothes or you'll catch your death." They both helped to take his friend across to his truck to lay him in the back. He gave her a shirt and trousers and while he turned aside to tend to Steve she took off her bra and briefs and put on the trousers that she belted and turned up the legs. The brushed cotton shirt was warm and tucked into the belt. "Here's a pair of boots and a dry blanket. "How long have you been there?"

"I don't know. All of yesterday and in the middle of last night I guess. Where are we?"

"<u>Last</u> night? You are just north of the Tanganyika border. Nobody came this way during daylight?"

"No."

"You poor darling," he said and hugged her again to keep her warm. He asked her if she bandaged Steve's head.

"Yes. I'm not sure I did the right thing. I just put on a compress."

He redressed the wound and said that in the circumstances she had done a marvellous job in stopping the bleeding. "He's concussed I reckon. I hope it's nothing more serious. We'll get you both to the Nairobi hospital. How are you feeling right now?"

"I'm Okay."

"Sure? You don't look it."

"I'm cold." she said.

From his truck he took out his British Warm greatcoat, put it around her and hugged her for a long time. She cried again and gave herself up to his closeness and warmth and wished it would go on – with him – for ever.

"Oh Peter," she said, "I prayed and prayed for you to come."

Eventually he kissed the tears away and released her. "My darling girl. Let's get you back to Nairobi. Do you feel fit enough to help me get the Land Rover hitched up?"

"Yes."

"Sit in, keep it in neutral and when I pull steer to that flattish place twenty yards down there," he said shining a torch and giving it to her. "When there, turn on to the road and I'll pull you to face up hill. Keep the rope tight with a soft hand brake. Don't try to start it there may be damage underneath. And don't use the lights." He retrieved the Springfield, and fixing a rope he hauled her, with one or two minor slips, down to the flat and on to the road to face up the rise. There he backed up, fixed two spare tyres between the vehicles and wire-winched the Land Rover's front wheels off the ground and released the handbrake.

"You must be hungry." He poured coffee and gave her a handful of dried fruit and nuts. "Best you ride in the back with Steve to keep an eye on him. Give me a shout if you need me."

While she was with Steve trying to get him to take some water, but failing, Peter tied a red storm lantern to the back doors of the stricken Land Rover then drove up the rise, the long haul to Athi River, and eventually pulled into the Nairobi hospital at about four a.m. The casualty staff X-rayed Steve, found no serious damage, cleaned and dressed his head wound, gave him a tetanus booster and put him in a private ward. Della was given a thorough check and a mug of hot, sweet cocoa from the nurse's restaurant. Steve regained his senses just before they left him, but he was somewhat dazed, told that he must rest, and given a sleeping draught. They were finished there at five thirty.

Peter made a telephone call before driving Della to the Norfolk Hotel to pick up her things and check out.

"I got Morrissey out of bed and told him what happened. Now, you are coming to my pad to get a bath and breakfast. I shan't let you out of my sight because I arranged to be responsible for you until you are called for at two pm. I am told you are still under curfew, and I promised I wouldn't let you go skiving off again," he said with a grin.

"How can I? I haven't gotten your pickup," she countered with humour. "Anyway, who would want to when I'm with a big white hunter who rescued me from a nasty end in Darkest Africa – for the second time?"

"You've been reading too many penny dreadfuls again," he said as he drove to the police compound to leave the Land Rover there.

"Ah, but I mean it," she said. "I've noticed you don't use your arm much. Is it badly hurt?"

"It's only that mosquito bite."

"Liar!"

At the Norfolk hotel she collected her remaining things and booked out. On the way to his apartment he asked her how she came to be trussed up in the pickup at Losiolo. She filled in the remainder of her story from the time when the apparition of the Masai appeared in the cloud when she followed the pointing spear. "That was weird, because if I had gone the other way I would have been caught by the police, and that would have meant curtains for sure. It was weirder still when up on the escarpment. Just before he turned nasty and hit me with a stone he stood on the rear of the pickup and became quite Shakespearean. He pointed with his spear down to what lay below in the valley and I remember very clearly what he said when he spoke in English." Shifting in her seat she struck a pose with hand pointing downwards and lowered her voice an octave. "Sianka goes back to the place where the beginnings of the Masai were seeded, before the time of the great ascent!"

"Did you say Sianka?"

"That's what the man said."

"Good God. I was right."

"Right? Don't tell me you know him."

"Yes I do . . . did."

"A friend of yours?"

"Anything but. I knew him briefly. Very briefly."

"One of the bad guys?"

"Yes. Bad."

"What is it with you and these Masai? Why so cagey? Steve tells me you have been a naughty boy. He was going to arrest you."

Peter smiled and would not be drawn. "We should be coming to the apartment soon," he said changing the subject.

\*

At the rear of the studio he put the truck in the lockup and carried all their gear up an iron fire escape to his back door and entered his apartment and switched on lights. She looked around wide-eyed. It reminded her of a lush penthouse suite in Bohemian Montrose in Houston except for the decor that was purely African.

His apartment had once been a nightclub. What had been a small dance floor surrounded by tables and plush, intimate seating with a dais for the musicians was now a thirty-feet-square drawing room with animal skins and rugs on a parquet floor. A log fire was laid in an iron grate with guard and copper chimney. Peter put a match to it. Half-drawn curtains revealed French windows onto a veranda overlooking Jeevanjee Gardens with its grassed public square with shrubs and flowers. On the walls were oil and watercolour landscapes by East African artists vying with action photographs of Masai in various stages of dance rituals. Shields and spears filled gaps between bookshelves.

Since her coming to Kenya Della had seen two sides of Peter. His extraordinary reaction to her noisy arrival that she put down to his frustration and tiredness, and then his pleasantness, ability to cope with a crisis and his playful, yet romantic attitude. Here, in his apartment she saw yet another side of him. Neatness and the domestic ability to make good use of space without clutter. Although large, this drawing room was cosy and inviting.

On looking around she saw other black and white photographs. An actress in performance poses. She thought she recognised her. Next to them were a head and shoulders portrait and a tastefully photographed artistic nude study of the same girl. She admired the modest poses and discreet lighting. "Well!" she murmured. "That's the redhead at the hotel desk who changed my dollars! So, I reckon our Peter's been quite busy with his camera and all!"

A low, table with tiled zodiac runes surrounded with scattered cushions carried in its centre a unique carving in mottled, pale brown hard wood of two facing lions up on hind legs with teeth bared and claws out. Obviously fighting. Flickering shadows from the fire gave them life and movement as though dancing together.

"Bathroom's here," he called, opening a door along a passage. "Plenty of hot water. Bath or shower. Towels on the rail."

"Peter doesn't do things by halves," she said as she kicked off his boots and removed his greatcoat, shirt and trousers in a large, tiled bathroom.

Selecting a bottle from a shelf she scattered the contents into rising hot water and sank down into utter luxury. She lay there relaxing for ten minutes savouring every comforting second while letting the events of the past days, or weeks, was it? to be washed out of her system. She had lost count. She would have slept she had not heard Peter moving and shutting a door.

He had put his gear into his bedroom and went to the rear of the apartment out on to a veranda and called down to Juma his elderly steward who appeared from a brick house beyond a courtyard. They exchanged words in Swahili and Juma came up the fire escape and collected her wet things. Further words were said and Juma was delighted and the last to speak before descending to his house. *"Asanti sana, bwana" (thank you).*

Back in his bedroom Peter took the three guns from the long holdall, locked them in the gun safe, then picked up the object of his protracted quest and ran his hand along the smooth, black wood of the Okiuka and stared into the gem while thinking jumbled thoughts. He moved the bed, pulled up a corner of a rug and exposed a floor safe. Wrapping the Okiuka in paper he put it under files he kept there, closed and locked the safe and replaced the rug and bed, then undressed.

Della wallowed in the bath, shampooed her hair, soaped herself all over, immersed her body and savoured sweet, luxurious moments. She wanted to linger but knew that he would need the bathroom. She pulled the plug, and when shampoo and soap had been showered from her she dried herself and wrapped a bath sheet around her glowing, revitalised body, used her own cologne and wound a towel around her head and went into the drawing room. On hearing her leave the bathroom Peter, in a robe, went there and turned on the shower.

Walking around the large drawing room she closed the curtains against the brightness of a dawn just breaking and turned out all the lights except for a table lamp to add a little to the glow from the fire on which she dropped a sprig of rosemary and pinches of musk she found in a large dish of potpourri, then sat on a cushion before the fire to dry her hair.

Peter had a relaxing shower, slicked back part dried hair, donned the robe and came out of the bathroom and called in her direction. "Do you think you could do something for me?"

She came to him and drew in a sharp breath when he slipped the robe from his shoulder.

"Wow! That's not what you would call a mosquito bite! Are you sure it wasn't a bespoke tailor who stitched that up?"

"Cover it with this dressing and stick it down."

She stuck down the strips of plaster and he pulled the robe straight.

"How on earth did you . . . ?"

"Anything you would like?" he asked, changing the subject.

She paused, then putting on an exaggerated Southern drawl said, "Yes . . . er . . . *Leti kahawa* . . . *er* . . . *mara moja*! Is that right my big white chief?"

"Yes, my squaw," he said, and with a bad attempt at the accent: "Cawffee coming up one time. *Sasa hivi* – right now."

She went back to the drawing room while reflecting he had affected not to notice her dressed in only a towel with the smaller one from her head now around her shoulders. He heated water enough to make two mugs of his favourite Kenya blend and laced them with honey and a generous dash of malt whisky. Taking them into the drawing room he discovered her sitting near the fire on a cushion with legs tucked under, sleeking hair back having dried it to catch with a decorated elastic band. She wore no make-up and the low, flickering light playing on her hair and creamy light tan on a smooth face and neck stopped him momentarily while he smelled the rosemary and musk coming from the fire.

"Er . . . ?"

"Come and sit," she said. "I don't bite." He handed her a mug and sat. She took a sip. "Delicious . . . Hey! there's more than coffee in this."

"We have a saying in Kenya that coffee should be as black as the devil, hot as hell, pure as an angel and sweet as love." He continued expansively "Add to that the virgin's kiss of a single malt whisky and you have in your hands the elixir of the savannah."

"Wow!" she said taking a large sip. "You are so right! May I quote you?"

"Be my guest."

"I reckon you've put a double single in mine."

"Here's to you."

She sipped again and reflected while staring wistfully into space. "It would be a privilege to return that virgin's kiss." When their eyes met again she said "You've already seen I can be as black as the devil . . . Could I be as hot as hell given half a chance? . . . Don't know . . . Pure as an angel?" . . . Their eyes were communicating. "Love is sweet too, I guess." She sipped at the nectar again while looking over the mug without taking her eyes from his. "What was that you called to your servant?"

"I gave him your wet clothes. They'll be clean and dry and ready for you in good time. Then I asked him to make lunch for us at one o'clock . . . I'll go and make some breakfast."

"No, not yet. I have something to say."

"Oh?"

She put down the mug and with elbows on knees and chin in her hands she gazed at him.

"You're quite something, don't you know. I haven't met anyone quite like you. You damned me to hell when we first met, but you helped me get the story of my career, which is all but buttoned up, and better darned well please my editor. Your pickup helped me see Kenya and its animals as I had never dreamed it. Most of it I liked – loved. What a fabulous place! Bits of it weren't much fun – that's for sure! I didn't know it could be so . . . fierce one minute and so gentle the next. You allowed me the most exciting time I've ever had. You gave me the run-around too! I'd give my right arm to know what you were up to, dashing all over the place – it certainly wasn't farming."

He smiled and shook his head.

"But you kept me out of custody with those extra photographs, well, for the time being anyway until . . . More importantly, you saved my life – twice. Then again, whatever mistakes I made – and I made a few believe me – you never once said 'I told you so' and you didn't scold me for purloining your pickup. That makes one female journalist feel darned good."

"I said use the pickup as you thought fit. It was you who had the guts to find out about this country. It's you who pulled the hair from the elephant's tail and is about to make the headlines. We didn't have our safari but your animal pictures are more than just first rate, especially the nose-to-tail elephants and that series of the cheetah making a kill. Particularly the shot of them both in the air at the strike with flying earth. That shot ought to make a good poster. It'll make you quite a few dollars. You certainly know how to use a camera. I am most impressed."

"Thank you. But then, I stopped you from getting your film of Bili making her kill . . . I shall complete what I have written already about my first impressions and include those pics for the centrespread."

"Our safari I doubt would have been as . . . savage as the one you have been on."

She looked him in the eye. "How about yours? I don't know of any mosquito that could cause a six-inch gash. You're still not going to tell me what you were doing? Off the record?" Again he smiled and shook his head. She finished the coffee, started to rise and said, "I'd better get dressed."

He raised his hand and she sat, He smiled and looked searchingly at her. She met his gaze with questioning eyes and rising heart beats. Then he stood.

"I have something for my lone safari girl. Come over here."

She took his hand to rise and looked at him enquiringly while being led to a long wall mirror. From his robe pocket he took a small parcel. "In memory of your brush with the Masai and my sincere apology for being bad tempered to a fabulously beautiful girl when we first met."

Gingerly she opened tissue paper and held up strands of beads and shells.

"What . . .?"

"It is a Masai woman's authentic headdress. This is how it goes . . ." He set it on her slicked-back shining hair for beads and trinkets to flicker and dazzle in the firelight. "I thought it would be something for you to wear as a cloche hat at a party with a flapper's frock, or just to remember your time here. There, it fits perfectly," he said kissing her nose, "even though you haven't shaved your head." She was blushing and saying thank you. She kissed the palm of his hand. He added, "All you need do now is to pierce your ear lobes and stretch them with silver dollars."

She laughed, turned and admired herself in the long mirror. He picked up a patterned Masai blanket from the back of a chaise longue, and stood behind her. "This is the other part of it." First he took the small towel from her shoulders and dropped it. "Raise your right arm." He put the blanket around her and with a twist he secured two corners over her left shoulder leaving the right one bare. She marvelled at the effect while seeing herself from top to bare toe. While standing close at her back and with an arm across her chest he could feel her heart beating quickly. She was acutely – and pleasantly – aware of his closeness.

He picked up her bare right arm and kissed the bruise on her forearm then brushed his lips up to a bare shoulder and caressed her neck until he reached her ear and said softly, "You are one darling girl and I am rather glad you came to find me and Africa."

"Mmmm!" she murmured with eyes closed.

His lips continued caressing her "But I ought to tell you that since you discovered Kenya there is one other very important thing you should know."

"And what is that?" she breathed, thrilling at his caresses. He was kissing her ear and neck again. Between breaths she said, "Tell me then . . . have I done . . . something else . . . very wrong?"

" . . . No."

"Was it something about Bili?"

" . . . No."

"Is it lions?"

" . . . No."

"Elephants?"

" . . . No."

"My photographs?"

" . . . No."

"My . . . driving all over?"

" . . . No."

"You are teasing me . . . Please tell me . . ." she was now breathing in snatches and her toes were digging into a zebra skin . . . her lips found his face and ear . . . "please?"

His lips were caressing her cheek and ear, and he whispered, "The true Masai wear nothing under the blanket."

She opened her eyes and they gazed at each other in the glass. Her blush was now caused by a different, intense feeling. They continued looking silently at each other for a moment longer, then she wriggled her body and the towel under the blanket dropped at her feet. She leaned back into him and his hand found a gap in the blanket. She did not resist but gave herself up to a most wonderful feeling. Like that he danced her slowly around the table while whispering the endearing words of a Shakespeare sonnet. Then they sank onto the scattered cushions on the floor in front of the fire while he loosened the blanket twist and she undid the tie to his robe. Through snatches of breath and rising heartbeats while kissing him she managed to say in the Texan drawl, "Peter, y'all is one heck of an S.O-ooo. ." She did not get to the 'B.'

*

Now looking delightfully feminine wearing a simple pink frock, court shoes and hair held by a silk cheetah spotted bandana, she sat with him on floor cushions at the low table tucking into a curry prepared by Peter's steward, and washed down with bottles of cold Tusker ale. She cleared a second heaped plate, drank the last of a bottle and picked up a second.

"That," she said with relish "I deserved. That was something else again. Best breakfast I've had since Davy Crocket's Diner in San Antonio – Not the same circumstances I hasten to add! . . . just touring! . . ." Then with a hand on his arm and a look in her eyes that spoke volumes she added with innuendo not lost to him "But now, I have never been so . . . full."

"Tell me, am I still a detestable stinker?"

"Well, not right at this moment. I'll keep it in reserve," she said with a grin. "And am I still a pain in the butt?"

He shook his head "Never! . . . I thought you said you didn't bite," he said fingering a sore ear.

"Sorry. Out of control . . . Oh, Peter, I must come back here and . . . go out and find Bili with you . . . I would have to call you by a name which I thought of this morning – I can't tell you right now, but it would be a better name than some I called you in private after we first met."

"You can call me anything you like, now that I have no need to go dashing all over the place. I have done what I set out to do. 'Mission Accomplished' as they say.

"<u>Now</u> he tells me!" she said with feeling . . . "and I have to be torn away from you. How cruel can life be! If I had gone with you to the 'Wide Blue Yonder' – wherever that was, and not in Pat's truck that night of the party things would have been so different! Poor Pat. And I would not have . . . Oh, I don't know . . . We would have had our safari . . ." Then she burst out, "Oh, why does it have to happen like this?" She had a tearful edge to her voice. "But I know I can't have what I want all my life. Fate has such horrible twists!" She looked down at her empty plate, bit her lip and looked up. "You said you'd take me to the coast if there was time . . . Oh, how I wish we could . . . But then having fallen in love with you utterly and completely you'll let me go back to Texas with a broken heart . . . Oh, hell, what am I saying? Am I such a dumb blonde? One more for you to add to your conquests? Oh, Peter! . . . why! . . . why!" Now there were tears in her eyes.

He was about to put an arm around her shoulder and say that he loved her when there was knocking at the door. "Damn!" he said as he went and opened it.

It was Superintendant Morrissey and a civilian. "Come in," said Peter. Morrissy said, "Good afternoon Miss Mitchell, Mr.Grant. This is Sir George Williams; Police Commissioner."

"How d'y'do," she said, offering her hand. "It's a five star General then for me?"

The Commissioner smiled. Morrissey said, "Sir, I believe you know Mr.Grant."

"Oh, yes."

"Sir," Peter said to Sir George, "Can she not stay? For just another week?"

"No. The law has been broken and the law has spoken. The law is the same for foreign journalists whatever gender or status. In any case, Miss Mitchell, your Embassy tells me you are wanted immediately for the editing of your dissertation and to be on hand in Houston for the release of the details of the arrest and trial. Before we go, I understand that you two have helped Inspector Harris out of a difficulty. For that I thank you. I have seen him this morning and he is recovering well. He has done a remarkably good job. As for you, Mr.Grant, if you had not been so wayward it would not have happened I am sure. And another thing; be ready for an appointment with Sir Rupert Stafford. His secretary will call you, and you are to go to Government house at Muthaiga. Now, Miss, if you would be so kind . . ."

As Peter was about to go with her she said, "No, Peter. I shall be surrounded by policemen, and I shall cry if you are there."

"Sergeant," said Morrissey. The driver came in and picked up her bags that were ready by the door. She was whisked away down the stairs.

Peter was stunned. Suddenly she was not there. No girl before had gone from his life in such bizarre circumstances. It was a few seconds before he dashed to the top of the stairs. "I . . . shall come to Houston . . . Love you!" he called. His voice echoed against the plain plastered walls of the empty stair well. He went to the veranda and looked down as she was being ushered to the police car. She looked up. He blew a kiss and she was gone.

As the police car drew away quickly Della's eyes misted over. She blinked a tear and her mind's eye saw the immense cliffs and escarpments of the Rift Valley peopled with the fabled Masai walking among their cattle. Volcanoes crowded her vision, some now dead, others sending ash and fire to the heavens. Under a relentless sun she had perspired and then had stood in freezing rain on ground that trembled when thunder roared. She had tasted some of the best food in the world and travelled through acres of regimented rows of crops waiting to burgeon on Peter's farm. The stark beauty of millions of pink flamingo and birds she had never seen before wading in immense lakes bowled her over, and she then heard Africans singing in gardens surrounded by vibrant colours of flowers and shrubs but a short safari from arid deserts and lush forested mountains abounding with elephants. As the image of the formal line of eighty-three elephants assailed her a tear dropped down her cheek then the image changed into the elephants at the Whistling Thorn camp site in the Ndoto Hills which brought an agonised sigh. Then she could not but weep uncontrollably with a different emotion – the unforgettable sound of the magical Kenya dawn chorus of birdsong waking her on sparkling mornings – a sound that would be with her wherever she travelled; a sound that would linger in her psyche for ever.

"We are here, Miss Mitchell."

Morrissey thought her tears to be those on leaving this way. They were, but mingled with tears of joy for having had the most amazing time of her life by experiencing Africa's extremes – from near-death to full emotional expression of love with Peter. During her short visit to Kenya she had lived life to the full. She dried her eyes on a small handkerchief before walking with the imposing men through the entrance of the airport. Here two Masai stood hand in hand, each on one leg, idly watching passers by, and looking disdainfully at the African police sergeant carrying Della's luggage.

While crossing the crowded concourse Sir George handed her an envelope. "Here, Miss Mitchell, your passport, and boarding card. You'll be travelling first class with the American Charge de-Affaires who is in the VIP lounge waiting for you. He has the other business in hand with all the relevant negatives and prints with a release date to coincide with court appearances here. Your personal photographs and negatives are here in this other envelope. I have read a copy of your other article of your first impressions which I think is most apt and I am sure cannot fail to encourage people to come here for their safaris. Your animal photographs are as good if not better than many I've seen. There is something original about them that catch the eye. Kenya will always welcome you in different circumstances. Perhaps your next visit here will be longer. Have a good flight."

"Thank you."

"Bon voyage, Miss Mitchell," said Morrissey. The two men did not wait for the 'plane to take off. They had matters to attend to such as the radio shack at the Tanganyika border post that had been struck by lightning and demolished.

When entering the VIP lounge she said to herself, "Now, Della Mitchell, pull yourself together. Yes, you are one hell of a dumb blonde to fall for and willingly be seduced by a Kenya White Hunter. I have a good job; have some superb photographs and the best two articles I have ever written. If that doesn't get me that editor's job I am after I shall . . . I shall . . ." she sighed deeply . . . "I know I shall have to come out here and find Bili with Peter."

\*

Peter sat in an easy chair in his apartment for a long time with his head in his hands while thinking of Della, of Pat O'Brien and of Sekento his childhood friend turned murderer. Of Olekowlish and his determined stride out into the rain to his end. Then of the five-year old boy that was to inherit the Okiuka. Snapping out of it he went to his bedroom, pulled aside his bed and took the staff from the floor safe. He took it to the veranda to see it in daylight.

At the sound of an aircraft he looked up. Her 'plane was rising and heading northwards to fly up the Rift Valley where rain-clouds were gathering. Overhead broken cloud was building up quickly into cumulonimbus. "Hmmm," he said looking at his watch, "rain at twenty past three today."

The Okiuka was heavy in his hand. "So," he said to it, "You are the fiendish thing that kept me from my amazing Della." He felt his temple where her fist had hit him, and had a fleeting image of her in the borrowed flannel nightdress, hair not done, red eyed and no make up. "That was when I knew I really loved her . . ." He looked down on the ornamental shrubbery in the gardens below while thinking of her impetuous chasing after the poachers, then shook his head with a smile. "What a girl! . . . I really must . . ." he murmured.

He straightened up. "And the Governor? Our Rupert Stafford can go hang. If he wants to see me then he can damned-well come out to Kinangop. Ah well, first things first. I think I had better get back there and set about planting some new coffee." As he went to move the sun came from behind a patch of cloud. Its rays angled down and struck the Okiuka which seemed to take on an aura he could not begin to explain.

The black gem winked at him as it did when he first shone a thin-beamed torch at it in a cabinet in Kamau's office, but this time, in the open air, it reflected the rays of Kenya's huge golden sun.

THE END

# GLOSSARY

| | | | | | |
|---|---|---|---|---|---|
| Askari | Soldier | Mahindi | Maize |
| Bao | Ancient board game | Manyatta | Enclosure for Ilmoran (warriors) |
| Banda | Cottage apartment | | |
| Barathea | Close woven Select cloth | Matata | Trouble, Argument |
| | | Moran | Masai warrior class |
| Biltong | Dried buffalo meat | Mpira | Vehicle tyre, Ball |
| Boma | Dwelling with protective border | Murram | Hard wearing earth road surface |
| Bwana | Master | Ngombi | Cattle |
| Dhobi | Laundry | Pole | (say as poli). Sorry |
| Donga | Depression or split In the earth. | Pole Pole | Slowly |
| | | Posho | Maize porridge |
| Duka | Store, shop | Pesi | Quickly |
| Engang | Masai village | Rondavel | Round dwelling |
| Fisi | Hyena | Rungu | Hardwood stick with knob |
| Ghari | Wheeled vehicle | | |
| Hodi? | May I enter? | Shamba | Farm, homestead |
| Kanzu | Long cotton shift Worn by men | Shenzi | Mean, disreputable |
| | | Shauri | Affair, Business |
| Karibu | Welcome, enter | Siafu | Fierce ants |
| Khali | Sharp, Fierce | Simi | Short sword |
| Kloof | Large fissure in rock Mountain pass | Shuka | Garment worn as Roman toga |
| Kongoni | Tasty game meat | Tommy | Thomson's gazelle |
| Kopji | A hill of rock | Toto | Child |

## Biography.

After serving in RAF Bomber Command in WW2 Ron Jameson became a professional actor/manager at Stratford East, the RSC and touring. Then, acquiring an old London taxi for £25 He motored to Casablanca from where he 'overlanded' mostly on foot via West Africa, the Congo and Uganda to Nairobi in Kenya. There he safaried extensively in East Africa's three territories and collected stories and legends of the Masai. He married a broadcaster there. Then later in South Africa he drew on his past knowledge of theatre and became Actor Manager and Director with The Performing Arts Council in Johannesburg. There he wrote plays and daily serials for broadcast on SABC. Back in the UK in Theatre senior management and with an award for "Best Director" under his belt he continues writing of East Africa.